2000

$2.<u>00</u>

SCAVENGER

Novels by Tom Savage

Scavenger
The Inheritance
Valentine
Precipice

SCAVENGER

TOM SAVAGE

A DUTTON BOOK

DUTTON
Published by the Penguin Group
Penguin Putnam Inc., 375 Hudson Street,
New York, New York 10014, U.S.A.
Penguin Books Ltd, 27 Wrights Lane,
London W8 5TZ, England
Penguin Books Australia Ltd, Ringwood,
Victoria, Australia
Penguin Books Canada Ltd, 10 Alcorn Avenue,
Toronto, Ontario, Canada M4V 3B2
Penguin Books (N.Z.) Ltd, 182–190 Wairau Road,
Auckland 10, New Zealand

Penguin Books Ltd, Registered Offices:
Harmondsworth, Middlesex, England

First published by Dutton, a member of Penguin Putnam Inc.

REGISTERED TRADEMARK—MARCA REGISTRADA

ISBN 0-525-94538-5

Printed in the United States of America
Set in Sabon
Designed by Leonard Telesca

PUBLISHER'S NOTE
This is a work of fiction. Names, characters, places, and incidents either are the product
of the author's imagination or are used fictitiously, and any resemblance to actual persons,
living or dead, business establishments, events, or locales is entirely coincidental.

FOR ANN ROMEO

ACKNOWLEDGMENTS

As ever, I am grateful to my family, my friends, and my colleagues at Murder Ink for their support of my work.

Stuart Krichevsky, literary agent extraordinaire, has worked his usual wonders for me, and this book—to say nothing of my career—would not exist without him. And his associate, Paula Balzer, provided constant help.

Two editors worked with me on this one, Danielle Perez and Doug Grad, and I thank them and everyone else at Dutton for their care and guidance.

Finally, the only rose without a thorn is friendship, and I can prove it. I have dedicated this book to Ann Romeo, but I must also acknowledge her contribution to it. For the long sessions listening to several variations of the story, for reading and commenting on the manuscript, for encouraging me to try something so different from my other novels, and for suggesting the perfect title, I thank her most of all.

scavenger:
1. an animal that feeds on dead or decaying matter
2. a person or animal that searches through refuse for usable articles

—The Random House Dictionary

PROLOGUE

START GAME

It was nearly dawn now, but still he continued to read. He was sitting in his favorite armchair in the living room of the house on the hill, glancing over occasionally as the pine trees beyond the windows became visible and took form. The big brass floor lamp beside the chair was almost unnecessary at this point, as the ever-increasing light in the eastern sky above the valley and the distant hills would soon be pouring in on him. It didn't matter: he was going to finish the book again, and then he would go to bed. Who knows? he thought. Maybe today I'll actually sleep.

Sleep.

He had known from the moment he'd first heard about this book that it would be important to him. That had been late yesterday afternoon. He kept the radio in the ancient home entertainment center switched on most afternoons, tuned to National Public Radio. Yesterday he had listened with growing interest to an interview with the author. It had been an animated discussion, and it had proved to be most enlightening. When the program was over, he'd driven down the hill into the village, arriving at the tiny bookstore on Main Street just at closing time. He'd tapped on the window, flashing his very best smile. The bookseller recognized him, unlocked the door, and sold him the last copy in stock. He'd known the man would open the door, because people were always overly solicitous of him. There had been a desire, quickly suppressed, to read the novel right there in the parked car. He had driven home again with what he thought was admirable restraint.

He started reading the book over his solitary dinner at the head of the long table in the dining room, oblivious of the silent comings and goings of his servant. He ate little from the succession of plates Ivan placed before him, and they were eventually removed and carried back into the kitchen. But the wineglass at his elbow was kept full, and he drank frequently from it as he read. When his meal was over, he carried the glass with him into the living room. Ivan placed the bottle on the end table beside him, built a fire in the big stone fireplace, and retired to his rooms on the top floor.

He finished the book sometime after midnight. He thought about what he'd just read for a long time, staring into the dwindling flames in the fireplace as the big living room grew steadily colder around him. Then, at nearly two o'clock in the morning, he got up to stoke the fire, poured himself another glass of wine, and settled down in the armchair to read the book again.

It was the plot of the novel that had attracted him, the thinly veiled fictional version of an actual series of events. Five families in various parts of America had been murdered over a period of two years, the last incident being eleven years ago. Twenty-four people in all, and seven pets. One killer, according to official FBI reports, dubbed "The Family Man" by some clever journalist or other. There had never been any real suspects in the case. The Family Man was never apprehended, and now, so many years later, he was generally believed to be dead. It was the only way the experts could explain his silence, because no serial killer in history had simply stopped before: it went against everything that was known about them. There was a compulsion to kill in these people that did not go away. So, presumed dead. But no one, not even the federal agents involved, knew this for certain.

The novel he was now reading stuck to general facts, changing names and locales just enough to keep it in the realm of fiction. The random sociopath in the story was never referred to as The Family Man, but the inspiration for the story was patently clear. The author of the novel knew a lot, an uncomfortable amount, about the real story. The writer had obviously followed the case, studied it.

As he progressed through the now-familiar material, he felt the excitement growing within him. He began rereading the last chapter, rapt, amazed. Yes, he knew it was a work of fiction, but even so, how on earth could this man know these things? He waited, putting his thoughts on hold while he turned the final pages, read the final words.

He closed the book and sat there with it on his lap, staring down at the glossy dust jacket. Then he opened the back cover of the book and reread the brief author biography on the back flap. The small, square, black-and-white photograph above the biography was now the object of his fascination.

It was a good face, he decided. This man would be in his mid-thirties. Handsome, certainly, but more than that. The large, serious, dark eyes stared out at the world, filled with a distinct, innate intelligence. There was a definite spark in them. The strong chin and the wide shoulders under the sports jacket and T-shirt denoted a man of more than usual power and endurance. The voice on the radio yesterday had been pleasantly low-pitched and remarkably clear. A man who was sure of himself, who wouldn't scare easily. Yes. . . .

He took in the face and the shoulders and the full, soft dark hair. A single lock was out of place, as if the wind had suddenly blown it down toward the thick eyebrows. He decided that the man was fairly tall, and his musculature would be well defined. He closed his eyes for a moment, removing the suit and tie in his mind, visualizing how this man would look naked.

Tied up.

Screaming.

He opened his eyes, raising his right hand to his chest to soothe his pounding heart. Don't be foolish, he told himself. I can't indulge in such fantasies; not now. Not yet. The point is that he is the one. I have found him at last.

There had been many times over the years when he had despaired of ever finding this man. It was a subject that had consumed him utterly, something he'd wanted, needed, ever since—well, he wouldn't think about that. Not just now.

He glanced again at the picture, and at the brief biography below it. New York City . . .

Okay, he told himself. New York City. So be it. If that is where this man is, I shall plan accordingly.

He closed the book and studied the front cover again. It was a hazy, indistinct artist's rendering in deep brown and sepia tones, an extreme close-up of a man's face. The face was half in shadow, so that all one could really see were the outline and one side of the nose and the large, staring right eye that dominated everything. The eye had a wicked gleam to it. The title of the novel was splashed across the book just below the staring eye in embossed, bright red letters, crudely painted to simulate a finger dipped in blood.

DARK DESIRE

At the bottom, the author's name appeared in smaller lettering, in a plain typeface, discreetly white.

MARK STEVENSON

Yes, he thought again, smiling to himself. Mark Stevenson is obviously the one. The name makes perfect sense, now that I think about it.

He wanted to play the piano. It was his usual reaction, the thing he always wanted to do in moments of great excitement, moments of triumph. He looked across the room at the corner by the big window where the beautiful black mahogany Bechstein concert grand stood waiting for him, as it always did. But no, he reluctantly told himself. Not now. It was far too early in the morning, and he would probably wake Ivan. No, the music would have to wait.

He stared at the piano for a long time. Then, as ever, he looked up at the wall of framed photographs and posters beside it. His parents smiled out from most of the pictures, in various stages of their celebrated careers. There were a couple of pictures of his brother with his cello and his sister with her violin, and one small photo of himself, many years ago, sitting at a Steinway piano at the Institute, awkward in his first formal clothes at his first and only recital. The posters announced his parents' many appearances in America and Europe: Lincoln Center, Carnegie Hall, Heinz Hall, the Kennedy Center, Albert Hall, Covent Garden, La Fenice, La Scala. . . .

The life-sized painting was on the big wall behind him, and he had to turn around in the armchair to look at it. His mother was wearing a low-cut red satin gown, her dark hair up, her famous Fabergé ruby necklace, a gift from his father, flashing at her throat. She smiled serenely out from the picture, her elegant hands poised above the keyboard of the Bechstein. The piano was part of the legend that had sprung up about her. It had always been shipped to wherever she was appearing: she had refused to touch any other instrument.

Now the Bechstein was his, and he thought about his mother whenever he played it.

He returned his attention to the book. He stared at the cover again for a long time, and then he picked it up from his lap and hugged it to his chest. He stood up, turned off the brass lamp, and made his way over to the staircase, giving the painting of his mother a last, brief glance as he passed it. He carried the book with him. It is time for bed, he told himself. I must rest now so that I will awake refreshed. There is much to do, much to think about, starting tomorrow. *Today,* he amended, glancing at his watch as he climbed the stairs.

Today he would begin planning his little game. And it would be perfect: he would see to that. He would plan every move, every moment, as only he could possibly plan it. It would take him weeks, perhaps even months, to prepare, but that was no matter. He'd waited a long time already, more than ten years. He could be patient awhile longer.

He paused for another long moment at the top of the stairs, smiling to himself. Then he went down the hall and into his mother's bedroom. Everything was there, just as it had been before she died. He went over to her vanity table, staring at the articles laid out upon it. There was a big silver hand mirror lying beside her combs and brushes. He picked it up and gazed into it, studying his own reflection. Smiling again and nodding to himself, he carried the mirror out of the room and down the hall to his own bedroom.

Yes, he thought again. It will be a perfect game.

The sun finally rose to fill the gray, overcast January sky as best it could, but by that time he was asleep, dreaming of New York City. Dreaming of the game. Dreaming of Mark Stevenson.

Naked.

Tied up.

Screaming.

Bleeding. . . .

ARTICLE #1

NEWSPAPER

FRIDAY

$$\boxed{1}$$

"Congratulations, Mark!"

"Thank you. Thank you very much."

"Such a wonderful book. Scared the hell out of me!"

"Yes, well—"

"*So* wonderful!"

"Thanks."

"Excuse me, Mr. Stevenson. Could you look over here a sec?"

"Uh, sure."

"Say cheese!"

Click. Click. Click.

"Oh, *there* you are, Mark! *Mazel tov,* darling!"

"Thank you, um, Jackie. . . ."

He smiled at the slim, dark-haired woman as she pecked his cheek and sailed on through the crowd. He hoped her name was indeed Jackie, but he couldn't really remember. He was beginning to think the party would go on forever. A quick glance at his watch—ten thirty-seven—informed him that he'd been standing in the packed room for nearly an hour now, grinning vacuously around at the people, mostly strangers, who were constantly surging forward to shake his hand and/or kiss him. The cocktail party had begun at six, followed by dinner at seven, followed by the long, long awards ceremony itself, the ostensible reason behind these festivities. And he'd had the good—or, perhaps, bad—luck to win one of the damned things. The big one, in fact: Best Mystery Novel of the Year. Despite his intense discomfort around crowds, to say nothing of strangers, he'd been obliged to come here tonight. So here he was, smiling and thank-you-ing and you're-so-very-kind-ing as he searched the packed room for Tracy.

"Hey, Stevenson! How's my fellow laureate!"

He turned in the direction of the raucous voice. Jared McKinley, his friend—and tonight's winner in the Best True Crime category—was at his elbow, brandishing his award statuette in one hand and a large glass in the other, grinning from ear to ear. He was extremely tall, seeming to take up enough room for two men, and he had a voice to match. Judging from his glazed eyes, it wasn't his first large glass of the evening, Mark decided, and it probably wouldn't be his last.

"Hi, Jared. How are you doing?"

"Fan-fuckin'-tastic!" the big, handsome Scotsman boomed, causing several heads to turn their way. Jared was always the center of attention. He threw back his head and laughed, executed a rather sloppy little timestep, and waved his award statuette in Mark's face. "Where's yours?"

"In Tracy's purse," Mark replied. "You haven't seen her around anywhere, have you?"

"Nope. Don't worry, she can't have gone far in this madhouse. Are we still on for tomorrow?"

"Sure," Mark said. "I'm looking forward to it. I could use it, after tonight."

The two writers lived near each other in Greenwich Village, and they'd joined the local health club together. Twice a week, rain or shine, they rode the stationary bicycles, worked out on the exercise machines, and did serious time in the sauna and steam room. The idea was that each man would spur the other into staying in shape, and so far it was working. Three years now, and Mark felt better than he had when he was twenty, sixteen years ago. Quitting smoking had helped considerably. And he had finally recovered from the divorce. There was something else in his past, of course, something that would never go away, but for once he wasn't thinking about it.

Now, at the party, Mark and his friend were joined by the proprietor of a local mystery bookstore, who congratulated them both and asked them to drop in soon to autograph more first editions of their books. The two men smiled, thanked him, and promised him that they would.

When the bookstore owner was gone, Jared said, "Hey, man, we're celebrities now. About fuckin' time!"

Mark shrugged. "It's no big deal, Jared. You were a good writer before tonight, and so was I. This is all very nice, but—"

"Oh, sure!" Jared McKinley's hearty laugh resounded through the ballroom. "That's easy for you to say. *You're* the one who's on the *New York Times'* bestseller list. Not that I'm envious, you understand. It couldn't happen to a nicer guy. Hey, any word from Hollywood?"

"Uh, yeah." Mark glanced around self-consciously. "I'll tell you all about it at the club tomorrow. Three o'clock?"

"Okay. Three o'clock. See ya then, buddy." With that, Jared took off in the direction of the bar.

Mark was again wondering if he'd ever get out of this place when he spotted Tracy at last. She was on the other side of the hotel ballroom chatting with two women, one of whom was Mark's editor. Tracy looked beautiful in her long white dress, her tawny hair cascading down around her bare shoulders. Now that he thought about it, that dress left a great deal of her bare, front and back. Good thing the room was warm. Now, in the first days of April, the weather in New York City was just beginning to be appropriate for spring. If the awards had been one week ago, she would have had to wear something else. Oh, well. The admiring glances of the men at the ceremony were a reflection on him, in a way.

Sexist pig, he reprimanded himself. He didn't own her, nor she him. But he was willing to try another marriage, which is why they'd agreed on it three months ago, on her birthday. He'd popped the question over dinner, and she had surprised him by accepting immediately, after only four months together. But they were comfortable with it—at least, *he* was. And she seemed pleased by the prospect. They'd both been married before. No big deal.

They'd met at a party not unlike this one, a cocktail party given by Jaffee/Douglas, the literary agency where she worked. His agent, Bill Steiner, also worked there. Mark had seen the tall, lovely blond woman across the reception room and asked Bill to introduce them. He'd wanted her immediately, and she seemed interested in him, so he'd pressed his luck and asked her to dinner. It had been the first of several dates, and soon they were sleeping together. Everything had happened rather fast, he supposed, but it just seemed right to him. To both of them.

Mark was essentially monogamous. His divorce had not been his idea, but Carol's. He would have happily stayed with her: it was she who wanted out. Mark rarely found women who truly interested him, and Carol had been one. Tracy was another, *definitely*. He thought this as he made his way through the crowded ballroom to her.

"Hello, there," he whispered as he arrived beside her.

"Hello, yourself," Tracy murmured, leaning over to brush her warm, moist lips briefly against his cheek. "How are you holding up?"

He grimaced. "Barely. I've had enough of the public relations thing for one night. I'm thinking about bed."

She raised an eyebrow. "Tired?"

"No."

Now she laughed. "I'll just say good night to my two hundred closest friends, and we'll be out of here. But first, you really should . . ." She waved her hand surreptitiously, indicating the other two women.

Mark nodded and dutifully embraced Fran Wood, his editor, who introduced him to the other woman, a writer whose name was vaguely familiar to him. She wrote bestselling murder mysteries that were solved by small, furry animals, if he remembered correctly. Cats—or was it dogs? Something.

He chatted with Fran and the domestic-pet-detective woman for several minutes, watching out of the corner of his eye as Tracy made the rounds, saying good night to various colleagues and clients. She seemed to know everybody, whereas he was only acquainted with about five people in the place. One of the intrinsic differences between writers and literary agents, he supposed. As an agent, Tracy was required to remember the names of virtually everyone in the publishing industry. Better her than me, he thought, smiling as she at last made her way back over to him.

"Okay," she said. "We can go now."

"Yes, Mommy."

"I'm not your mommy." She took his hand and led him toward the exit.

"I'm glad to hear it," he said. "Are you my French parlormaid?"

"No."

"My porno movie star?"

"Maybe. Play your cards right . . ."

He grinned at her. "How do I do that?"

She grinned right back at him as they arrived at the cloakroom. "You can start by getting my coat."

He got her coat very quickly, almost as quickly as he managed to hail a cab.

2

Tracy was still awake three hours later. Mark had been asleep for nearly an hour, but she had not been able to relax enough to drift off. Well, she was relaxed enough physically, she supposed, smiling to herself as she remembered the lovemaking that had very nearly begun in the backseat of the taxi. But now she was once again tense, anxious.

She was staring up at the ceiling, watching the shifting shadows caused by the tree outside her window swaying in the light of a nearby streetlamp. Mark was on his side, his chest against her left arm, a well-muscled arm and leg carelessly draped over her. She felt his warm, dry skin against her, and she could feel the rhythmic beating of his heart just above her elbow. His soft, dark hair brushed against her neck every time he inhaled. She turned her head on the pillow to look at him.

His face in repose was somehow even more handsome than it was when he was awake. No lines or creases, and there was the hint of a smile on his lips. She smiled, as she always did when she studied him like this. He rarely moved or made noises when he slept, and she fancied she could set her watch by his breathing. She wondered once again that anyone over the age of five could sleep so soundly. He was the heaviest sleeper she'd ever encountered. But there was something reassuring about that. She liked having him beside her in bed. It felt safe and comfortable. It felt *right*. And yet . . .

He was a big, strong, handsome man; brilliant, talented, financially secure, heterosexual, and available. He drank in moderation and never took drugs. He was well-known, soon to be downright famous. He was tender, ardent, and always polite. She enjoyed sleeping with him—not merely sex, although that was certainly wonderful, but *sleeping*. He had even passed her mother's ultimate test: perfect teeth and perfect table manners. Her girlfriends would gladly trade places with her. Every other single woman in New York—in the *world*—would kill for such a specimen.

So what was *her* problem?

She'd been asking herself that for three months now, ever since they'd decided to make it legal. And now, fingering the beautiful engagement ring on her left ring finger, she still hadn't come up with a decent answer. She wondered for the hundredth time in two weeks if she was crazy. She wondered exactly what it was she wanted, if not Mark Stevenson.

With a little sigh, she carefully extricated herself from him and got out of the bed. She put on her terry robe and moved silently out of the bedroom and across the darkened living room into the kitchen. Only then did she turn on a light. She filled the kettle with water and rummaged in a cabinet for the box of Sleepytime tea. Maybe that would help.

Waiting for the water to boil, she went over it again in her mind. He was thirty-six, two years her senior, and he was originally from the Chicago area. He'd moved to New York twelve years ago. When she'd asked him about his parents, he'd told her they were both dead. He didn't have any siblings, either. He'd worked for the *New York Post*, first as a city reporter and later progressing to his own column on books. New books, new authors, what was happening in the publishing industry. She remembered reading the column occasionally, because those were the days when she'd been trying to establish herself as an authors' representative. He'd quit journalism when his first novel was accepted for publication. He was married for three years, to a magazine editor. The divorce was five years ago, and he and his ex-wife were still on speaking terms, so it had apparently been amicable. He didn't want to talk about it, he'd told her, and he didn't want to talk about his life before New York.

She poured the water into her favorite mug, thinking, He's very secretive. Very quiet. In seven months with him, she'd met exactly one friend of his, Jared McKinley. He didn't seem to have any other friends. He had his agent, Bill Steiner, with whom she worked, and Fran Wood, his editor, of course, but his relationships with the two of them seemed to be limited to their professional dealings. He did not see either of them socially.

She turned off the light and went over to stand at the front window in the living room, gazing down at Gramercy Park as she sipped the tea. They were to be married in the first week of June, two months from now, and she really knew very little about him. Less than she'd known about any other man with whom she'd been involved.

Well, almost. She thought, inevitably, of Alan, her first husband, remembering with a grimace how very little she'd known about *him*. For six years she'd tried to make the marriage work, finally concluding that she was the only one trying. But Alan had been an immature runaround whose late nights at the office had involved secretaries and chorus girls and at least one airline hostess. As little as she knew of Mark, she knew instinctively that he didn't have that problem.

Enough of this, she decided. She would go ahead with it, wedding plans and all. Mark was a good man, she was certain, and he obviously cared about her. The questions she still had about his past would be answered in due time. After they were married, he would have her circle of friends, to make up for his apparent lack of them. Everything was going to be all right, for one simple reason: she was in love with him.

She thought back over her marriage to Alan, wondering whether she'd ever felt this way about him, and finally deciding in the negative. She had even decided early in her first marriage not to have a child with Alan, although she wanted children. She and Mark had already talked about that, and he seemed to like the idea. She could now have children with Mark, and the thought of it was comforting. No, she realized, Alan wasn't Mark, not by a long shot.

Go to bed, she told herself, moving back into the kitchen and washing the empty mug. She glanced at the clock on the microwave oven: two-fifteen. It was Saturday now, and a good thing, too. She didn't have to go in to the office today. But she did have work to do, two manuscripts from clients to read over the weekend. One of them, the medical thriller, was part of a seven-figure, multiple-book deal with Doubleday. Her percentage of it would help to finance the summer house in the Hamptons she'd always wanted. Mark seemed to like that idea, too. There were other things, big things, to think about. She'd worry about it all later.

With this resolve, she went back into the bedroom and joined him, finally, in sleep.

SATURDAY

3

Mark wasn't prepared for it when it happened. That, he later decided, was the main problem with it. One minute his life was under control, and the next minute—well, it wasn't. It didn't take him long to realize that his life would never be the same again.

If there was anything Mark hated, it was surprise. He always planned things, down to the smallest detail. His day, his week, his writing schedule. He'd done it ever since he'd reached adulthood after a reckless adolescence. Anal retentive; that was what an analyst would have called it, but Mark simply regarded it as being in control. And he now insisted on being in control of things. He was no longer any good at being spontaneous.

He was about to get a lesson in spontaneity.

It happened the evening after the awards ceremony. He'd met Jared at the club at three o'clock, and they'd worked out until about five-thirty. At six, he'd arrived at an Italian restaurant in Chelsea just minutes before Tracy. It was her favorite place, and it was geographically desirable, being equidistant from his Village home and her Gramercy Park apartment. They weren't staying together tonight because she had some manuscripts to tackle and he was supposed to be completing his new novel, already overdue at the publisher. Fran Wood was waiting for it. So after dinner he had come straight home.

He checked his mailbox in the vestibule of the apartment house on Bedford Street before unlocking the interior door and pressing the button for the elevator. His one-bedroom co-op was on the top floor of the five-story brick building that shared an intersection with the narrowest house in the city, once the residence of Edna St. Vincent Millay, and the storefront, now a restaurant, that had previously been a recording studio for the Beatles, among others. Directly behind his building, in the cul-de-sac at the intersection of Barrow and Commerce, were the identical two-story townhouses known as the Twin Sisters, and across the street from them was the apartment building where Jillian Talbot, the suspense novelist, had lived before her famous run-in with the violent stalker who'd called himself Valentine.

Jillian Talbot, oddly enough, was the reason he lived here. When he and Carol had split up five years ago, he'd left her in their West End Avenue condo and taken a temporary sublet, an ancient railroad apartment in Hell's Kitchen that he shared with a recently divorced sportswriter from the *Post*. The only good thing about that place had been its proximity to work. He was there about one year, writing his book column by day and secretly working on his first novel at night, when he'd gone to Talbot's apartment one afternoon to interview her. It had been a good story, one of his better ones, but the best thing about the experience was her neighborhood. He'd never really noticed Greenwich Village before. After the interview he wandered the streets near Jillian Talbot's building, staring delightedly around at everything. When he saw the sign reading CO-OPS AVAILABLE on the handsome red brick apartment house on Bedford Street, he took it as a personal message.

One month later, he left Hell's Kitchen for good. He always looked back on the move to Greenwich Village as the turning point in his new, post-divorce life. After that, only good things happened to him. He completed his first book and showed it to Bill Steiner, who immediately got him a two-book deal with Random House. The books did very well, critically and commercially, and another contract followed, this one for more money. Now his fourth work, *Dark Desire*, had made the bestseller lists and brought the award and the movie offers. And, of course, he now had Tracy Morgan.

Mark was smiling as he stepped out of the elevator and approached his apartment. One of Mrs. Liebman's identical black cats—Tevye or Golde, he could never tell the male from the female—stood mewing uncertainly in the hallway in front of his door. The two cats were always in the hall. A glance over at the open hall window confirmed the usual *modus operandi*: the fire escape. He scooped up the animal, looking around for its partner in crime as he headed for his next-door neighbor's door, which opened before he reached it.

"Oh, *there's* my little Golde!" the elderly widow cried. "How on earth did you get out *here?*" She took the cat in her arms. "Sorry to trouble you, Mark."

"No trouble," he replied, smiling at his neighbor and turning to insert his key in his lock.

He stopped, arrested by the sight of something taped to his door. It was a manila envelope, five inches by seven. His name was printed across it in capital letters with a thick black marker. There was nothing else, he noted; no return address, no postmark, no stamp.

"Hector put that there a few hours ago," Mrs. Liebman offered as she disappeared into her apartment.

Mark grimaced, wondering for the hundredth time if anything could possibly happen in the building that Mrs. Liebman missed. He doubted it: the only thing she *didn't* seem to know was the whereabouts of her pets. He detached the envelope from the door and carried it inside.

The computer stood waiting for him on the desk in front of the living room window, the animated fishes blowing bubbles among the strands of seaweed as they swam about the screen. He dropped the envelope on the desk and went into the kitchen to make a pot of coffee. Only after he had returned with his mug and ensconced himself in the executive chair before the electronic aquarium did he bother to open the envelope and remove its contents.

It was a single, plain diskette with no label, merely the manufacturer's stamp informing him that it was from AT&T, formatted for Macintosh. Intrigued, he slid the disk into the floppy drive and touched his keyboard, banishing the fish to cyber-limbo. He opened the only file on the disk, noting that it was untitled, the only official logotype being that of Hackers, a chain of computer-nerd coffee bars with branches all over New York. For the price of a cappuccino and a nominal fee, anyone could use the keyboards and screens that were the chain's principal decor. That was apparently where the file had been created. The usual flashing and whirring gave way to an image on the screen: a letter.

Oh, he thought. Someone—someone who knows me, and knows I have a Mac—has used this distinctly modern way to communicate with me. But why? Why not e-mail, or a phone call, or a plain, old-fashioned letter? He glanced at the opening paragraph: fan mail. Terrific. Someone was delivering electronic fan mail by hand to his home. Annoyed, he began to read the words on the screen, bracing himself for fulsome, meaningless praise.

But it was not a fan letter. Not at all, as it turned out. His first reaction was confusion, followed almost immediately by a cold, growing sense of dread.

Dear Mr. Stevenson,

I am writing to you regarding your excellent novel, <u>Dark Desire.</u> It is truly extraordinary, and I understand you have just received an award for it. Congratulations!

My purpose in writing, however, is somewhat more provocative. You see, it is obvious to me—and, I presume, everyone else—that the novel is based on the "Family Man" case of a few years ago. You never stated that; in fact, you went to great lengths to stay in the realm of fiction. But your final chapters, in which the serial killer is tracked and apprehended, were entirely your own contribution. As we all know, the real-life prototype of your character was never brought to justice. And that is what I want to address.

I have always been a lover of games, Mr. Stevenson, and I would like to propose that you play one with me now. I could never find anyone who was willing to play chess or Scrabble with me, as I always seemed to win, and yes, I am one of those annoying people who do the Sunday <u>Times</u> crossword puzzle in ink. But the game I propose is one of my own devising. You are obviously as fascinated by The Family Man as I am, and I think you may find my game amusing, not to mention enlightening.

You see, I know a great deal about The Family Man, more than anyone else. And I am willing to share my knowledge with you. You are a wonderful writer, and I think it is time The Family Man—well, went public. I realize that he has long been presumed dead. For purposes of our game, let us both agree right now that this is true. But his story should be written down, and there is no one more suitable for the job than you.

Are you interested? I hope so. But, for reasons that should be obvious to you, I can't simply approach you directly with the information I wish to impart. That is why I have come up with my game, which I have designed along the lines of a scavenger hunt. I will provide you with a series of instructions that will lead you to certain locations, where you will be responsible for finding certain articles. Each instruction will have a time limit for completion. They will eventually lead you to—well, to what you may want to know. Total playing time, if all goes well, will be one week. Today (as you read this) is Saturday: the game will begin at midnight tonight and end next Saturday at midnight. There will be some expense involved, but I am willing to provide for that.

As I cannot approach you, and as you do not know who I am, I realize that there is no way for you to answer me. So here is what I propose we do: I will give you your first clue now. If you wish to play—if you are interested in the "prize" to which I have obliquely referred—simply begin. This will indicate that you are willing, and I will contrive further communication. How does that sound?

Before you begin, I must point out to you that there are three rules in my game that must be followed at all times. Failure to do so will mean you automatically forfeit, and the game will end then and there. And you will never, ever hear from me again. I trust I make myself clear. These are the rules:

1) You must follow my scenario strictly, as it is presented to you. You may not at any time deviate from the order in which the clues arrive and the articles are retrieved.

2) No one else may know about the game. No one. Of course I mean the authorities, but I mean everyone else as well. Your friends, your associates—everyone. This is strictly between you and me.

3) Once you have begun to play, you cannot stop for any reason until the game is over.

So, now you know the rules. I hope I have piqued your interest with this. It will be a most entertaining game, I promise. And your prize for successfully completing it is certainly all that a former journalist such as yourself could want. Without boasting, I can safely say it is one of the truly big "scoops" of the century.

If you choose not to play, I thank you for your time and attention regarding this missive, and I wish you all the best in your future writing career. But I will be presumptuous and assume that you want to continue. If so, your first instruction is quite easy:

*YOU ARE LOOKING FOR A NEWSPAPER, AT A PLACE IN NEW YORK
CITY THAT WAS DEAR TO THE FAMILY MAN.*

*You have twenty-four hours, beginning at midnight tonight.
Happy hunting!*

You may call me:

SCAVENGER

He sat there, stunned, staring at the screen before him. He couldn't grasp it, couldn't take it all in. He couldn't breathe. Nearly ten minutes passed before he snapped out of his trance and summoned the motor skills necessary to scroll the electronic letter back to its beginning and read it again, this time more slowly. No, there was no mistake: it was exactly what he thought it was.

A message from someone who was "obliquely"—to use the person's own word—hinting that they knew the identity of The Family Man. Someone who was, perhaps, obliquely hinting that they—he? she?—that it *was* The Family Man.

What else could the letter possibly mean?

He wouldn't think about that right now, he decided. There was a more immediate mystery, and that, at least, was something he could solve. Ejecting the disk and dropping it on the desk, he stood up and went out to the elevator.

Hector Ramos was not in his apartment. Mrs. Ramos directed Mark to another part of the basement, where he found the superintendent tying stacks of newspapers and flattened cardboard boxes with twine, the usual unlit, half-smoked cigar clenched between his teeth. He was a small, burly man of indeterminate middle age, and he panted with the exertion of his chore. He barely looked up when Mark spoke.

"Hector, that envelope you taped to my door—where did you get it?"

"*Que?*. . . oh, yes. Envelope. Man come, 'bout four o'clock."

"What man?"

A shrug. The super flicked a sharp box cutter across the twine and tied off another bundle. He spoke around the stogie. "Man come. Ring my buzzer. Marisa go up to lobby and he gib her mail for you, ast her to tape it to your door. 'Urgent,' he say. She bring it to me and tell me do it. I always do what Marisa say." Another shrug, accompanied by a man-to-man grin. He reached for another pile of cardboard.

Mark restrained himself from yanking the boxes from the man's hands. Patiently but firmly, he said, "Please, Hector, this is very important. I have to know who the man was."

His distress was noted. Hector straightened up, dropped the twine and the box cutter, and removed the wet cigar butt from his mouth. He regarded Mark a moment, then led the way down the ill-lit basement hallway to his apartment door. He opened it and called, "Marisa!"

Mrs. Ramos appeared in the doorway almost immediately, wiping her wet hands on her apron. Her husband spoke to her in Spanish. She listened, watching Mark all the while, a look of concern on her pretty face. When her husband paused, she said something to him, also in Spanish.

"She say he not the postman or UPS," Hector translated. "He speak Spanish, but he not Spanish. He offer her money, but she refuse."

"What did he look like?" Mark asked.

More Spanish.

"Tall," Hector said. "*Very* tall."

Mark looked at the woman. She pointed at Mark, then measured a length of about six inches with her hands. He understood the pantomime: the man was that much taller than he, making him about six feet eight inches in height. Mark searched his mind. No, he didn't know any basketball players, and Mrs. Ramos knew Jared McKinley, who was nearly that tall.

"What else?" Mark asked.

She thought a moment, then spoke. *"Blanco."* She pointed at her own hair. *"Negro."* She mimed a mustache, then pointed at her own face and made a very stern expression. She narrated this, and Hector chuckled and said, "She say he scary-looking, like Frankenstein."

Mark blinked, thinking that this was no time to correct them. Frankenstein was a handsome scientist; she obviously meant his creation. "Boris Karloff?"

"Si!" Marisa Ramos cried. "Borees Karloff!" She fingered the gold cross that rested on her bosom, as if her staunch Catholicism were all that would protect her from such a person. Then she pointed at her eyes and said something Hector translated as, "Very pale gray, almost clear."

"How old was he?"

She pointed at her husband, then wiggled her right hand in the international sign for "more-or-less." Mid-fifties.

Mark smiled, thanked her, and turned to go. He was almost to the elevator when she stopped him.

"Meester Stevenson!"

He turned around.

"He hab—" she began. Then she turned to her husband and unleashed a torrent of Spanish, lifting her right index finger to the outside corner of her right eye and drawing it slowly down past her mouth, all the way to her chin.

Hector raised his bushy eyebrows in obvious surprise. "She say he hab a scar. An old scar, very long, thin, whiter than his skin, down the side of his face. Like from a knife."

Mark stared at them a moment, then smiled again, nodded, and got in the elevator. As he rose to the top floor, he put all the details of the man who had delivered the envelope together in his mind. He went back into his apartment, carefully locking the deadbolt behind him, and inserted the disk in his computer again.

He read and reread the letter long into the night, trying to imagine the scarred face of the tall stranger who had obviously terrified Marisa Ramos. And all the while, he repeated the same three words aloud, over and over.

"Who are you?"

4

A chill wind whipped down the narrow Greenwich Village street, and he felt cold despite the solid thickness of his long black coat. Oh, well, he thought, grinning to himself in the darkness and reaching up to run his finger slowly down the thin white scar on his right cheek, I've been in colder places than this. Far, far colder. This is nothing compared to where I've been. . . .

He moved slightly forward out of the doorway of the townhouse just across Bedford Street from the red brick apartment building he had briefly visited this afternoon, and gazed up at the fifth-floor corner window. Yes, the lights were still on there, practically the only lights still on in the building at this late hour. He consulted his watch: three-forty. He wasn't remotely tired, had never had much use for sleep. And he knew that the man in the apartment on the fifth floor would not be getting much sleep tonight, either.

Still smiling his cold, enigmatic smile, he glided away down the street. There was an all-night delicatessen at the next corner, on Seventh Avenue. He'd noticed it when he'd been studying the neighborhood around the author's home. He went inside and ordered a large black coffee, taking care not to show his amusement when the man behind the counter, a stocky type of Middle Eastern origin who could probably have gone ten rounds with LaMotta, glanced into his pale gray eyes, blinked, and began instinctively to reach under the counter. There would be a gun there, presumably, or a baseball bat. Something like that. This was New York, and you never knew who was going to walk through the door. He smiled at the man, who paused, considering his options, then withdrew his hands from the hidden shelf and went off to fill the order. He waited patiently for the trembling proprietor to pour the coffee, thinking, If only you knew. . . .

He was used to this reaction from people, inured to it. He'd noticed it just this afternoon, from the pretty superintendent's wife to whom he'd handed the first package. He'd spoken to her in her native tongue, Spanish being only one of several languages in which he was fairly fluent, and attempted to mollify her with a smile. It was vital that she— or someone in this place—deliver the envelope. But even the familiar language and the smile had not allayed her obvious discomfort. He had reached out to give her the envelope, and their fingers had briefly touched. She had drawn back her hand with the package as if she had been scalded, and reached absently up with her other hand to grasp the gold crucifix at her neck.

But she had done what he'd asked her to do.

That much, at least, was obvious. He'd manned his post in the doorway of the empty townhouse across the street, holding the tiny earpiece up to his ear, listening to the sounds inside the writer's rooms. He'd heard the computer keys clacking, and the harsh intakes of breath as the man read the letter he'd so carefully typed on the machine in the crowded coffeehouse on the Upper West Side, constantly consulting the written script in his notebook. Then the man had muttered something and left the apartment. He had not left the building, however, which indicated the logical next move: he'd gone to pump the super's wife for a description.

Well, that was fine. Now the writer had at least a hazy picture of his opponent, which made the game that much more interesting. Besides, if all went as scheduled—and it would—the two of them would be seeing quite a bit of each other in the next seven days.

He carried the hot coffee back to his post. Yes, the lights were still burning in the fifth-floor apartment. He reached inside his coat and pulled out the listening device again, holding it up to his ear. When he heard what the writer was mumbling over and over, he smiled again.

"Who are you?"

Who am I? he thought. Well, Mark Stevenson, you'll find out soon enough. And you'll wish you hadn't. This I promise you. You'll wish you had never written that "novel," *Dark Desire*. Dark desire, indeed.

He smiled and sipped the coffee. He had killed before, many times, and one more killing would make very little difference to him. But *this* one was going to be special. This one would be a work of art.

The suitcase was in the trunk of his rented car, which was currently in the parking garage a few blocks from here, on Seventh and Morton. And in that suitcase were the props he would use tomorrow, *at a place in New York City that was dear to The Family Man*. All the writer had to do was figure it out and go there. Everything would be waiting for him, and the game would truly begin.

The game. . . .

He smiled again. Because he couldn't resist, because it pleased him to do so, he raised the device to his ear again and listened. He stood there on dark, chilly Bedford Street for a long time, listening to the writer's whispered mantra, noting the wonder and undisguised fear in his words.

"Who are you . . . ?"

S U N D A Y

$$\boxed{5}$$

YOU ARE LOOKING FOR A NEWSPAPER, AT A PLACE IN NEW YORK CITY
THAT WAS DEAR TO THE FAMILY MAN. . . .

The house was in a row of almost identical buildings, brown brick
and gleaming windows, on a fashionable street in the westernmost section of Brooklyn. Time and the weather had made no inroads here because the residents of Cobble Hill were, at least in recent decades, an
upscale crowd. Everything on this street was well maintained, and
shady trees stood at regular intervals along the smooth sidewalks. The
block was lined with expensive cars. It was a quiet, clean, relatively
safe area, perfect for upper-middle-class urban families with children.
Violent crime was a remote consideration here—or, rather, it should
have been.

Mark stood on the sidewalk in front of 125 Kane Street, gazing up
at the curtained bay window beside the polished, decoratively carved
oak front door, thinking, Murder has no business here. Not on this
street, not in this neighborhood. Not *that* sort of murder, at any rate.
A crime of passion, perhaps, or a robbery gone awry: these could happen anywhere. But not, no, most definitely *not* what had happened to
the Banes family. That, he knew, was why the crime had been so perfect, and why it was still unsolved. Why they were *all* unsolved, the
five incidents attributed to The Family Man.

All five crimes had occurred in just such neighborhoods as this, to
upscale, Caucasian, Christian families of identical makeup: father,
mother, two young adult sons, one young adult daughter. All five families had owned at least one pet, also dispatched, and in two of the five
cases a live-in housekeeper had died, as well. Only three people had

survived, not having been with their families at the times of the attacks: the daughter in the first incident, the elder son in the third, and the younger son in the fourth. And all five crimes had occurred on national and/or religious holidays.

The Banes family had been killed on Easter Sunday, eleven years ago, the last of the five incidents. Dr. George Banes had been a well-known surgeon, and his wife, Alma, had been active in the Catholic church the family attended. Their friends, the Rosses, who were perplexed when they didn't show up in church for the Easter mass, had tried calling them, to no avail, and finally had driven to the house. Mr. Ross remained in the car while his wife went up to the front door, which was uncustomarily unlocked. When there was no reply to her repeated ringing and knocking, she went inside. The overwhelming stench and the sight of the drying blood in the living room and on the stairs sent her immediately outside to fetch her husband. As she called the police from the pay phone at the next corner, he took the tire iron from the trunk and, thus armed, went into the house.

He found them in the dining room. All of them, including the cocker spaniel. George and Alma were seated at either end of the table, dressed in their Easter Sunday best. The three children—Joel, twenty; Brad, eighteen; and Heidi, seventeen—were in their usual places at the sides, and the dog lay underneath it. The table was covered with a brightly printed paper tablecloth, white and yellow and lavender, with the words HAPPY EASTER! splashed rampantly among the comical pictures of eggs and fuzzy chicks and Easter bunnies with baskets. Matching paper plates, drinking cups, and napkins were set at each place before the bodies, along with pink plastic cutlery. In the middle of the table was a big, multicolored basket overflowing with purple plastic grass and plastic Easter eggs. George Banes's severed head rested in the center of the basket, a macabre centerpiece for the macabre *tableau vivant*—or *tableau mort*, depending on how one looked at it. A happy family celebrating the holiday together around their dining room table, one of them headless and all the others with their throats slashed. . . .

Now, eleven years later, a chill breeze whipped down Kane Street, and Mark shivered and pulled up the collar of his leather jacket. He knew that his shivering was not caused by the wind, but by the cold fury that suffused him as he stared up at this house. The fury that had prompted him, after all these years, to write *Dark Desire*. The fury he felt when he thought of the diskette that had arrived at his home last night. The fury that brought him here now, today.

He was here, as instructed. A PLACE IN NEW YORK CITY THAT WAS DEAR TO THE FAMILY MAN. That could only be 125 Kane Street. But it wasn't the same house that had made the headlines. The same building, but changed, as such a crime would inevitably change anything. Some subsequent owner had evidently split up the three floors of the building into separate floor-through apartments: there were now three mailboxes and three intercom buttons beside the big oak door. He had no idea what he was supposed to do now.

YOU ARE LOOKING FOR A NEWSPAPER . . .

The curtain in the bay window before him moved aside, and a pretty young woman peered out at him. He caught her eye and she frowned, and then the face disappeared and the curtain fell back in place. Two women walked by on the sidewalk on the other side of the street, glancing over at him as they passed. He couldn't stay here much longer, he knew. He'd been standing here for nearly twenty minutes already, and the natives were getting suspicious. But what was he supposed to do?

A newspaper . . .

He had just decided to give up and retrace his steps to the Borough Hall subway station two blocks away when the man with the newspaper arrived from the direction of Smith Street. He was extremely tall and muscular, white, and black-haired, and he had a mustache—but he was in his mid-twenties, not his mid-fifties, and his face was unscarred. He was wearing a football jersey, jeans, and sneakers, and he was balancing a cardboard tray from Starbucks on his upheld right hand, two large coffees and various expensive pastries.

Under his left arm he carried the Sunday *New York Times*.

The young man frowned at Mark as he approached down the sidewalk, and as he came abreast of him, he apparently made the born-and-bred New Yorker's decision as to how to deal with the stranger in front of his building. Pointedly ignoring Mark, he turned and started up the steps to 125.

"Um, excuse me," Mark called to his retreating back.

The big man turned on the steps. "Yeah?"

Mark tried to smile, but found that he couldn't. "Is—is that newspaper for me?"

Now the man frowned again. He looked down at the paper under his arm, then up at Mark. When he finally spoke, he uttered Mark's words of a moment before—"Excuse me?"—but it was the born-and-bred New Yorker's reading of the line. Rough translation: *Screw you.*

Mark actually took a step backward on the sidewalk. "I—I'm sorry, it's just—I thought maybe—a friend of mine sent me here to look for a—I think he's playing a practical joke on me. . . ."

He trailed off, the words of instruction flashing in his brain. *No one else may know about the game.* He stood there, writhing with uncertainty, when three things happened simultaneously.

He heard music. From somewhere behind him, he heard the approaching sound of a familiar female voice singing a familiar song. It registered, fleetingly, that the singer was Judy Garland and the song was "Easter Parade."

The door behind the man opened, and the pretty young woman Mark had glimpsed through the curtains arrived on the stoop. "Billy, what's going on . . . ?"

And a rolled newspaper materialized from thin air and landed with a soft thud at Mark's feet.

All three of them stared down at the missile. Mark whirled around and looked behind him. For an odd, frozen moment, he thought perhaps he was hallucinating. A young boy, maybe twelve, was sailing silently by down the street on a red bicycle. The music came from a boom box in the wire basket attached to his handlebars. The boy turned his head briefly, his curly brown hair streaming, and shot Mark an impish grin. Then the hallucination vanished as instantly as it had arrived: the song faded away as the red blur sped to the corner, turned sharply, and disappeared from sight.

As the woman watched from the doorway, the man came back down the steps. He was reaching for the package when Mark knelt and snatched it up.

"Hey, buddy," the man protested, "I think that must be for one of our neigh—"

"No," Mark said with certainty. "It's for me."

It was not the Sunday *Times,* or anything nearly that size. It was one of the tabloids, rolled into a neat tube and tied with a black silk ribbon, like a college diploma. In one swift move, Mark slid the ribbon off and unrolled the tube. It was a *New York Post,* and not a recent one. That fact barely had time to register when Mark had a second hallucination: as the paper flattened, a yellow-and-purple plastic Easter egg that had been wrapped inside slid out and slowly, slowly fell down to land on the sidewalk, cracking open as it struck. A fuzzy yellow stuffed chick went skittering across the cement.

"What the hell?" the young man cried, nearly dropping his own packages.

The two men were staring down at the front page of the newspaper. George and Alma Banes were smiling up at them from a grainy photograph just under that day's bold headline: FAMILY MAN STRIKES IN NEW YORK! The date was Monday, the day after Easter, eleven years ago.

The big man—Billy, she'd called him—bent to put down the tray and the *Times* on the sidewalk, grabbed the paper from Mark's hands, and quickly folded it over, concealing the headline. He turned and called over his shoulder, his voice jocular, artificial. "It's okay, Nan. Go back inside."

Without a word, Nan complied, closing the door behind her. The man named Billy handed Mark the folded paper and viciously kicked the plastic egg halves into the gutter. The fuzzy chick followed them. Then the man turned to face Mark, his huge body unnaturally close, his eyes on fire. Mark could feel the heat, the outrage, the dangerous power of the man, and he shrank involuntarily back from him.

"You'd better leave now," the young man growled. "Nan doesn't know about what happened here, and I don't want her to. It took me forever to find a place we could afford. She wouldn't want to stay here, she'd want to move, and I *like* living here. That Family Man stuff was a long time ago. You said a *friend* sent you here for this? Well, I think your *friend* has a real creepy sense of humor. Now get the hell out of here!" He picked up his packages and bounded up the stairs to 125 Kane Street.

"I—I'm sorry, I . . ." Mark clutched the newspaper to his chest as he turned and fairly staggered away down the street in the direction of the subway that would return him to Manhattan, to his home, to sanity.

6

The tall, dark-haired man with the scar raised the field glasses and watched Mark Stevenson staggering away down the sidewalk. Then he lowered the glasses, a glint of amusement briefly lighting his pale gray eyes.

The writer was definitely upset, that much was plain. Unsettled and embarrassed, with that couple from the building intruding on the otherwise perfect setup. But the package had been delivered as instructed. The local boy had been only too glad for the twenty dollars and the new boom box, although his brief mission was never explained to him. He would boast to his friends about it, and about the strange, huge man in black with the scar down his face, but that was all. He was no problem.

And Mark Stevenson was playing the game.

That was the important thing, he knew. Everything that had been planned for the next six days, the elaborate setup that would move the pawn around the enormous chessboard—it all depended on the pawn playing the game. But he had known beforehand that the writer would play, and why.

So, on to the next round. If Mark Stevenson was as smart as all that, he would read the newspaper he'd just received very carefully. He would put together the next clue, and the next move. And tomorrow, Monday, he would be on his way to the next location.

The big man moved forward out of the shadows of the doorway where he had concealed himself to watch 125 Kane Street, and glided toward his parked Lincoln Town Car. He gave the appearance of *gliding*, he knew. The long black coat, what in more romantic times had been called a "duster," swirled around him, concealing his legs. The voluminous coat was also good for concealing other things, such as the field glasses, and the power pack and headset that monitored the listening device he'd planted in the writer's apartment. Not to mention his special medical kit. And the knife.

The eight-inch, stainless steel blade was something he knew how to use. His father had given it to him when he was twelve years old, and he had first killed with it when he was fifteen. Since then, it traveled with him. It had become an essential part of him, a defining characteristic. The custom-made leather sheath was attached to a shoulder holster, and the knife fit comfortably against the left side of his rib cage. It was there, always, waiting to be put to use.

He preferred the weapon to a gun, although he prided himself on the fact that he could use any firearm in existence if the occasion arose. He was an expert marksman. That, too, had been part of his early training. He could kill a man with his bare hands, if it came to that, and had done so. Violence was second nature, part of his everyday reality, and it always had been. He didn't even think about it anymore.

And he had big plans for Mark Stevenson.

He would follow Mark—or "*the* mark," as he had come to think of him—back to Manhattan. He would resume his post outside the brick apartment house on Bedford Street and wait for the next discovery, the next flurry of activity. And the forthcoming week would be fraught with activity.

Yes, he thought again. It will be a perfect game. . . .

Dark as a shadow, silent as the grave, he glided into the car and glided away down the street, toward the avenue that would lead him to the Brooklyn Bridge.

7

There had to be some mistake.

Mark had known from the moment the newspaper, that mocking gauntlet of challenge, had been cast down before him that this game, this scavenger hunt, was inevitable. He knew—as this person, this "Scavenger," apparently knew—that he would be compelled to play along. He was already playing, in fact. And for this, he was going to need money.

He had credit cards and a checkbook, but he would probably need cash as well. His next stop was Washington, D.C., and he had decided to rent a car. He'd come here, to the bank at Sheridan Square three blocks from his building, to check his account balances and withdraw some cash, and as he stared down at the illuminated screen of the automated teller machine he repeated his first, incredulous thought, now spoken under his breath.

"There has to be some mistake."

But there was no mistake; he knew that, too. The last time he had noted the balance in his account had been four days ago, Wednesday. At some point between then and now, his checking balance had grown by exactly ten thousand dollars.

Even as he accepted the fact, he accepted that there was no point in following it up. Like the diskette taped to his door, it was simply *there*. Anyone could deliver an envelope to an apartment building, and anyone with ten thousand in cash could deposit it in someone else's bank account without arousing suspicion. Scavenger hadn't tried to *withdraw* money from Mark's account, which would be questioned, and some teller in any one of hundreds of branches of his bank would only be able to provide the same description Mrs. Ramos had already given him: tall, dark, scarred. Tracking down the teller could take days, and Mark didn't have days. He had obtained the newspaper in half of his allotted twenty-four hours, and tomorrow, Monday, he would be in Washington. He'd been given twenty-four hours there, too, beginning at midnight tonight. Time was a big factor in this demented game.

Washington was the next apparent destination, but he wasn't looking for a specific article this time. He was looking for a man. He thought about this as he withdrew several hundred in cash from the ATM and stuffed it into his wallet. Then he proceeded home, to get ready for dinner with Tracy. He'd called her and asked her to come to the Village this evening. He wanted to say good-bye in person, not on the phone. He'd do it over dinner in a restaurant, and he would take her back to his apartment for the night. She didn't know it yet, but it might be their last night together for at least a week.

He showered and changed at home, thinking all the while of the eleven-year-old copy of the *New York Post* that was now folded into his suitcase.

The breaking news concerned the Banes family, of course, and it had covered the first few pages of the paper that day. The details of the slaughter were related, with photos of the covered bodies being carried down the steps, the very steps where Mark had stood this morning. The paper had been careful to include as much information as could hastily be gathered about the victims, the actual people behind the sensational tragedy. The family's status in the community, Dr. Banes's distinguished contributions to the medical profession, the children's schools and colleges, Mrs. Banes's many charity activities. A brief sketch, a hurried overview of the lives of five perfectly decent, perfectly innocent people.

Nobody had seen anything on that holiday morning. The neighbors on the block near 125 Kane Street were not the sort of people who spied on each other, and the Christians among them had been preoccupied with church and Easter egg hunts in backyards and preparing feasts for their families and guests.

If there had been a commotion in the house, or screams, nothing had been noted. There were no unaccountable fingerprints, no footprints in the blood. The FBI and police had speculated on that, the apparent ease with which the shocking deed had been done. Five grown people do not simply *allow* themselves to be killed, one cop was quoted as saying. The best guess was that it had been done very early, while the family had still been asleep, exactly as in the other four incidents. The forensic evidence supported this: four of the five members of the Banes family had been killed in their beds upstairs and carried down to the dining room. Only Alma Banes had apparently been downstairs at the time: she was killed in the kitchen.

The red Magic Marker highlights had appeared on a related story on page five—a sidebar, really—detailing the ongoing FBI investigation and recapping the earlier four attacks by The Family Man. Accompanying that story was a photograph of a big, imposingly handsome, powerfully built African-American man in his mid-forties. He was Ronald O'Hara, the FBI special agent in charge of the Family Man case. He and his team had arrived from Washington to work with the NYPD as they had earlier worked with the police in the other four locations.

The head shot of Agent O'Hara was circled in red marker, and a big question mark had been drawn in the margin beside it. In the text of the story, the word "Washington" had been underlined three times, and a big exclamation mark accompanied it. Near these markings had been scrawled, *24 HRS. STRTNG MDNGHT TNGHT!*

And there was something else. Across a department store advertisement beside the article, in the same red marker, was the sentence:

> *Newspapers were very important to The Family Man,*
> *because they reported what he wanted them to report.*

So Scavenger had conveyed his new instructions. Mark would go to Washington tomorrow, to look up O'Hara. That was obviously the next move. After that—well, he had no doubt Scavenger would provide further directions.

Mark would not call O'Hara, or in any way forewarn him of his arrival. He knew the agent was retired, had been for several years now, and he had his address in Georgetown. Last year, when Mark had been preparing his notes for *Dark Desire,* he had called the man and requested an interview. The former agent had refused to discuss the Family Man case, certainly not for a novel based loosely on the facts. He had refused to see Mark outright, and Mark knew why.

That was going to be the big problem, Mark thought as he dressed for dinner. He would surprise O'Hara at home—if he was at home—

and he would have to get the man to invite him in. To cooperate with him. To talk to him now, despite his earlier refusal. . . .

The intercom buzzer sounded, interrupting his reverie. Tracy. Right on time, as usual. And she must not know about this, any of it. He loved her, and he didn't want her to be frightened or to worry about him. She had enough on her mind at the moment, he knew. In a couple of months, they were going to be married, and even a small City Hall ceremony took planning. By that time, Scavenger would be a thing of the past.

He hoped.

With a sigh for the difficult task that awaited him in Washington tomorrow, he forced a smile to his lips and went over to the door to let Tracy in.

8

"Washington?"

"Yes."

"For a week?"

"Well, I'm starting there, anyway. I think I may have to go to a couple of other places as well."

"Where?"

"I'm not sure yet."

"You're not sure. You're doing research for your novel, but you're not sure where you're going to be?"

"Something like that."

Pause. Then the woman said, "Mark, is—is something wrong?"

At that moment a car horn blared loudly before the vehicle tore through the intersection beside him, obliterating the reply. When the car was gone, he heard her say, "Okay, okay, you're right. I'm beginning to sound like a wife. Of course, that's what I'll be in two months, don't forget. I'm sorry. But please call me from wherever you are from time to time, so I won't worry."

"I will."

"Okay."

"Okay. Now, where do you want to have dinner?"

The woman laughed. "That place around the corner, the one with the Cobb salad I like so much. . . ."

He smiled to himself and switched off the receiver. They would emerge from the building in a few minutes, he reasoned, and he would shadow them while they were out. Then they were coming back here to spend the night: they'd already discussed that, too. He wouldn't listen in on that part of it. Well, *probably* not, anyway. . . .

And tomorrow, the mark—"Mark"—would go to Washington. Perfect.

9

It was over dessert and coffee in the restaurant that Mark first conceived the idea.

Tracy looked beautiful, as ever. She'd smiled and laughed all through dinner, her glowing face and sparkling blond hair reflected in the muted light of the candle between them. She'd had her famous Cobb salad, and he had ordered filet of sole, but he hadn't really been able to eat, being so distracted, so preoccupied. He pushed the fish and potatoes and string beans around on his plate, hoping she wouldn't notice that he was barely eating any of it. If she did notice, she didn't say anything, and for that he was grateful.

He had to do something.

Tracy ordered more white wine and launched herself into a couple of amusing stories, one about her mother's obsession with international bridge tournaments and the other about one of her authors. Mrs. Morgan was soon going to play in some high-stakes game somewhere, and the author, a mousy young woman named Edna Clapp who wrote gushing, semipornographic romantic fiction under the glamorous pseudonym Stella Verlaine, had decided on cosmetic surgery. This had struck Tracy as being hilarious, because the woman was cross-eyed: all the nose jobs and chin remodelings and boob jobs in the world would not improve her most distinctively unattractive feature. . . .

He could not go to the police.

Tracy finished her anecdote and looked over at him expectantly. He laughed perfunctorily. She finished her salad and said something he didn't quite catch, something about hot pecan pie with whipped cream. . . .

And he could not tell anyone; not Tracy, or Jared McKinley, or his agent, or his editor. No one.

The waiter arrived again, and Mark realized that Tracy had been telling him what she wanted for dessert. She ordered the pie for herself and coffee for both of them. . . .

But he had to be ready for this, ready for Scavenger.

Then the dessert and coffee arrived, and he suddenly realized what he was going to do. It frightened him, filled him with an alien coldness. But Scavenger—whoever he was, *whatever* he was—had not mentioned it in his instructions. And after the scene today on the sidewalk in front of 125 Kane Street, Mark wasn't going to take any chances.

Yes. . . .

He looked over at Tracy again, forcing himself back into the here and now, to this table in this restaurant. She mustn't suspect, he thought. She must not know what I am doing, or why. I must behave as normally as possible with her until I leave tomorrow morning. But tonight, while she's asleep, I will prepare myself for the game. For Scavenger.

He wondered, even as he planned, just how prepared anyone could be for a shadow, a phantom. He wondered what this madman had in store for him. Judging from today, the newspaper and the music and the Easter egg, it promised not to be very pleasant.

Mark took a deep breath and smiled again at Tracy. He had a sudden overwhelming desire to make love to her. He signaled for the check and paid, and the two of them went out of the restaurant into the cool April evening.

It was dark in the street, with only the occasional street lamp to light the way. They had just reached the one on the corner, waiting in a pool of light for a moving van to pass by in front of them, when Mark happened to glance across the street at the opposite corner.

There was no streetlight there: the entire other side was dark. Yet, for a single second, Mark had the impression that he saw something, a tall figure darker than the surrounding darkness. A very tall figure standing unnaturally still in front of the building on the opposite corner. It was only a second, not even that, but Mark's already frantic mind filled in the rest; the black hair, the pale eyes, the uncanny resemblance to Boris Karloff, a long black coat. And a scar: a long, thin white line down one side of the gaunt, staring face.

He would later reason that he could not have seen any of this, not in the darkness and shadows. It was, he would decide, something he had *felt* rather than seen, the knowledge of a presence across the street, watching him.

Then the van rattled noisily by in front of them and rumbled off down the street.

Mark blinked and looked again. The opposite corner was empty.

He turned immediately to Tracy. "Wait here."

"Mark, is something—"

He didn't hear the rest of what she said. He was already halfway across the street, dodging to narrowly miss the yellow taxi that whizzed by behind the van. He reached the opposite corner, peering into the gloom.

Nothing, anywhere. The corner, the street, all the stretches of sidewalk that he could see were empty. He blinked again, his heart racing. No, his rational mind told him, there had not been a man here a moment ago. It was impossible.

With that, he turned around and headed back to the light of the street lamp, to Tracy.

"What's up?" she asked. "You look like you've seen a ghost!"

"Sorry," he mumbled. "I thought—I thought I saw—someone I knew. I guess it *was* a ghost."

She smiled and placed her hand in his.

"Take me home, Mark," she said. "It's cold out here."

10

They made love that night. Tracy would remember that later, when she was trying to sort everything out in her mind. She and Mark made love, and it was wonderful, as usual, and shortly after that she dozed off. Then, somewhere in the early hours, she woke with the distinct sensation that someone was moving around the bedroom.

She sat up on the bed, aware of the dim light coming from the clothes closet on the other side of the room. When her sleepy vision cleared, she saw that Mark was silhouetted in the closet doorway, and he was doing something there. He was reaching up to pull something down from the shelf above the rack. Two things, she now saw: a small black box and a smaller red one. As she watched, he carried the two boxes across the room to the open suitcase on the chair in the corner and carefully laid them inside it. He stood there, his back to her, staring down at the suitcase.

"Mark?" she said. "Is something wrong? Why aren't you asleep?"

He whirled around to confront her, obviously startled by the sudden sound of her voice. And there was something else about his face: an odd expression she could barely make out in the dim light from the closet, a look she'd never seen there before. It was the look of a child who has been caught doing something naughty. That was her impression of it, at any rate. But the odd expression dissolved in an instant, to be immediately replaced by a smile.

He shrugged. "I can't seem to go to sleep tonight. I always get restless when I'm nearing a deadline. You should know that right now, before you marry me. You still have two months to change your mind. I was watching you, though, a little while ago. You're beautiful when you're dreaming."

Now she smiled, too, disarmed as she always was by him. "Thanks, I guess. But I wasn't dreaming—not that I recall, anyway. What time is it?"

"Nearly four," he replied. "I'm sorry I woke you. Go back to sleep."

She thought about arguing, about asking him what was preoccupying him, but she immediately thought better of it. He was being evasive about this sudden trip, about his work in progress, and she was going to have to respect that. She wouldn't pry, even though there was something about the two boxes she'd seen in his hands that bothered her, something she couldn't quite place. . . .

She settled back against the pillows and drifted off again.

When Tracy woke at seven-thirty, he was gone. She got out of bed, wrapping herself in his discarded bathrobe as she made her way around his apartment. She brushed her teeth and showered in his bathroom and dressed for work. She thought about the busy day ahead as she went into his kitchen to make coffee. She was having breakfast with a new client at nine, followed by two meetings, then lunch with an editor from Ballantine, and two more meetings. After that full itinerary, she was having dinner with her mother.

She was staring distractedly around Mark's immaculate, orderly kitchen, wondering for the hundredth time why this room and the rest of his apartment didn't seem to have any personal touches, when she recalled the earlier scene. She had been awakened by his moving around the bedroom, and he'd carried two boxes over to the suitcase. Now, awake and alert, she remembered clearly. A black box and a red box, just like the ones her father had kept in his bedside table in her childhood home. She'd found them there once, when she was seven or eight years old, and their contents had fascinated and chilled her. She'd never been able to ask her father about them, because she'd been snooping in her parents' bedroom, something she never, ever did again. The two boxes had scared her too much.

The black box had contained a big black gun, and the smaller red box had held ammunition. Bullets.

She raised a hand to her chest, wondering what had been in the two similar boxes Mark had packed and taken with him to Washington.

MONDAY

11

Ronald O'Hara would be in his mid-fifties now, Mark thought as he drove the rented Chevy Lumina through the suburbs of Washington. He was retired from the Federal Bureau of Investigation, and Mark knew all about that, too. He had apparently resigned in a fury when his superiors had suspended the file on the Family Man case due to a complete lack of new developments.

O'Hara had been obsessed with the case from the moment he had become involved in it, in Los Angeles thirteen years ago. He had led the FBI team that had been sent there following the Fourth of July massacre in the Hollywood Hills. Popular television actor Ian Webster and his family had been found on the holiday, four months after the first incident, the Mardi Gras murders near New Orleans. The first case had been a matter for the New Orleans police, but the L.A. incident occasioned the arrival of the Feds when it became apparent that the two cases were related. It was then that someone coined the name "The Family Man."

The Bureau could hardly be blamed for having brought the investigation to a halt. The two cases and the subsequent incidents in Illinois, upstate New York, and New York City had yielded nothing but bodies, holiday decorations, and only one brief suspect. Mark grimaced as he remembered this, and as he remembered O'Hara's well-documented rage at the director's decision to put aside the file. The Family Man had gradually faded from the public consciousness, except for the obligatory quickie true crime books and cheesy TV movies inspired by the case. And Mark's novel.

Now Mark was on his way to find the man who had given up his high-profile job, not to mention a good chance of promotion, over a case he probably never wanted to hear about again. And Mark was going to try to talk to him about just that. Add to that the fact that Mark was already one of O'Hara's least favorite people, and the forthcoming interview—if he found the man—was not something he approached with any joy.

No one else may know about the game.

He'd printed out the letter from the disk, and the pages were in his pocket. He'd practically memorized it by now, but he figured that particular instruction had been waived in the case of the former agent. The markings in the *New York Post* had indicated this action—at least, he hoped that was what it meant.

Mark slowed, a result of the steadily increasing number of cars before him. He was approaching the city proper, and he was doing it at three o'clock on a Monday afternoon. He'd only been to Washington three times before—once in his travels while in college, once as a *New York Post* reporter, and once recently for background, "local color" for his second novel. He had only the haziest memories of various landmarks, impersonal hotel rooms, and horrible traffic on virtually all roads at all times of the day. But not at night: this, unlike New York, was a daytime town. Even the cars disappeared at night. His most vivid memories were of the Lincoln Memorial, the Vietnam wall, the Kennedy Center, and the Smithsonian. He was always impressed by Washington's cleanliness. The public sections, at least, were immaculate, giving huge portions of the capital city the appearance of a lovingly tended public park, which, in a way, is precisely what it is.

At least the weather was good today, Mark mused. The sun shone brightly down from a blue sky only marginally dotted with clouds. The temperature was still brisk enough to warrant his leather jacket, but hat-and-glove season was definitely over for another year. He looked around at the city basking in the bright sunshine, realizing that the beautiful day was doing nothing to cheer him.

The highway gave way to streets, and the streets became hilly as he entered Georgetown. He passed the university and turned up a steep road, first checking his newly acquired gas station map to be sure it was the correct one. It was. He found the address halfway up the street, in a row of graceful townhouses that reminded him of Kane Street in Brooklyn yesterday. Parking was a problem: he had to turn around and search down another street before he found a space. Then he proceeded back up the hill on foot.

He stood before the building, remembering why all of this was familiar to him. One of the steep blocks nearby was well-known to everyone, courtesy of Hollywood. The Devil had once visited this place, years ago. In *The Exorcist*, Ellen Burstyn and her unfortunate daughter had resided in a townhouse just a short walk from here.

O'Hara's wife was Wanda Morris, the famous singer and actress, and it was she who owned this house. A federal agent, no matter how highly placed, could never have afforded it. Mark thought this as he went up the steps to the front door and rang the bell. He waited a minute, idly examining the black carriage lamps that flanked the door, then rang again. No response.

Great, he thought. A long drive for nothing, a day wasted. And he only had until midnight tonight, though he wasn't sure what he was to learn from the man. But Scavenger obviously wanted Mark here, so here he was.

He turned from the door and went back down the steps, trying to remember the name of a hotel in the area. The Watergate was the only name that sprang to mind, for obvious reasons, and he couldn't afford that. Some little place near the university where he had stayed three years ago on the research mission—Whitney? Whateley? Something like that. He'd find it and get a room for the night. A meal somewhere, then he'd come back here and try again. He started down the sidewalk toward the street where his car was parked, aware of a sudden feeling of relief that the interview would not take place just yet.

Then he stopped, staring, and the chill of anxiety returned. A large, powerfully built, middle-aged African-American man was coming up the hill toward him. The man was jogging, dressed in a light poplin jacket over a sweaty T-shirt and a pair of blue shorts. White socks and Nikes. He was panting from his exertion, pumping his huge arms as he ran.

It was O'Hara. He was older than Mark remembered, which stood to reason. His close-cropped hair was more gray than black now, and his mustache was nearly white. But the fierce eyes beneath the thick brows were the same, as was the scowl of his lips. As he approached, he looked up toward his destination and slowed, taking in the sight of the man who waited at the base of his front steps.

By the time he arrived before Mark, he had slowed his pace to a walk, and he was eyeing him with trepidation. And something more, Mark knew: distaste. He came to a stop, still panting slightly, not five feet from Mark. He continued to regard Mark as he removed a small towel from his waistband and wiped his gleaming face. The two men stood there on the sidewalk in Georgetown, staring.

"Well, well, well," O'Hara muttered at last. It was the menacing *basso profundo* voice Mark remembered all too well. "Matthew Farmer, as I live and breathe."

"Yes," Mark said.

Ronald O'Hara was not pleased to see him. His voice, his expression, everything about him conveyed that message. Mark wasn't surprised: he had been expecting it. He would have been surprised by any other reception.

Now the man glanced up at the house, then back. "Looking for me?" It was barely a question.

"Yes," Mark said again.

"Why?"

It was a perfectly simple question, but Mark had no simple way to answer it. He had to think a moment. "I—I have to talk to you."

The thick brows above the fierce eyes shot upward in grim amusement. "Writing another—*book*?" He managed to make it sound like a dirty word.

"No," Mark whispered. "But I—I have to talk to you about The Family Man."

The big man made a guttural sound that might have been a laugh. Then he shook his head, turned away from Mark, and went up the steps. He pulled a key ring from the pocket of his shorts and unlocked the door. In a moment he would be inside.

"Please!" Mark heard himself say to the man's back, wincing at his own impotence in this situation.

Ronald O'Hara turned around to face him. "There's nothing to talk about, Mr. Farmer. The Family Man is dead. The case is *closed*." He started to turn away again.

"No," Mark said. "It isn't. Not anymore."

O'Hara paused now, turning slowly back to stare at him. "What makes you say that?"

Mark shrugged, looking away. "Someone—someone has contacted me. I think they know who The Family Man is. *Was*. Whatever."

He saw O'Hara step forward, could almost hear the sudden intake of breath. "When?"

"Two days ago."

Another step. "Who?"

"I—I don't know. He's sending messages. I haven't seen him."

"How do you know it's a he?"

"I got a description of the man from my super's wife. She saw him."

O'Hara was obviously intrigued, but he was still wary. "What makes you think this guy knew The Family Man?"

Mark shrugged again. "Because he's sending me all over the place, collecting clues that are supposed to lead me to The Family Man's identity. He sent me here."

"He sent you to *me*?"

"Yes."

"Why?"

The burning gaze was too much for Mark: he looked away from the man. "I think you're supposed to help me figure out my next move."

Now the agent leaned back against the doorframe. "What do you mean, your 'next move'? 'Collecting clues'? Sounds like some kind of treasure hunt."

"It is. He's playing a game with me, a scavenger hunt. He calls himself Scavenger."

There was a pause. Then the man said, "Uh-huh. And why is he suddenly interested in *you*?"

"He read my novel, *Dark Desire*."

O'Hara grunted. "Yeah, I read it, too. You made me a white man in the story, thank you very much! What does this Scavenger want you to do now—write the *real* story?"

"Yes," Mark said. "That's exactly what he wants me to do."

The eyebrows went up again. "Why you?"

Mark forced himself to look into the fierce eyes and hold the gaze. "Why do you think?"

O'Hara held the gaze, too. "Are you telling me he knows who you really are?"

Whatever reply Mark might have been about to utter flew from him as the equilibrium flew from his body. He felt it in his ankles, his knees, all the way up his spine. His vision blurred, and he reached out with his arm to grab on to something, anything, but he clutched at empty space. One moment he was standing there, confronting O'Hara, and in the next instant he was not standing at all. He was lying on the sidewalk.

He recovered almost immediately. He sat up, blinking, aware of the harsh curse and the pounding as O'Hara came down the steps. The big man reached down and helped him to his feet. Mark stood there, still blinking, feeling the first surge of embarrassment at his ridiculousness as he sagged helplessly against the other man's shoulder.

"You'd better come inside, Mr. Farmer," O'Hara muttered.

He nodded and took a deep breath to clear his head. Then Mark Stevenson of New York City, formerly Matthew Farmer of Chicago, the only living member of the Farmer family, one of only three survivors of The Family Man, climbed the steps behind the former federal agent in charge of the case. The man who had once suspected him of the crimes. The man whose accusations had led to the eventual disappearance of Matthew Farmer and the birth, twelve years ago, of Mark Stevenson.

He nearly stumbled at the top of the steps. O'Hara reached out his hand to steady him, and the two men went into the house together.

12

He was beginning to enjoy this.

The man had collapsed. Fainted. That was what it had looked like, anyway. He wondered vaguely if there was something he didn't know about "Mark," about his general health. Perhaps he was diabetic or anemic. But nothing in the available information that had been amassed indicated any such problem. He guessed—and he was probably right—that it was simply the strain, the emotion of this meeting with this particular person from his past. Former FBI Special Agent Ronald O'Hara. . . .

O'Hara. He thought about that, about the two men who had just disappeared into the house. Had this part been a mistake? It was the most questionable, in some ways the weakest element of the plan. But no: human nature being what it is, Ronald O'Hara would probably offer the next logical information, the next move in the game. He was counting on it.

If not—well . . .

He smiled, giving the pretty brownstone up the hill a last, satisfied glance before proceeding down the side street toward the rented Chevy Lumina, reaching inside his black duster as he walked. When he arrived at the car, he scanned the sidewalks and windows up and down the quiet street for possible witnesses. No, there was nobody watching him. Good.

Popping the lock on the passenger side took mere seconds. He opened the door boldly, forthrightly, so that any casual observer would have no reason to suspect him. But no one entered the street or emerged from a building as he briefly leaned inside the car, and his task took less time than opening the door. He closed the door again, making sure it was once again locked.

Then, with a last glance around, the tall man in the black duster glided away down the sidewalk. In a moment he had disappeared.

13

"Here," O'Hara said.

Mark took the brandy glass from the big man and sipped. The reviving warmth flowed through him as he settled back into the overstuffed armchair in O'Hara's living room, gazing around. O'Hara went upstairs to take a shower, so Mark had a few minutes to himself.

This was—or had been—the home of a woman. Definitely. The creamy walls and polished wood floors, the muted Oriental rugs, the heavy drapes at the big front windows, the carefully chosen furniture—everything in this room had been coordinated by someone other than the gruff, volatile man who now dominated it: O'Hara's wife, better known as Miss Morris. Wonderful Wanda, to music lovers everywhere. But when Mark had asked after her before sinking weakly into the chair, the former agent had muttered, "She's not here anymore."

Photographs, Mark thought. There are no photographs in this room, although it cries out for them. Several bookshelves and tables were bare of the expected silver-framed pictures: frozen moments of happiness in the lives of a family. Miss Morris had two grown sons by her first husband, now deceased, a jazz trumpeter as famous as she, and the two boys had been brought up in this house, by this man. Yet there were no mementos of them or their beautiful mother anywhere. Their absence was conspicuous.

Perhaps Mark had been wrong about who owned the house. He wouldn't ask; not now, not under these circumstances. But he wondered if Ronald O'Hara's twenty-plus-year marriage was yet another victim of The Family Man.

As Mark was thinking this, the big man came back into the room. He'd changed into a pair of old jeans and a faded black T-shirt with a bold message in white lettering on the front that read, STRIP SEARCH SPECIALIST. Mark blinked at the whimsical joke, briefly imagining the rowdy male colleagues on some beery, smoky, long-ago occasion, presenting their stern colleague with the entirely inappropriate gift. He could almost hear their raucous laughter, and he wondered if the man who now lowered himself to the couch across from him had so much as smiled when they presented it to him. Probably not. But he wore the shirt, had obviously worn it many times, which was interesting.

"So, tell me about this Scavenger," O'Hara growled without preamble. He leaned forward, elbows on knees, studying Mark's face, waiting for the witness to give his statement.

At least Mark was a witness now, as opposed to a suspect. Their relationship was improving. He stared at the man a moment, remembering his home in Evanston that cold, rainy Christmas Day thirteen years ago. The bodies of his parents and his brother, Joshua, and his sister, Mary, and the housekeeper, Mrs. Tornquist. And the dog, the collie Sam, which his sister had persuaded their silent, fearful mother to let her keep in the garage, despite Reverend Farmer's displeasure. The winking tree and the garlands, and the carol that played over and over on the portable cassette player on the table in the living room. "Jingle Bells." His father had not allowed a tree or decorations in the house, to say nothing of music, because the commercialization of Christ's birth by the nonbelievers was an abomination. It had all been placed there, part of the staging, a theatrical set for the bodies on the couches and chairs around the room. The four slashed throats—five, counting Sam. And his father, sitting in his usual easy chair, his severed head in a garish holiday box beneath the tree several feet away from his body, staring up from the blood-soaked tissue.

He remembered the freezing rain, and the ride in the backseat of an unmarked black car to the nearest precinct, and the spare, airless, cork-lined room where he had been interrogated for several hours by this man and four others. The popping flashbulbs from the press as he was taken in, only to walk out again nearly twelve hours later. Mark did not believe in God; not then, and certainly not now. God was something his family had believed in, and look where it had gotten them.

He thought all of this in a matter of seconds. Brief flashes, freeze-frame images from his memory. He pushed them away again and confronted O'Hara. In answer to the former agent's question, he took the folded printout pages from the inner pocket of the worn leather jacket that now lay across the arm of his chair. He unfolded Scavenger's letter, smoothing out the paper, and handed it over, briefly explaining about Hackers, the coffee bar where the letter had been written. Then he sat back in the chair again, watching the man as he read, wondering what he was thinking. This was a futile speculation: he had never known, would probably never know.

"Hmm," O'Hara breathed at last. "Saturday. Then what?"

Mark told him about 125 Kane Street, and the newspaper with O'Hara's photo circled by a red marker, punctuated with a question mark. The mysterious ten thousand in his checking account. The rented car and the drive here to Washington.

O'Hara nodded. "Describe the man."

Mark described him, just as Marisa Ramos and her husband had done.

"Hmm," O'Hara muttered again. "Not familiar." He leaned back on the couch, and his permanently angry gaze wandered over to the front windows. "Could be an employee."

"Employee?" The moment he echoed the man's final word, Mark cringed, remembering his father's long-ago exhortation never to do that. It made a person sound half-witted. Reverend Jacob Farmer had been big on his children not sounding half-witted.

"Working for someone else," O'Hara supplied, as if Mark were indeed stupid. "This tall man with the scar could be legs."

Mark suppressed his instinct to repeat the final word again. He could figure out what "legs" meant.

"The point is," the former agent went on, "to find out who's behind it. Someone connected to the case, I should think. They sent you to the last murder scene, and to me. Now you and I are apparently supposed to guess the next move."

"I don't want you involved," Mark heard himself say. "He may have sent me here for a consultation, or whatever, but if you actually *do* anything, he may stop."

O'Hara shot him a look, and Mark was once more reminded of his father, the Fundamentalist minister. "I know that." Then he leaned forward again, studying Mark. "Matthew: Mark. That's easy enough. And Stevenson was"—he thought a moment, apparently remembering old police reports—"your mother's maiden name. Yes. So Mark Stevenson wrote that book, and someone with a great interest in the case figured out who you were." He examined Mark again, his dark eyes sweeping him from head to foot, like a searchlight. "You had long blond hair then. Bleached. And you had that beard and that earring. That's how you looked in all the published pictures. You were, what? Twenty-two? Twenty-three? You're quite different now. And you've lost that dazed, glazed look. You're not on drugs anymore."

Mark forced a thin smile. "Thirteen years, one day at a time."

"Good," O'Hara said. "You don't look like the same person."

"I'm not the same person. Matthew Farmer died with—with the rest of his family."

"Yes, I can see that." O'Hara looked him over once more before returning his gaze to Mark's eyes. "The Family Man is dead. I'm certain of it. He would have—he would have continued, otherwise. Perhaps he killed himself, or perhaps it was a car crash or a barroom brawl or an earthquake. Whatever it was, I hope he died screaming. I hope it hurt a lot. But he's gone."

Mark nodded, returning the gaze. "I think so, too."

"So why now?" O'Hara asked the air between them. "Why you, *now*? That's what we have to figure out. Someone—a relative, a neighbor, one of the cops, or—or one of my people. *Someone* knew something about him. Has known all these years. They waited until you surfaced, until you wrote that novel, before coming forward. Which makes me wonder. . . ."

Mark drained the brandy glass and set it down on the coffee table between them, coughing slightly at the unfamiliar burning sensation in his throat. He avoided alcohol, as he avoided the cocaine and pills that had once been such a big part of his life. Once. Before The Family Man. He watched O'Hara stand up and wander over to the nearest front window, waiting for him to continue.

The big man gazed out at the darkening view, his back to Mark. He would be able to see the houses across the way, Mark supposed, but not much more than that. The darkness was entering the room. Mark reached over and switched on the standing lamp beside his chair.

"Okay," O'Hara said at last. "What did we have? The Tennant family in New Orleans, Mardi Gras. The Webster family in L.A., Fourth of July." He turned to glance at Mark. "The Farmers in Evanston, Christmas." Then he looked back out the window. "The Carlins in Green Hills, New York, the following Halloween. And the Banes family in Brooklyn, the Easter Sunday after that. Two years, start to finish. Five local forces. And us, the Bureau. I had, let's see, about forty people working for me, one way or another, and maybe a dozen field people in each location. A hundred federal people, or thereabouts. Some were on the case exclusively, but most of them were doing several things at once. Most of those people are still with the Bureau, and none of them had any personal ties to the case. Ditto the local cops. If we cross off the professionals, that leaves three people. Well, *two*, actually."

He stopped speaking abruptly, turning around to face Mark again. He appeared to be thinking, coming to some kind of decision. After a moment he blinked, glanced at his watch, and crossed the room to the archway leading to the front hall. "Come on."

Mark stood up and followed the man as he crossed the hall into the dining room, switching on lights as he went. They made their way through the swinging door on the other side of the room into the kitchen. The lights were bright here, gleaming on the modern metal fixtures and the white tile and porcelain. There was a butcher-block-covered island workspace in the center of the room, with copper and cast-iron cookware suspended from a grid attached to the ceiling above it. The curtained back window above the double sink afforded a view of the rest of Georgetown. A beautiful room, a woman's kitchen: the offstage presence that was Wanda Morris asserted itself yet again.

He watched in fascinated silence as O'Hara reached into the refrigerator and produced an enormous, raw sirloin steak on a platter. Next came lettuce and tomatoes and onion and cucumber from the crisper compartment. A box of seashell pasta from a cabinet. A large pot was filled with water and set on the range to boil, and the broiler beneath the oven was set to preheat. The vegetables were placed on the island, followed by a big plastic bowl. Then O'Hara pulled a long knife from a rack near the stove. He hesitated a moment, glancing from the shiny blade to Mark and back again. There was a brief flash of something unreadable on his face. Then he extended the knife to his guest and jabbed a thumb at the bowl.

Mark nodded, took the potential deadly weapon the former agent had thought twice about giving him, and began to make the salad. "So, I guess this means you don't suspect me anymore."

"I never did, really," O'Hara said as he measured coffee into a filter and placed it in the coffeemaker. "We were desperate by that point. But don't expect an apology. I apologized formally at the time—and to the media, no less. I'm not sorry for interrogating you. You *were* a suspect, however unlikely."

Mark looked up from slicing the cucumber. "What do you mean, unlikely?"

"Okay, you were a runaway college dropout junkie who had a hate on for your dad. And you were only twelve miles away at the crucial time, with your girlfriend. We knew that much. But we were certain it was Family Man. Besides, Ms. Barlow alibied you. And I observed you later, at the funeral." He slid the steak into the broiler. "And I talked to your sponsor in Narcotics Anonymous. He said you were planning to reconcile with your family at the time of—well, at the time." He glanced over at Mark as he poured pasta into the boiling water. "That's why you went home that Christmas morning, right? You were going to bury—I beg your pardon, I mean you were going to try again with them."

Mark nodded, noting the other man's discomfort at what he'd almost said: *bury the hatchet.* In the circumstances, it would have been a horrible thing to say. "I told you that when you questioned me." He'd been thinking of Judy Barlow, his girlfriend and fellow former addict, when something else O'Hara had said registered with him. "You talked to my sponsor? Wow, so much for the *A* in N.A. . . ."

O'Hara shrugged. "He was working for me."

Mark paused again in his chopping. "Nick was a *Fed*? Funny, he told *me* he was a heroin addict."

"He was." O'Hara was getting dinner plates and silverware from various cabinets and drawers. "He's still with the Bureau. He now has the job I used to have."

Mark almost asked him if he missed his job, but thought better of it. Instead he said, "Back in the living room, you said something about three people, or two, actually. What were you talking about?"

O'Hara was checking the broiler. "How do you like your steak?"

"Rare."

"Good. As soon as you finish with the salad, dinner's ready." He drained the pasta and added butter and parmesan cheese to it. As he worked, he said, "I was thinking about the three survivors. The daughter in New Orleans, the son in Green Hills—and you."

Mark tossed the greens in the bowl and took the oil and vinegar O'Hara held out to him. "Yes, that makes three of us. Why did you say, 'Two, actually'?"

O'Hara shrugged as he sliced the steak in half and transferred it to the dinner plates. "Seth Carlin, the guy in Green Hills, New York, is dead. I heard he did himself, with sleeping pills or something, not long after his family was murdered. And then there were two, as Agatha Christie once observed. You and Sarah Tennant."

He added pasta to each plate before picking them up and heading for the swinging door. Mark followed with the salad.

"Sarah Tennant," Mark said as they went into the dining room. "Tell me about her."

"Let's eat first. I'm hungry, and I'm sure you are, too. Then I'll tell you about Sarah." He met Mark's gaze as they sat down at the table. "You should know about her."

"Why?" Mark asked.

O'Hara picked up his fork before replying.

"I think she may be your next stop."

14

Mrs. Morgan picked up her fork before replying.

"I think she may be your next stop."

Tracy reached for her water glass, hoping the action would mask her grimace. This was the last thing she needed, advice from her mother. But her mother was concerned, and her argument, in this case, was legitimate. Mrs. Morgan had liked Tracy's first husband, Alan. She had trusted him and believed him, as Tracy had, and she was as disappointed as her daughter when she learned that her trust in him was misplaced. Once burned, twice shy: Mrs. Morgan had actually used that phrase a few minutes ago, as they had sat down to spaghetti at her dinner table overlooking the East River.

Even so, Tracy had to wonder about her mother's advice. She would have to think about it, assess the possibilities of it. She was also a bit surprised that the perfectly simple solution had not occurred to her.

Well, it wasn't perfectly simple. Nothing was.

"It's just a suggestion," Mrs. Morgan added, handing her daughter a warm slice of garlic toast. "I mean, how many women have your option? You're getting married in June, committing yourself. *Again.* And you yourself admit that you don't know anything about Mark. Well, what I mean to say is, you don't know *enough* about him. I must say he's charming—but so was Alan. Your father and I—"

"I know, Mother," Tracy offered quickly, hoping to stem the tide before the floodgates opened. "You and Dad were crazy about Alan."

"Yes. Your father didn't live to see your divorce, but if he were here, I know he'd agree with me on this."

Tracy nodded distractedly, wondering how her mother was so uncannily able to zero in on the very subjects she was trying to avoid.

They'd been talking about dresses for the simple civil service she and Mark were planning, and the small reception after the ceremony. Then, somehow, the discussion of designers and restaurants had given way to this one, the What Do You Really Know About This Man speech. It was a mother thing, obviously.

"Okay, Mother," she heard herself saying. "I'll think about it. I really will. Now let me tell you about my new client, the one I met this morning. . . ."

With the deft finesse she usually reserved for negotiations with publishers, Tracy guided the conversation away from the danger zone to safer waters. Her new author, the first novelist whose book was sure to be a big hit. The various publishing houses that were already calling with offers. Mrs. Morgan's own news, the upcoming international bridge tournament she and her friends were planning to attend.

But all the while, as the spaghetti gave way to ice cream and the lights of Queens across the river appeared beyond Mrs. Morgan's picture window, Tracy thought about her mother's suggestion. It would be difficult to do. It might be impossible. And it would certainly be embarrassing. But it would answer some questions, she was sure of it. And for that alone, it might be worth it.

She regarded her mother as she spoke, and she remembered her late father. Henry and Irene Morgan had been the best kind of parents, she knew: loving and attentive and nurturing. They had provided her with everything a child and, later, a young woman could possibly want or need. Private schools, tuition to Harvard, trips to Europe, a car. They'd even helped her finance the Gramercy Park co-op. They'd entertained a long line of friends and boyfriends, never once objecting or balking at her choices. As a child, she'd announced the usual assortment of professions to which she aspired: actress, ballet dancer, Olympic gymnast, policewoman. Her parents had smiled and nodded enthusiastically, knowing that things would change.

And they had. She'd always loved books. From early childhood she'd read voraciously, anything she could get her hands on. When, in her junior year of high school, she'd told them she wanted to be a writer, they were delighted with the choice. Her father had immediately suggested Harvard, his alma mater, and offered to pay for it. She'd insisted on augmenting his payment with her own contributions, and she'd found babysitting jobs and waited tables and tutored other students in English. When she graduated *cum laude*, her parents beamed. She'd soon decided that she didn't enjoy writing as much as finding and promoting other writers, and they had supported that decision, too. Her first job as an editor's assistant at Bantam, her eventual employment by the Jaffee/Douglas Agency, her early author clients, her first bestselling writer, her various romances, her wedding to Alan: all had been approved of and applauded. And now, with her father gone, her mother was continuing the tradition alone.

Tracy loved her mother, and she knew that the suggestion had been a kind one. She had also been wondering all afternoon about the two boxes she'd seen Mark putting in the suitcase, which led inevitably to the next question in her mind. She smiled at her mother and nodded, only half listening to the details of the bridge tournament, thinking:

Where are you, Mark?

15

Mark was back in the living room of O'Hara's house, and the two of them were drinking coffee. After their meal, they had cleaned up the kitchen and loaded the dishwasher. From the way O'Hara did these things, Mark was certain that the man was unused to living alone, unaccustomed to fending for himself in the kitchen. Miss Morris's departure was apparently very recent, and any maids or housekeepers there might have been had evidently departed with her.

O'Hara lit a cigar and settled back on the couch. He regarded Mark silently for a long while, and Mark knew instinctively not to break the silence. Whatever the big man had to say, he would say it when he was ready. That was his way, and there was no changing it. Mark knew this, as he knew that it had cost the man dearly to invite the former suspect into his house and discuss a case that was obviously still painfully frustrating for him.

But he *had* invited Mark in. Mark had succeeded in what he had been instructed to do, and he shook his head now as he remembered his trepidation yesterday, in his apartment in New York City. Now, twenty-four hours later, here he was with the man he was supposed to see.

At last O'Hara said, "I believe Sarah Tennant is still in New Orleans. She was nineteen when the murders occurred, a student at Yale, majoring in drama. She and a couple of her student friends were staying at her family's house outside New Orleans on the weekend before Mardi Gras. On Monday night, Lundi Gras, she and her friends went into town, and they crashed with another friend who lived there. They did the whole Mardi Gras thing the next day, the parades and all that, and they came back to the Tennant house at about two o'clock Wednesday morning. That's when they found the rest of her family. They'd been dead nearly twenty-four hours. I guess you know that much; everybody does. And you wrote the book, so to speak."

Mark nodded.

"Well, Sarah had a bad time for a while," O'Hara continued. "She was treated for shock, and later for depression. She went to live with an uncle, her father's brother, in downtown New Orleans, and she never completed her education. She joined an amateur drama group while working in her uncle's law firm as a secretary. I understand she married a young local lawyer. But she's had recurring psychological problems. Anyway, she and her husband are still in New Orleans, so far as I know."

Mark leaned forward. "Mr. O'Hara—"

The former agent held up a big hand. "Ron. You might as well call me Ron. I'll call you Mark, I guess, seeing as that's the name you use now."

"Okay. Ron, you resigned from the FBI—when was it? Six years ago?"

"Seven."

"Seven. Okay. So how do you know all this about Sarah Tennant?"

O'Hara shrugged and relit his cigar. "I'm still interested in the case. I guess I've kept up with all the players. I kept up with *you*, as soon as I found you again—or, rather, *you* found *me*—last year. You used to be a journalist, and you were married to a woman named Carol Johnson, now Carol Grant. You've just announced your engagement to a literary agent named Teresa Morgan, or Tracy, as everyone calls her, and the two of you are planning to marry in June. I've read all four of your books—which are quite good, by the way. But did you have to make my character in *Dark Desire* a honky?"

Mark stared at the big man with the cigar, and their eyes met over a plume of smoke. Then they both began to laugh. Mark had never seen Ronald O'Hara laugh before; he gave himself over to it, his whole body shaking from the force of his deep bellows of mirth. For the first time since his arrival in Washington, Mark actually relaxed.

"Lawsuits," he explained when he had caught his breath. "My publisher's legal department thought it was a good idea. They told me to keep everyone—especially you—as far from reality as possible. I had to make some changes in the manuscript, and that was one of them."

O'Hara's deep laughter had diminished by now to a low chuckle.

"I wouldn't have sued you. Hell, you even let my character *catch* the guy, which was a damn sight more satisfying than—well, than anything that actually happened. Thank you for that, I guess."

"You're welcome," Mark said. "I wrote the book as a sort of catharsis, I suppose. You know, closure, to use the popular new term. I guess I wanted that fictional ending more than anybody—even you. But tell me, why did you say you thought Sarah Tennant was my next stop?"

O'Hara put down his cigar and leaned back on the couch again, watching Mark across the coffee table. He frowned and licked his lips, as if trying to form words in his mind. His hands fidgeted in his lap.

"You're not going to believe this," he said at last. "Hell, *I* don't believe it. I think—I think your friend Scavenger told me."

"*What?*" Mark's coffee cup landed on the saucer with a clatter. O'Hara stood up and reached over to take them from his hands. He placed them on the table and went over to the front window, as he had done earlier. Mark got up from the armchair and followed him. He stood behind the big man, looking over his shoulder at the lights of Georgetown, waiting for him to explain his extraordinary statement.

He did. Without turning from the view, he said, "It was about a week ago. I didn't think twice about it until today, when you arrived here and explained your business. I—I got a phone call. I answered the phone, and I heard a man's voice say, 'Tell him to talk to Sarah.' I said, 'What?' and he repeated it. Then he hung up. I thought it was a wrong number. I didn't recognize the voice, and I don't know anyone named Sarah. I never thought of Sarah *Tennant*. It was only when I remembered her today that I remembered the phone call. But I'll bet the farm it was Scavenger."

"So will I," Mark whispered.

Now O'Hara turned around to face him. "Whoever this is, whatever they think they're doing, they seem to have it all planned down to the last detail. What I don't understand is, why didn't they just go to the police or to the Bureau? Why the elaborate game?"

"I don't know," Mark said.

"Hmm. Neither do I. Well, we may be able to clear up some of it, at least. The telephone's over there, next to the couch. You can call Sarah Tennant in New Orleans. Maybe she knows something."

Mark blinked. "No, I can't call her. I—I have to go there. You saw the letter: that's the way it works. Whatever he—she, it—whatever *they* have planned for me, I have to do it in person. I'll have to retrieve the next object, whatever it is. Those are the rules."

O'Hara shook his head and looked back out the window. "So what are you going to do now, tonight?"

Mark shrugged. "There's a little hotel near the university—"

"You can stay here tonight if you want," O'Hara said.

"No," Mark said quickly. "Thanks for the offer, but I don't think that's a good idea. You've already given me enough of your time. Besides, I have to assume that my actions are being monitored. If I stay here too long, Scavenger might not like it."

O'Hara turned back to him again. "You think someone's following you?"

"Yes," Mark said. "I do."

The two men looked out the window again at the lights of the city. Then O'Hara reached up and quickly closed the curtains. Without a word, Mark went over to collect his jacket, and the former federal agent led him out of the living room and down the hallway to the front door. Only when they arrived there did Mark finally bring himself to ask the question he'd been wanting to ask all evening.

"What do you do now, Ron? I mean, now that you don't work for the FBI."

"I'm a consultant for a corporate security firm. I test security equipment and train others how to operate it. But I—I'm talking to another former agent about opening a private detective agency."

Mark nodded. "You'd be a good private eye. Good luck with it."

"Thanks." O'Hara opened the door, and Mark stepped out into the surprisingly cool evening air. "Be careful, Mark. I don't know if the people you're dealing with are actually dangerous, but don't count on them being nice. What they're doing is definitely *not* nice. Do you have any protection?"

"Yes," Mark said. "I have a gun. It's licensed, and I know how to use it."

"Okay," O'Hara said. "Watch yourself. I wish I could help you more. Hell, I wish I could go with you. But I think you're right about me scaring them off. I just want you to make me a promise. If you find out who The Family Man was, you let me know first thing."

"I promise," Mark said.

O'Hara pulled his wallet from his pants, rummaged in it, and handed Mark a card. "That's my number, if you need me for anything. Don't hesitate to ask. I've got a lot of spare time on my hands these days. And I've still got friends with the Bureau who may be able to help out, too."

They stood there in the doorway for a moment, regarding each other. Mark studied the man's face for signs of what was going on behind it, but, as usual, it was an inscrutable, unreadable mask. He felt that he should say something, ask something that would somehow strengthen the link he thought they had forged together in the past few hours. He'd never have imagined this imposing, authoritative man as a possible friend before today. And now he was surprised and disconcerted by the prospect. He was surprised most of all by the sudden certainty that this man's friendship might be invaluable, something to be desired.

Yet he did not speak. He could not think of anything to say. As if sensing this, Ronald O'Hara was the one who broke the silence. He looked away down the dark street for a long moment, lost in thought. Then he put his arm on Mark's elbow, drawing him back inside the house, and shut the door.

"Come with me," he said. "Before you leave, I want to show you something."

He led the way back through the living room and down a hallway beside the staircase. At the back of the house, across the hall from the kitchen, was another door. He opened it, switched on the light, and motioned Mark forward. He stood aside in the doorway as Mark walked past him into the room.

Mark stared around him. This place was obviously Ron O'Hara's private sanctum. It was his office, but it was more than that. There was a desk with a computer on it near the only window, and one wall was lined, floor to ceiling, with crowded bookshelves. But it was the other three white walls of the room that arrested Mark's attention. Framed photos and newspaper clippings covered almost all of their surface. The houses in New Orleans, Los Angeles, Evanston, Green Hills, and Brooklyn. O'Hara, somewhat younger, surrounded by agents and technicians and medical personnel, in several of the places, including Mark's own living room. The headlines of the clipped, framed articles were similar to each other in that every one of them included the same two words in various sizes of bold typeprint: FAMILY MAN. There must have been thirty or forty clippings, and nearly as many photos.

In the center of one wall, dominating everything else, was a large map of the United States, with pins and labels clustered around the five crime areas. As Mark gazed at it all, drinking it in, he was aware of a rising sense of otherworldliness, of a passion, an obsession, the extent of which he would never had suspected had he not seen this place. And he was aware of something else: the silence behind him, and the sensation of eyes studying him as he studied the shrine. He felt a cold trickle of sweat break loose from his temple and course slowly down the side of his face.

He stood there for a long time, staring, unable to will himself to turn around and face the man in the doorway. When Ron O'Hara finally broke the eerie silence in the room, his voice seemed to be coming from far away.

"You know, it was the worst thing that ever happened to me. I lost my parents before that, and several friends—a couple in the line of duty. But none of those things compared to the loss of The Family Man. There wasn't the embarrassment, the humiliation. The constant, never-ending *frustration*. They called it a resignation." He laughed bitterly. "I didn't resign; they *fired* me. Because I wouldn't give it up, even after they told me to. I just knew I *had* to find him. Bring him in. Make him pay for what he did. Twenty-four people slaughtered like the animals that died with them—many of them young people, practically children. And those are just the people we knew about. My only consolation is the knowledge that the son of a bitch is dead. He must be dead." Mark heard him draw in a long, deep breath. "He'd *better* be dead."

Now, at last, he came into the room and walked around to stand before Mark. "Someone—this Scavenger, whoever it is—says they know who he was. I want to know, too. I have to know. I lost my job, my wife, my stepsons. Everything. All I can do now is dance on his grave. At least give me *that*."

Mark forced himself to look up at him. Ron O'Hara stood there, and at last the mask had fallen away. His face reflected all the pain of which he had just spoken. Mark put a hand out to rest on the man's arm and nodded.

"Okay," Mark said.

O'Hara motioned for Mark to leave the room. He switched off the light, closed the door, and led his guest back through the house to the entrance. Mark walked out into the cool evening and turned around on the doorstep. He looked at the big man, then at the big, empty house behind him. Before he moved, he said, "Are you going to be all right?"

"Sure," O'Hara said, smiling. "And so are you. We're both going to be just fine. Good night, Mark."

"Good night." Mark forced a smile, too, and then he went down the hill in the direction of his car. After a moment, he heard the heavy oak door close firmly behind him.

16

When Matthew Farmer came out of the house, he was waiting for him. He stood in the shadows of a doorway down the street, watching the exchange between the two men. The FBI agent looked sad, and Matthew Farmer looked concerned. He couldn't make out their words, but he got the gist of it from watching the pantomime.

O'Hara had obviously done his job, mentioned the phone call to the writer, and now he would be on his way.

Good.

He would follow the man now, back to his car. His own car was parked just up the street. When Matthew Farmer began to drive, he would be right behind him.

And here he came now. He descended the front steps of O'Hara's house and approached down the hill, while behind him O'Hara went inside and closed the door.

The tall man in the black duster shrank back into the doorway, watching as Matthew Farmer passed within mere feet of him. He noted the look in the writer's eyes: he was obviously preoccupied, thinking hard about something. "A million miles away," as his wife, Anna, used to say.

Anna . . .

No. He wouldn't think about that now. Now there were things to do. He put the thought away, storing it in the sealed vault where he kept his most vivid memories.

He would wait until the writer turned the corner into the side street where he had parked his car, and then he would steal closer. He wanted to let the man feel his presence, be aware of him. He wanted Matthew Farmer to be afraid.

He wondered what the man was thinking about that would cause that odd look, that preoccupied, million-miles-away expression in his eyes.

He left the doorway and glided silently closer, reaching up inside his coat to finger the eight-inch blade in its sheath at his side. Perhaps I should forget about the game, he thought. Perhaps I should just finish it, right here.

Right now. . . .

17

The rain was the image that would not leave him. It had snowed for several days before, but then the snow turned to freezing rain. Not quite sleet: it was definitely liquid in form, falling uninterrupted throughout the night of Christmas Eve, and it continued on Christmas Day. Whenever he thought about it, which was every day of his life, he remembered the rain. That, and the bitter cold.

He had been in the warm bed in the warm apartment in Old Town, with the warm body of Judy beside him. He had gotten up and made breakfast for both of them, and it was all he could do to wake her. She had stood in the doorway waving, wrapped in a blanket, as he drove her battered old VW away through the cold rain, and he knew she would go back to bed as soon as the car was out of sight. But she had been the one to talk him into going to see his family on this holiday morning, and she waved from the doorway as a sign of encouragement. Dear, sweet, perfectly nice Judy, whom he would leave behind as he left Chicago behind. As he left Matthew Farmer behind. And all as a result of what he would find at the end of that morning's twelve-mile journey. The end of his life. The end of Matthew Farmer. . . .

Mark came to a halt now at the corner of the side street where he had parked his car, and the memories of thirteen years ago abruptly left him. He stood there, feeling the chill of the evening. And something else, something he couldn't quite define. He turned slowly around in a circle, his gaze sweeping the houses that lined the hillside street he had just descended. Porch lights glowed at the tops of picturesque steps, and he could see the two carriage lamps that framed O'Hara's door, now far away up the hill. There were streetlights as well, and he could hear the low sound of voices from a television in the corner house beside him. Somewhere, away down the street he was just entering, a dog barked. He couldn't see the dog or anything else in the darkness that surrounded him, the darkness punctuated only by those little porch lights. But everything seemed still, at peace: he was alone in the street.

Yet not alone. In that moment, as he stood there blinking at the darkness around him, Mark was overwhelmingly aware of the other presence. He was certain of it, as certain as he had ever been of anything.

Scavenger was here. Scavenger was very close by, watching him from the shadows. The tall man with the black hair and the scar down his face, the man who had reminded Marisa Ramos of the horror movie star. Mark could feel the man's gaze boring into his skin. He fancied he could almost hear the man's breathing, his heartbeat. He felt his malevolence, coming at him from everywhere at once, everywhere in the dark.

The writer in Mark came suddenly forward, filling his mind with vivid scenarios. Perhaps the man was waiting in one of the doorways, or crouched behind a car, clutching a long, sharp blade as he watched Mark's progress down the street. Perhaps he would leap suddenly, silently, out of nowhere, everywhere, to grasp Mark in a viselike hold, forcing his head back as he whipped the cold steel across his throat. The blood would gush silently out, and Mark would fall to the sidewalk, choking, dying, as the huge, dark figure of Boris Karloff slithered quietly away into the darkness—

Mark took a slow, deep breath and let it out, thinking of the gun in the suitcase, locked in the trunk of the rented Chevy. Willing himself not to run, not to display anything that could be construed as panic, he walked forward through the deep shadows toward the car. It was parked halfway down the street, perhaps a hundred yards from the corner, and the walk seemed to take forever. The echo of his footsteps resounded in the quiet, empty place, bouncing off the houses and parked cars as he passed them, doubling back on him. His own footsteps seemed to be following him.

Despite his best effort at composure, he actually ran the final few steps to the car, pulling the keys from his pocket as he went. He hurried around the car, and he was reaching down to unlock the driver's door when he stopped short. He leaned over and pressed his face against the rear window, peering into the backseat. No, there was no figure concealed there. Of course not, he told himself. The car was locked. He actually chuckled to himself as he opened the door and slid onto the driver's seat. The well-maintained engine came to life with the first turn of the key in the ignition. He switched on the headlights and reached for the gearshift.

He froze, staring. There, in the passenger seat next to him, was a little box wrapped in shiny black paper, decorated with a shiny black ribbon identical to the one that had wrapped the newspaper in Brooklyn yesterday. A big black bow was centered on the top. A bizarre, deliberate, cruel burlesque of the usual form: it was a funeral gift.

A gift from Scavenger. Scavenger had been here, in his locked car.

Mark moved. He would later wonder at his action, because he did not hesitate, did not even think about it. He slipped the car in gear, pulled out of the space, and drove quickly away down the hill. He turned left at the corner, then right at the next one. He made several more random turns, finding himself at last in a wide, well-lit avenue. He had no idea where he was going, or even in which direction. He was only aware of his sudden, overwhelming need to get away from here, to put distance between himself and Scavenger.

Somewhere very close to him, a telephone rang.

He slammed on the brakes, nearly causing a collision with a car pulling out from a street just ahead of him. He swerved to avoid the other vehicle and pulled over to the side of the avenue. He sat there, staring down at the black gift-wrapped box on the passenger seat. The ringing was coming from there.

He waited a moment until his heart stopped pounding. Then he grabbed the package and tore it open, sending black paper and ribbon flying all over the front of the car. The black-laquered box followed the paper, and the black tissue paper as well. He was now holding a black cellular telephone, and it was still ringing. He pushed up the antenna, turned the phone on, and pressed it to his ear. He said nothing; there was no point.

"Hello, Mr. Stevenson—or should I call you Mr. Farmer? Well, no matter. I'm sure you know who this is."

It was a deep, resonant voice, as Mark had known it would be. There was something assured about it, direct, almost to the point of being sinister. Now it continued.

"This phone is a little token of my gratitude for playing the game with me. I want you to keep it with you, and to keep it on at all times. That way, we can talk to each other whenever we wish."

Mark found his voice. "Whenever *you* wish, you son of a bitch!"

"Oh, come, now, Mr. Stevenson. Don't be that way. But yes, that is correct. Whenever *I* wish. But you *will* be rewarded, remember. I promised you certain . . . information, and I always keep my promises. Always."

"*Who are you?*" Mark shouted into the instrument. He knew the man was somewhere nearby; he wondered if the man could actually hear his frustrated cry without the phone. It was entirely possible. With this man, anything was possible.

"All in good time, all in good time," came the smooth reply. "Do you know where you're going next?"

"Yeah, sure," Mark spat. "O'Hara delivered your message. What are you, some kind of phone freak?" Now Mark actually giggled.

"*This game will not continue if you are rude to me again!*"

The commanding voice reverberated throughout the small space of the car. It seemed to echo on and on, and when it finally died away, it was followed by an ominous silence. Mark froze again, staring at the flimsy instrument in his hand. The heavy, even breathing of the other man continued to emanate from it. After the long, horrible silence, the voice resumed, once more low, mellifluous, in perfect control.

"I trust we understand each other, Mr. Stevenson. You know where to go next. You are looking for a mask. You have twenty-four hours, beginning at midnight tonight. I'll be in touch. Good night."

The line went dead.

Mark stared at the phone again, and then he dropped it back onto the passenger seat. He sat perfectly still, staring ahead through the windshield at the nearly empty expanse of what he now realized was Pennsylvania Avenue. A few blocks ahead of him down the wide boulevard was the White House, the home of the President, the center-piece of civilization. The symbol of democracy, of power, of control: all the things that he no longer had for as long as the scavenger hunt continued.

Then he started to scream. He shouted every foul word he'd ever heard, and he began rhythmically beating his fists hard against the steering wheel. He filled the car with deafening sound, possessed of a sudden, utterly uncontainable madness. A fury that had to be released, unleashed, on something, anything. The wheel, the seat, the entire car vibrated from the force of his blows. The cell phone slid from its place and landed with a thump on the carpet under the glove compartment. When he ran out of words to shout, he still continued screaming, uttering piercing, meaningless sounds from deep within him until he was out of breath. He saw spots in front of his eyes, and he knew that he was hyperventilating. And still the noise and the pounding went on and on, until they could go on no longer. The shouting gave way to whimpering, the pounding to soft, ineffectual slaps of his palms against the hard plastic wheel. His hands were numb, his voice hoarse and ragged.

The whimpers diminished into hard breathing as his impotent rage dispersed. The windshield and side windows were now a misty gray, fogged from his exertion. He dropped his heavy arms to his sides and sat there, drained, shaken, sweating. Defeated.

But not for long. He thought of his family, and of the other families; of what this meant. This game, this grotesque mockery of him, of all he had been through. The mist on the windows dispersed, clearing the way for him. He knew where he must go, what he must do. And he would do it: he would see this through.

Alone in the car on an avenue in Washington, D.C., Mark Stevenson drew himself up. He shifted the gears, grasped the steering wheel, and drove away into the night. Past the White House toward Union Station, where he would turn in the car and purchase a ticket on the overnight train to New Orleans. He could not fly with a gun in his suitcase, but he would get there as soon as possible. He would find Sarah Tennant, do whatever else Scavenger instructed. He had twenty-four hours to complete the next round.

He was going to win this game.

ARTICLE #2

MASK

T U E S D A Y

18

Finding Sarah Tennant proved to be easy. Getting to her was another thing entirely.

New Orleans a few weeks after Mardi Gras has the distinct aura of a town that has recently been vacated. There is an unmistakable, unavoidable feeling that one is in a place where the parade has just passed by. Still, the local populace is reluctant to admit this: the streets are always colorful and charming, and the strains of zydeco and jazz and the tang of crawfish and jambalaya emanate from the brightly lit clubs and restaurants on every downtown corner. It is an inland port, surrounded by miles of wide river and dense forest punctuated with bayous that serve to give it an isolated feeling, even when it is brimming with revelers. Isolated, but never quiet. The truth about the city is that when the public party for guests is over, the private party continues throughout the year.

This was the town in which Mark arrived at noon on Tuesday. He emerged from the overnight train disoriented, trying to get his bearings, to remember what he could about the city. He'd been here once, years ago, but he barely recognized the place in what was essentially the off-season. He knew that the French Quarter was east of Union Passenger Terminal, where he was, and that he would find many small guest houses there in a wide variety of price ranges. He had already decided on looking for a good one in the medium range. That was his first task.

He found it on a relatively quiet little row off Decatur Street near Jackson Square. Mullins Guest House was just what he was looking for, and he thanked the cab driver for recommending it. There was a small foyer, actually a living room, and a dining room beyond it. One little downstairs room was a bar and cocktail lounge. Mrs. Mullins, a cheerful elderly woman with several cats, led him up the staircase and down a hall to an immaculate single room with a balcony above the front porch. She informed him that breakfast in the dining room was part of the package, and left him alone.

He took a quick shower and put on a clean shirt. Then he sat down on the bed and reached for the phone directory beside the guest telephone on the night table. He glanced at his watch: one-fifteen. He had exactly ten hours and forty-five minutes to find a mask.

He had some immediate luck. There were three Tennants listed in the phone book, and the first one he tried, a Mrs. Ada Tennant, was Sarah's aunt. She and her late husband had taken Sarah in after the murders thirteen years ago. She sounded like a friendly woman, and she was perfectly nice at first. Then Mark told her that he was writing a nonfiction account of the crimes and that he wanted to speak with Sarah. At this point, Mrs. Tennant became more guarded.

"Oh, dear," she said. "You obviously don't know about Sarah. Well, she's Sarah Gammon now. She married Robert Gammon, the lawyer. Perhaps you should talk to him. I don't have his office number nearby, but it's in the book. Chalmers and Gammon, over on Gravier. Call him, okay? He—he may be able to—to help you. Enjoy your stay in New Orleans, Mr.—uh—good-bye."

She hung up so abruptly that Mark didn't have time to thank her. He looked up the law firm, wondering why the woman had become so flustered. He dialed, wondering what Mrs. Tennant had meant, what it was he didn't know about Sarah.

He was about to find out.

It took him a few minutes to get through to Gammon. He'd apparently just returned from lunch, and he had a client already waiting for an early afternoon appointment. The secretary who answered the phone was obviously the overly organized, fiercely protective type, and she was initially reluctant to let Mark speak to him at all. Mark finally prevailed by mentioning that he was a journalist working on the Family Man story. After a moment Robert Gammon came on the line. Not that it mattered.

"Absolutely not!" was Sarah's husband's immediate response when Mark had explained his errand. He had a low-pitched Southern drawl, the voice of a well-bred, educated, moneyed professional. There was also a band of iron in it: Mark was aware of that, too. When this man said no, he meant no.

But Mark had to try. "Mr. Gammon, this is very important to me, or I would never—"

"Look, Mr. Stevenson, that was the worst ordeal of Sarah's life. She—she's very fragile, and I can't have anyone upsetting her. Especially now. I'm sorry, but your request is out of the question."

No one else may know about the game. The words jangled in Mark's mind once more, but he pushed them away as he made an impulsive decision born of desperation. As briefly and concisely as possible, he told the man about Scavenger, and about the "game" they were now playing. He went so far as to tell Robert Gammon that the mysterious Scavenger had as much as promised to reveal the identity of The Family Man.

There was a long pause then, and Mark knew that the man was considering all this. Mark could only imagine how Gammon and his wife would react to the prospect of learning the killer's name. He held his breath, daring to hope for the best.

But it was not to be.

"I'm sorry," Gammon said again. "I don't want my wife involved in this."

"Okay," Mark said. "I understand. But I'll leave my number here with your secretary. Please think about it, Mr. Gammon. I'll be in New Orleans overnight. Call me if you change your mind. Thank you for your time."

He was transferred back to the secretary, and he gave her the number of the guest house telephone. The cellular phone didn't seem to have a number that he could find, and Scavenger had told him to keep the line open, anyway.

He was beginning to play the game almost automatically, he realized. A series of clues, a succession of locations, constant time limits: these things demanded a nimble brain, an ability to adapt quickly and efficiently to a variety of situations. He knew, as every journalist knows, that the first attempt to get a story may not be successful, and that fallback plans are often necessary. The people with the information were not always predictable. They had their own histories, their own agendas, their own ways of doing things. So it was with Robert Gammon, and Mark would have to adapt himself to that. He knew he could do it, and he knew that the mysterious, offstage character known to him only as Scavenger would expect it of him as well. So he would play the game as well as—better than—his opponent.

Now, in the room in the guest house near Jackson Square, Mark began to formulate Plan B. He had the address of the law firm from the directory, but no home address for Gammon. He figured that Gammon would leave the office between five o'clock and five-thirty. He intended to be outside the firm then, and he would follow him home. He reasoned that it would be much more difficult for Gammon to get rid of him on his doorstep. Besides, Sarah would be there, he presumed, and she might agree to speak with him.

Plan B was never finished, as it turned out. Exactly fifteen minutes after he'd completed his call to the law firm, the bedside telephone rang.

Robert Gammon had changed his mind, or, rather, his mind had been changed for him. But when Mark heard what the man had to say, he felt a thrill of apprehension.

Interviewing Sarah was definitely not going to be easy.

19

The mark—Mark Stevenson, once Matthew Farmer—came out of the guest house and strode swiftly, purposefully down the lane to Decatur, where he hailed a cab. It was only by running into the street behind the departing taxi and flagging one down himself that he was able to follow. But he was grateful that they were on the move again.

He'd followed his quarry, first from New York and then from the former FBI man's house in Georgetown last night. He'd boarded the train moments after Stevenson, concealing himself in a sleeper for the duration of the journey. Then he'd shadowed him from the station to the Mullins place, and he'd used the half hour after that to find his own lodgings nearby, assuming that Stevenson would be settling in and using the telephone to locate the woman. As it turned out, Stevenson took considerably longer than that inside. The tall man with the scar had waited outside the guest house until now, nearly four o'clock, when Stevenson had finally emerged.

He tailed the taxi to a Hertz rental agency not far away, and waited in the backseat of his own cab, safely across the street, while Stevenson was given a shiny, bright red Ford Taurus. Good: the car would be easy to follow.

His cab driver was delighted when he was offered the bonus to follow the red Taurus. The man actually seemed to enjoy the suggestion, finding something romantic in the idea of being a detective. But the man with the scar was far from intrigued, himself. He was fairly certain he knew where Stevenson was going. He just had to be sure. . . .

Yes. He smiled as the two cars headed north, in the general direction of Lake Pontchartrain. My, my, he thought. Stevenson certainly is resourceful, not to mention a fast worker.

He was beginning to get a sense of how the man's mind worked, and he decided that Mark Stevenson was a worthy opponent. He'd known that the former Matthew Farmer—to say nothing of the former journalist—would be unable to resist a chance, however difficult, to solve this particular mystery. But he hadn't expected the speed, the efficiency, the cool intelligence that defined Stevenson's every move. This made the enterprise infinitely more provocative for both sides. There were several more phases to the game, and setting them up for this resourceful man would be a pleasure. Of course, it would be very interesting to observe how Stevenson would handle the little surprise that awaited him before he left New Orleans tomorrow. . . .

He continued to smile as the red Taurus turned off into the street that would lead Stevenson to the next stop in the game. Then he gave his driver new instructions. He noted the man's confusion and disappointment as he turned the cab around and carried his mysterious fare back to the Hertz agency. The wild, possibly dangerous adventure the cab driver had apparently imagined was coming to an abrupt, unsatisfactory end. He paid the man his bonus and went inside to rent a car for himself. He had big plans for this evening, and he would need transportation to get him to the next destination. But there was something else he had to do first. He had to set up the first really *big* surprise for Mark Stevenson.

Patting the reassuring bulge of the sheathed, eight-inch stainless steel blade at his side, he drove to Gravier Street and turned in the direction of Robert Gammon's law firm.

20

Mark had never been in such a place before, and he didn't know what to expect. His work in journalism had never included it, as he had been limited mostly to literary subjects. He admitted to himself that he was as full of preconceived notions as everyone else, vague—and presumably false—images culled from films and novels. It won't be anything like that, he assured himself as he parked in the appropriate lot and followed the discreet signs through the lush, well-tended gardens and lawns toward the big, attractive building near the shore of Lake Pontchartrain. Well, *probably* not, he amended with a grim smile.

The sky was clear blue now at four-thirty in the afternoon, and the temperature was comfortably in the low sixties. He was aware, as he had been outside Ronald O'Hara's house in Washington yesterday, of his good fortune: he'd been in New Orleans a grand total of four hours, and here he was, well on his way to completing the next play in the game. He wondered briefly at that, at the apparent ease with which he was succeeding at his assignments, but he thrust that line of thought from him and continued. He would analyze everything later, when it was over and he was back in New York with Tracy.

Tracy. He would have to call her, and soon. He made that mental note to himself as he went up the sidewalk to the imposing front entrance of the Pontchartrain Clinic.

He had been expecting a hospital setting, so the reality surprised him. When he entered the doors, he found himself in a big, airy space that looked much more like an elegant hotel lobby than any hospital he'd ever seen. He stood just inside the entrance, taking in the lush carpets and draperies, the French doors that would open onto the gardens, and the gleaming oak and mahogany furniture. The lighting in the room was subdued, old chandeliers and shaded, tasseled standing floor lamps. Potted plants and several large bowls and vases of spring flowers were everywhere. Soft music—Beethoven's *Pastoral*—emanated from hidden speakers. An archway beyond led to another large room, from which he heard laughter and the distinctive sounds of a billiard game.

There were five or six people here in the lobby who were probably patients, seated on plush couches and chairs. They were all Caucasian, and they varied in age from a thirtyish man reading a newspaper to two seventyish women conversing quietly while they sipped tea from delicate cups. All were well dressed in what Mark could only think of as street clothes: he'd half expected standard-issue hospital gowns, robes, and slippers. The only uniforms in the room were on the two people present who were obviously not patients, a big African-American man who sat in a corner, glancing casually around at everyone, and a pretty young white woman with improbably blond hair who was seated behind a big mahogany writing desk near the entrance, a jarringly modern computer terminal before her, speaking quietly into a telephone. The man wore blue-green hospital scrubs, and the young woman was clad in a white nurse's uniform and cap.

Mark waited until the nurse had put down the phone before going over to stand before her desk. She looked up at him and smiled.

"Good afternoon," she said in a musical New Orleans drawl. "Welcome to Pontchartrain. May I help you?"

"Uh, yes, I hope so," Mark stammered, trying to return her smile. "My name is Mark Stevenson, and I'm supposed to—"

"Oh, yes." The girl nodded, picked up the phone receiver, and pressed a button. "Mr. Gammon called us and explained. One moment." Now she spoke into the receiver. "Millie, Mr. Stevenson is here to see Mrs. Gammon. Can you come get him and take him up? Great. Thanks." She hung up, still smiling at Mark. "Nurse Call will be with you in a moment." She turned her attention to the computer and began to type.

"Thank you," Mark said. He stood there for a few moments, looking around again, until another pretty young woman in a nurse's uniform and a white sweater, this one African-American, materialized at his elbow. She, too, was smiling.

"Mr. Stevenson? Come with me, please."

This woman—Nurse Call, he presumed—led him through a side archway into a hallway of some sort, and over to a bank of elevators. They got in one, and the woman produced a key, which she inserted in a lock just below the four buttons clearly labeled for the basement through the third floor.

"Fourth floor," she murmured, as if in explanation. As the car rose swiftly and silently up, Mark looked again at the control panel, just to be sure. No, there was no button for a fourth floor.

It was his first certain indication since his arrival here that he was in a mental institution. He leaned back against the wall of the elevator cab, bracing himself. Sarah Tennant, now Sarah Gammon, was not in the plush lobby, sipping tea or playing pool with the other patients. She was on the top floor, the one the elevator serviced only with a special key. He closed his eyes for a moment, thinking, Uh-oh. . . .

A soft giggle made him open his eyes. The nurse was watching him, laughing.

"Don't worry," she said. "It's not—I mean, Mrs. Gammon is perfectly—well, you'll see. The fourth floor is just medium security, that's all."

Mark smiled weakly. "So where's *maximum* security?"

She laughed again. "Not here. We don't have the facilities for that, I'm glad to say. State hospitals take care of that."

It was with a profound sense of relief that Mark followed Nurse Call out of the elevator into a gleaming white foyer, on the other side of which was a stainless steel door. A small camera was mounted on the white wall beside the door, and the nurse looked into this, raised her hand, and waved. There was a soft electronic buzzing sound, and she pulled down the handle on the door and pushed it open. Mark followed her through the door, his earlier trepidation returning.

As well it should return, he decided. Beyond the cold door was a cold, impersonal white room, the sort seen in any big-city hospital. A large, circular desk, a nurses' station, stood in the center, occupied by two women in nurses' whites and a man in a navy blue security uniform. There were computer terminals and several small television monitors arranged in front of them. Beyond the station was a barred gateway, and through the bars could be seen a long white hallway with many doors. Mark noticed three things immediately: the eerie silence of the place, the distinct smell of floral disinfectant, and the fact that the security guard who lounged beside the women, reading a magazine, was armed with a nightstick, a phaser or "stun gun," and a pistol. The hotel-like atmosphere of the downstairs rooms was nowhere in evidence here.

Nurse Call smiled at the people behind the desk and led Mark past them to the barred door. There was a low buzzing sound as one of the nurses released the electronic lock. The two of them passed through the door, which she closed firmly behind them. The click of the lock echoed in the silent place.

"She's in the dayroom," Nurse Call said as she led him down the corridor.

Mark followed. He thought he now understood the reason she wore a sweater over her uniform: the temperature on the fourth floor seemed to be twenty degrees colder than elsewhere in the clinic. He shivered as she stopped at a steel door on their left. Another humming sound, this one more muted, informed him that all the locks on this side of the gate were also operated by the people at the console in the reception area behind them. The nurse opened the door and led him inside.

They were now in a large room with pale blue walls and curtains, intermittently streaked with sunlight through a bank of windows along one wall. The overhead lights were not on, and there were deep shadows between the patches of sun. There was thick blue wall-to-wall carpeting, several overstuffed couches and chairs, and an odd-looking coffee table. The table seemed to be upholstered, the edges and legs actually padded with pale blue Naugahyde. He stood behind the nurse, staring at the table, thinking, No sharp edges. His gaze then traveled over to the row of tall windows, and he noted the tight wire mesh embedded within panes of presumably unbreakable glass. Other than the furniture, the room was bare of adornment: no flowers, no knicknacks, no anything. The low hum of air-conditioning was the only sound, and the artificial floral Lysol odor was stronger here than elsewhere. Mark took in every sinister detail of the room—the calming blueness, the protective padding, the dark spaces between bright bars of sunlight, the cloying scent—before he focused on its only other occupant.

She was sitting on one of the couches, clad in a cream-colored silk bathrobe or dressing gown over a pink flannel nightgown and soft pink slippers. Though she was seated, Mark could tell that she was a tall woman, about his age, with long, lustrous dark hair that hung rather limply around her shoulders. Large, dark eyes stared out at him from a pale face—a pretty, well-formed face bearing an expression he could only interpret as great sadness. She wore no evident makeup, but she didn't need it. She sat erect, knees together, her pale hands resting in her lap. A well-bred, upper-middle-class woman, the wife of a successful New Orleans attorney, the sort of darkly beautiful lady his sister, Mary Farmer, might have become if she hadn't been . . .

He stood there, awkward, gauche, uncertain, wondering why he was thinking of his sister. He and Sarah Gammon regarded each other for a long, silent moment. Then Nurse Call stepped forward, breaking the odd spell in the room.

"Mrs. Gammon, this is Mark Stevenson, the writer your husband told you to expect. I've ordered tea for you, and I'll be in the corner over there." She waved toward a nearby chair. "Let me know if you want anything else, or if you don't wish to continue the interview." With a fleeting, apologetic smile for Mark, the nurse went over to the corner and sat down.

Mark forced a smile to his lips and leaned across the coffee table, extending his hand. The woman regarded him silently for a moment, then frowned slightly and extended her own hand for a brief handshake. That was when Mark noticed the bandage. It circled her wrist, and it appeared to be fresh, as if it had just been changed. A surreptitious glance at the other hand confirmed his suspicion: there was an identical fresh bandage on her left wrist. He managed to continue smiling as he sank into the overstuffed chair across the table from her.

"Thank you for allowing me to see you, Mrs. Gammon," he said.

The woman returned her hands to her lap, concealing the wrapped wrists in the voluminous sleeves of the robe in what appeared to be an unconscious effort. Then she leaned slightly forward and spoke in a low, surprisingly clear voice.

"My husband seems to think this is a bad idea, but Dr. Graham disagreed with him, so he gave in. I understand you're writing a book about—about what happened to my family." She glanced over at the nurse in the corner, then back at him.

"Yes," he said, realizing that he was leaning forward, too. Now that he was here, facing her, he had no idea how to conduct the interview. "I—I thought maybe you could—"

"I don't want to talk about it," she said abruptly, cutting him off. "That is not why I agreed to see you. You're here because I want *you* to tell *me* something, Mr. Stevenson. I want you to tell me about the man with the scar."

Mark blinked. Sarah Gammon was still leaning forward, and now she was staring intently at his face, a steely cold glint in her dark eyes. He leaned back in his chair, away from her, and his breath left his body in a long, slow exhalation. So, he thought, her husband told her what I told him. He hadn't expected that of Robert Gammon.

"Perhaps I should explain that," Sarah said, a faint note of humor in her voice.

"Yes," Mark breathed. He continued to lean back in the chair, watching her.

She was about to speak again when the door behind him opened and another nurse came in with the tea.

21

It was one of those plush, dark, discreet, aggressively tasteful Upper East Side places that Tracy usually sought to avoid. Yet here she was in a sleek padded chair before a sleek marble-topped cocktail table near the translucent smoked glass picture window, sipping from an enormous chilled goblet of white wine, waiting.

This elegant Art Deco bar was in the lobby of one of New York's best hotels, and it was nearly empty now, just after four-thirty on a Monday afternoon. It would soon be full, she imagined, when five o'clock came and went and everyone stopped in on their way home from the office or out to dinner. The air would soon be humming with quiet conversation and redolent of expensive perfumes. No smoking, she noted, except at the bar itself. That streamlined structure ran the length of the wall on the other side of the room, eerily lit from behind, attended by an unsmiling, red-jacketed young man who silently mixed drinks for the lone businessman before him and the two beautifully dressed, impeccably coiffed middle-aged women at a table in the farthest corner. The two women were surrounded by shopping bags, and their muffled chatter was the only noise in the room. The big piano near them would be put to use soon, she supposed, after cocktail hour had officially begun, but now it was unattended. She gazed around, thinking of the shadowy hotel bar in the film *The Shining*: these people could be waxwork figures, or revenants of the long dead.

As if to emphasize the bizarre comparison, an unsmiling, well-dressed young couple, a pretty blond girl and a handsome blond man, came silently into the room and took the other table by the window, next to her. The barman, who seemed to have expected them, moved quietly over to them and placed two goblets of red wine on their table.

Then he went back behind the bar, and the new mannequins sipped their drinks, their voices never rising above whispers.

She had been uncertain what to wear for this, and she had agonized over the selection. After much deliberation she'd chosen Chanel's cure-all, a little black dress with black pumps and a single strand of pearls, and her blond hair hung loose about her shoulders. Her makeup had been carefully applied in an attempt to create the illusion that she wore none at all. She knew that her appearance this afternoon would be scrutinized, judged.

She was not looking forward to this meeting. Her mother had been persistent, following up her original suggestion over dinner yesterday with two late evening phone calls repeating it. Tracy had made the awkward, embarrassing call this morning, as much to please her mother as to set her own mind at ease. If, indeed, that was what was going to happen. She had no idea what to expect now, which was why she was dreading it.

Well, she was here now, and she was dressed for it. She was as ready as she ever would be. And here the woman came now, as sleek and shiny and elegant as this room in which she had so suddenly, inevitably appeared. She scanned the dim place from the doorway for a moment, until her gaze fell on Tracy. She nodded, apparently to herself, produced a bright smile, and moved forward through the room as a model glides down a Parisian runway. She was certainly beautiful enough to be a professional model, if a little old for it. Tracy noted with a brief flash of humor that the woman was also in the preferred uniform, a little black dress under her open leather coat, with gold chains rather than pearls. But the woman had had no choice of apparel: Tracy had called her at her office this morning, and she had presumably come directly here from there. She'd worn these clothes to work.

Tracy stood up, she wasn't sure why, as the tall, attractive woman with the short dark hair arrived at the table. She smiled at the woman, aware of the pounding of her heart and the sudden tingling sensation all over her body. She drew in a slow, careful breath.

"Hello," she said, nearly wincing at the high-pitched, unnatural squeakiness of her voice. She cleared her throat and tried again. "Thank you so much for—well, for agreeing to, uh—"

"Oh, sure," the woman said, her genuine smile as bright and cheerful as her speaking voice. She shrugged slightly when she said it, as though she wanted to get this part over with as much as Tracy did. She continued to grin, dispelling the odd mood of the room by her mere presence in it, as she dropped into the chair across the table and pointed down at Tracy's virtual fishbowl of white wine. "I'd like one of those, and pronto! What a day I've had! Well, here we are, anyway. Hi, Tracy, I'm Carol. Carol Grant."

Tracy sank into her own chair, raising an arm to summon the unsmiling young man from behind the bar, but her eyes were on Carol Grant. "You're, um, remarried." Dumb, she thought. Why did I say that?

"Yup," the woman said. She stopped the barman halfway, merely pointing a red-lacquered nail down at Tracy's glass, then at her own chest. He nodded and retreated to fill the order. "I've been married for two years now. I'm not Mrs. Stevenson anymore. I guess *you're* about to inherit that title. That's why we're here, isn't it?"

Tracy blinked. Then she relaxed, smiled.

"Why, yes," she said. "I suppose it is."

Carol Grant nodded. "Yeah, well, we've never worked together, but I certainly know who you are. I know a couple of your authors, too. Stella Verlaine did a couple of articles for me, but I guess that was before you were handling her. Are you Mark's literary agent?"

"No," Tracy said. "His agent is a colleague of mine at Jaffee/Douglas, and Mark and I sort of mutually decided not to work together professionally. We figured that a setup like that could get in the way of our private relationship, and we don't want that to happen."

"Good idea," the other woman said. "But I can't help wondering why you wanted to meet me. I mean, I'm glad you did, but—"

"Carol," Tracy said, using the woman's first name for the first time, "I—I don't know quite how to put this, but I guess I have a few unanswered questions. About Mark, I mean. He's very, I don't know, *mysterious*. About his life, his past. I don't know anything about his childhood, or his family, or what he did before he came to New York. And I'm curious about him. You see, I—I was married before, to a charming, handsome son of a bitch, and . . ." She searched for words, wondering how best to convey her anxiety.

As it turned out, an explanation was unnecessary. Carol Grant nodded again, sipped her wine, and leaned forward, a friendly smile on her face.

"I see," she said. "You don't want another dud. We know all about *them,* don't we? I guess every woman does, eventually. Well, I can put your mind at ease in one respect: Mark is a very nice man. He's honest and decent and moral, I think, and that's after four years with him, start to finish. *That* wasn't our problem—*my* problem, I mean. My problem with him was just what you've been saying, oddly enough. I didn't know anything about him at first, and it took me forever to get anything out of him about his life. When I did, I understood why he was so quiet, so uncommunicative with me. But it didn't help; by then, it was too late for us. I left him. Well, that sounds more dramatic than what actually happened. It was perfectly civilized, really. But it was I who decided to get divorced, not Mark. I don't regret that decision—but you may be surprised when I say I think *you* should give marriage to him a try."

Tracy reached for her wineglass as Carol Grant leaned back in her chair, smiling. The two women sat in companionable silence for a few moments while Tracy absorbed what she had just been told.

"Thank you," she said at last, smiling back at the woman across the table. "But tell me, if you don't mind, what did you learn about him?"

Carol raised an eyebrow, and her smile disappeared. She was quiet a moment longer, apparently making some sort of decision. Tracy studied the woman, noting that the decision, whatever it was, was apparently not a pleasant one. She felt another frisson of anxiety. At last, Carol leaned forward again.

"First, let *me* ask *you* a question," she said. "Well, two questions, actually. Otherwise, this could just be—I don't know—*needless,* and I wouldn't want to upset you needlessly. So I have to ask. Do you love him?"

Tracy answered immediately. "Yes."

"And are you going to marry him, no matter what you may learn about him?"

Again, Tracy did not hesitate. "Yes."

Carol studied her face a moment. Then she nodded again and took a deep breath.

"Okay," she said, "here goes. What I guess you should know first is that his name was not always Mark Stevenson. It was Matthew Farmer. . . ."

22

The tea was in white Styrofoam cups, and the plastic stirrers and packets of sugar and artificial sweetener were on a paper plate. Mark took in these details with something approaching humor, but he remained silent. Another surreptitious glance at Sarah Gammon's wrists was all he needed to remind him that china cups and plates were probably not a good idea. Of course, Sarah didn't really look as if she would suddenly shatter something and attempt to reopen her wounds, but then again, she didn't really seem the type to have done it in the first place. Besides, he hadn't seen any of the other patients on this floor, and he trusted the wisdom of the staff.

As soon as everything was placed on the table between them and the nurse was gone from the dayroom, Sarah Gammon leaned back on the overstuffed couch, her body in relative darkness between two slanting rays of light streaming in through the windows behind her, and began to talk.

"Your reaction tells me that you know about the man with the scar. I'm glad to see it. I was beginning to think I'd imagined him." She glanced over at Nurse Call in the corner with an expression that seemed to mix equal parts contempt and triumph.

"I—I don't understand," Mark said. "Did your husband tell you about my conversation with him, or—"

"My husband didn't tell me anything," she replied. "Only to expect a writer named Mark Stevenson at four o'clock." She shrugged then and leaned forward, holding out her hands—and her wrists—to him for the first time. "*This* happened, let's see, about three weeks ago. I woke up in the hospital, and then they brought me here. I've been here before, at Pontchartrain, but never mind about that. For a week they kept me in my room here, and they wouldn't let me out at all. So I started smiling and chatting with the nurses, you know, playing the game. Pretending to them I was real grateful to be here, and alive, and all that. So they finally let me out. I don't mean *out*, mind you. My husband wouldn't hear of that; not yet, anyway. But they let me go downstairs and out to the lawn in the afternoons, with the other . . . *guests*." She emphasized the word, as if it were the local polite euphemism, which it probably was. "There was always a nurse or an orderly with us—except this one time, on the third day, which would be about ten days ago. I was sitting in a chair on the back patio, near the rose garden, with one of the other *guests*, and she became—well, the orderly, Jake, had to take her back to her room. I was alone in the garden for, I don't know, maybe five minutes. That's when it happened."

Mark stared. "What happened?"

Sarah Gammon shuddered. "I was looking at the roses, watching a bee that was flying around them, when I suddenly felt very cold, as if a shadow had come between me and the sun. And I realized that this is exactly what had happened, that someone was standing over me. I looked up." She raised her eyes toward the ceiling, reliving the moment. "There was a man standing there, looking down at me. No, *staring*. That's the only word for it. He was nearly seven feet tall, and he was all in black, a black suit and a long coat nearly to the ground, like those coats they wear in western movies. Black hair and mustache, and very peculiar eyes, pale gray and, I don't know, piercing. But the most remarkable thing about him was the scar, a long white line down one side of his face. He just stood there, scowling at me, the most sinister-looking person I've ever seen. My first instinct was to get up from the chair, to get away from him, but he was standing too close, right in front of me, actually leaning over me. I looked around, but Jake wasn't back yet. He and I were alone in the garden."

"Did you speak to him?" Mark asked.

She shook her head and returned her gaze to him. "I couldn't speak. I could hardly breathe. Besides, he didn't give me a chance. He leaned down closer, and he took my hand in his. Then he reached out with his other hand and pressed something into my palm. And he spoke to me, barely a whisper. He said, 'Give this to Mark Stevenson. Mark Stevenson.' He said the name twice. He took his hands away, and I looked down at what he'd given me. I remember being confused, not really getting it. I looked up again to ask him who Mark Stevenson was, to tell him that I didn't know anyone by that name, but he was gone. Just like that. I mean, he was *nowhere*! It was as if he'd never been there at all." She shook her head again, then jerked a thumb to indicate the woman in the corner. "*They* didn't believe me. They thought I made the whole thing up. Dr. Graham told my husband that I'm delusional." A shrug, accompanied by a sad little smile. "Delusional. Isn't that a lovely word? It doesn't even sound like another word for *crazy*, does it?"

There was a long moment of silence in the room as the two of them regarded each other across the table. The sunlight was weakening now as dusk approached, the slanting rays through the windows growing gradually dimmer on the floor around them. Finally, Mark spoke, choosing his words with great care.

"I believe you," he said. "I don't think you're delusional, Mrs. Gammon. The man you described really exists, and *I'm* Mark Stevenson. He's—he's helping me with my research for the book, and I'm sorry if he frightened you. But tell me, what did he give you?"

She blinked. "Oh, yes." With another swift glance over at the nurse, she dug in the pocket of her robe and extended her hand across the table, palm up. "This. Of course, *they* said I made this up, too, that I'd had it with me all the time."

Mark looked down at her hand. She was holding out a large gold key. It seemed to be brand-new, unused, as if it were freshly minted. He reached out and took it from her.

"I don't understand," he said, inspecting it. "How could you have had this all the time?"

Another shrug, another sad smile. "Well, I have one just like it, don't I? It's a key to my house."

Mark stared at her, and his fingers closed around the key. "Are you sure about that?"

"Of course. I can't imagine how that man got ahold of one. As soon as I get out of this place, I'm changing the locks."

Now Mark was completely confused. "But your husband should—"

"Oh, not *that* house," she said, cutting him off. "It is a key to my family's house in Destrehan, the house I grew up in. I own it now, you know, and nobody's lived there in years, not since . . ." She stood up abruptly and walked a little away from the couch, apparently as an alternative to finishing the sentence. "I suppose you'd like to see the place. Research. For your book."

Mark stood up, too, still clutching the key in his fist. "If you wouldn't mind—I mean, if—"

"Sure," she said. "Whatever." She was over at one of the windows now, looking out, her back to the room. "It's on the river, not far from Destrehan Manor. Take the main highway about twenty-five miles west of here. You can ask for the turnoff at any gas station: just ask them for directions to the haunted house. They'll know what you mean." She laughed again, one sharp, ugly bark of derision.

"Mrs. Gammon," he said, going to stand behind her at the window, "I'm sorry if all this has upset you. I—I'm writing a book about it because I—"

"*Don't!*" she cried, whirling around and raising her bandaged hands up as if to ward him off. "Please, don't. I told you I don't want to talk about that. Not now. Not *ever*! Go look at the house, write your book, do whatever you have to do, but please go away now. I just want to be left alone!" She turned away from him again, toward the window, but not before he saw that her eyes were glistening with tears.

"*Mr. Stevenson!*" The voice of the nurse came from behind him, a firm command. He turned around to see that she was already at the door, holding it open. "You'd better go now."

"But, I—"

"*Now,* Mr. Stevenson, if you don't mind. This interview is over."

He looked at the woman, so coolly efficient in her starched white uniform and sweater. Then he nodded weakly and went to join her at the door.

"I'm sorry," he whispered. "I didn't mean—"

"It's all right," Nurse Call told him. "You can find your way out, I think. She'll be all right."

With a last glance over at the weeping woman by the window, Mark nodded to the nurse and went out. As she closed the door behind him, he heard Sarah Gammon's sudden, shouted words, her voice sharp with despair.

"I *won't* be all right!" she cried. "Nothing will ever be all right again!" The door closed with a click, cutting off all further sound.

He stood outside the door, his eyes tightly shut, feeling the edges of the key biting into his clenched fist. Then he opened his eyes and moved, walking forward down the cold white hallway to the cold metal gates. The foyer, the elevator, the lobby: he passed through all of them as swiftly as possible, with fleeting smiles and nods to the various staff members he passed. By the time he reached the front entrance, he was running. He ran out into the waning light of day and down the sidewalk toward the parking lot. Only when he reached his car did he stop, sagging against it, taking in huge lungfuls of fresh air. It took him several long, painful minutes to get his breath back again. He bent down over the hood of the car, pressing his hand down against its warm, reassuring solidity. The real world came creeping back, even slower in coming than his respiration.

She had not shared her family's fate, he thought, but in a way she had. She survived, and yet she did not survive. Not at all. She was dead, buried with her family.

And so, in many ways, was he.

He had gone there, to that awful place, the sort of place he most feared, not knowing what to expect. That had been his first thought upon entering, he now remembered. What he had perhaps expected least in all the world was to confront that empty shell of a woman, to gaze into those eyes so like his own. To hear that weary voice, so lost, so defeated by the vagaries of fate. The cruelty she had seen, had known. She had encountered The Family Man, and nothing in her world would ever be all right again. They had been her final words.

But now it was time to go. To get away from this place, the last refuge of the wounded, the broken, the discarded. He looked down at the gold key clutched in his fist. This key would open a door, and it was time to open it.

Slipping the key into his pocket, he got in the car and drove back to the guest house, glancing over occasionally at the cellular phone on the passenger seat beside him. He half expected it to ring at any moment, but it remained silent.

23

The two women had moved from the gloomy Art Deco bar into the relatively bright lights of the hotel's dining room. Dinner had been Carol Grant's suggestion, and Tracy had been unable to come up with a decent reason to refuse. She couldn't think, could barely even breathe. What was she learning from this friendly, well-meaning woman chilled her, dulled her senses, rendered her passive. She followed Carol Grant into the restaurant as a sheep follows the shepherd into an abattoir.

She listened to it all, the whole, terrible story of Matthew Farmer and his unfortunate family. There was more wine with dinner, but it didn't seem to have any effect on her. The cool, sweet alcohol failed to dull her senses to the horror she was absorbing, and her grilled chicken breast and salad went largely untouched. As Carol spoke, Tracy gazed around the dining room, at the waiters and the well-dressed diners and the attractive blond couple from the bar who were now eating at the table next to her.

Matthew Farmer was the oldest of three children of Reverend Jacob Farmer and his wife, Charlene. Reverend Farmer was the pastor of the Chicago branch of a nationwide Fundamentalist sect known as the Church of the True Believers, as his father had been before him. He had a local cable television show, and he frequently traveled to national gatherings of the church in other states. His wife and children accompanied him, and they participated in televised church activities, Mrs. Farmer playing the organ and the children singing and passing collection plates. The daughter, Mary, and the younger son, Joshua, were both students at a religious college in Oklahoma at the time of the murders, preparing for careers in the church.

Matthew had been the rebel. He hated the church, and he hated his family. His father had been very strict, even abusive, and Matthew had run away from home at eighteen, after barely making it through high school. He'd joined a group of runaways in Chicago, drifting into petty crime and drug addiction. This hadn't lasted long, as far as Carol Grant could tell. He and his girlfriend, a young woman named Judy something, had gotten jobs and a place to live, and they'd started taking classes at a local university. Judy was a waitress, and Matthew worked for a national market research firm. For three years, he mailed and received questionnaires, feeding results into computers that informed the company which brands of toothpaste and shampoo and breakfast cereal were preferred by families in various parts of America. Not challenging work, perhaps, but he had done well enough to pay the rent.

It was his self-improvement, he would later explain to Carol, that had made him reevaluate his family. He knew that he was an atheist, and he had no use for any religion, to say nothing of the Church of the True Believers. But they were his family, and he had not seen or spoken to them in nearly five years. He said he missed them. A couple of tentatively successful phone calls to his parents had inspired him to take Judy's oft-repeated suggestion: he would go to see his family on Christmas Day.

Carol Grant paused here, warning Tracy that the next part of the story was extremely unpleasant. Then she told her what Matthew Farmer—Mark—had found at his home that Christmas morning. She told her about The Family Man.

Tracy listened. She'd certainly heard of The Family Man, but she'd never made the connection. She wasn't sure how she felt about the information. She couldn't seem to react properly, couldn't arrange her thoughts into any coherent pattern. She didn't know what to say, so she remained quiet, staring blankly at the woman across the table from her. When the story was over, the two women sat in silence for a long time, Carol finishing her meal and Tracy recovering from the shock.

She was thinking about Mark's novel, *Dark Desire*. She remembered it vividly, having read it twice, and her new knowledge seemed to accelerate her memory until she thought she could remember every page, every sentence. Suddenly the novel took on new meaning, new weight, new resonance. Mark's guilt at the fate of his estranged family had obviously prompted him to write it. It was horrible, in light of what Carol Grant had just told her. She would have to think it through when she could think clearly again . . .

Now, with their places cleared and coffee before them, Tracy came to a decision. She would get through the rest of this meeting as politely as possible; on automatic pilot, if necessary. Then she would go home and make a cup of Sleepytime tea and sit quietly in her apartment. There, in the cool darkness of her living room, she would assess everything. She would decide what she was going to do next.

At last the meal came to an end. Carol Grant smiled at her and led the way out to the sidewalk and the fresh air.

"I hope you can deal with all of this," Carol said. "I mean, it isn't what Mark *is,* but what he *was.* It's something that happened to him. When I first met him, I romanticized his quiet standoffishness, but he finally told me the whole story. I thought I could find a way to handle it, to stay married to someone who was so damaged, so consumed by guilt, but it eventually became too much for me. I guess I was selfish. I needed something more, or something different, in a marriage, and that's what I have now. But that's no reason for *you* to change your mind. He's a good man, Tracy, and I hope the two of you will be very happy. I really do."

Tracy smiled at Mark's former wife because it seemed to be the proper reaction to her kind words. She was beginning to feel as she'd always imagined a robot would feel. That was ridiculous, she knew: robots felt nothing. Yet it was the best way, the only way to describe the numbness that was spreading through her, permeating her. She continued to smile absently, watching the blond couple from the dining room who now stood beside them, talking softly together as the hotel's doorman hailed a taxi for them. Before she was aware of having made the decision, she gave in to a sudden impulse. She turned to Mark's former wife and blurted out her next question.

"Did Mark have a gun when you were married?" she asked.

Carol studied her face for a moment before replying. "Yes. Yes, he did. I found it once, by accident, in the top of the bedroom closet. It gave me a shock, I must say—I've never liked the things, and the thought of having one in my house was unsettling, to say the least. But I never asked him about it, never even mentioned it. In light of what I've just told you, I think you can understand that. I didn't lose my entire family to a serial killer, and you and I can only guess at what that does to someone. Why did you ask me that? Does he still have it?"

"Yes," Tracy whispered. She knew in that moment that it was true, and that she had seen what she'd thought she'd seen the other night.

The two women regarded each other in silence. Then Carol said, "Just remember my two questions, and your answers. That's all that matters, really." She briefly embraced Tracy, kissing her cheek, before turning to the doorman, who handed her into a cab.

Tracy stood on the sidewalk in front of the hotel, watching as the cab pulled away. It wasn't until the car disappeared in the traffic that she realized what Carol had meant.

"Do you love him?"

"Yes."

"And are you going to marry him, no matter what you may learn about him?"

"Yes."

She knew it was the truth. Still . . .

"Would you like a cab, miss?"

Tracy blinked. The doorman was watching her. She nodded to him, and he raised his silver whistle to his lips.

24

The second time Mark saw the man with the scar, he recognized him instantly. And he knew he was not a ghost.

It was just after dinner. Mrs. Mullins, the proprietor of the guest house, had recommended a restaurant a few blocks north, on Bourbon Street, where he would find what she assured him was the best jambalaya in New Orleans, in the entire state of Louisiana. She became so rhapsodic about it that Mark briefly wondered if the guest house was her only financial concern, but he thanked her and took her advice.

As he was getting ready to leave, he picked up the room phone and dialed Tracy's number. He'd been gone two days now, and he wanted to hear her voice. But he wasn't going to tell her where he was; she thought he was in Washington, which was good enough for him. She didn't answer the phone in person: her recorded voice went through the familiar litany, and then came the beep. He'd drawn in a breath to leave a message when he remembered that she'd just installed caller ID, which would record the number in New Orleans. He quickly slammed down the receiver and left for the restaurant.

The food, not surprisingly, was everything Mrs. Mullins had promised, and the terrific Dixieland band in the packed, boisterous room was the perfect antidote to the clinic—the *asylum*—of the afternoon. The party extended out into the street itself, where there seemed to be some sort of festival in progress. Of course, every day in New Orleans was some sort of festival, he realized. Now, in spring, there were probably all kinds of saints' days and historical observances. All of them were observed, with bells on, because the locals knew that any tourist coming to the city expected Mardi Gras, even when that particular holiday was gone, and they were nothing if not accommodating.

It was perhaps for this reason that there was a parade coming down the street as Mark emerged from the dining room onto the crowded sidewalk. He stood in the restaurant's doorway, momentarily unable to move through the wall of human flesh around him, acutely aware of the heavy revolver in the inside pocket of his bomber jacket pressing against his rib cage. He'd planned to go directly from dinner to the Tennant house, and he wasn't going there without the gun. The red Taurus was parked nearby, and he would head north to Claiborne Avenue, then west out of the city. He could find his way from there.

It was not a particularly big parade, more like an impromptu gathering. There were perhaps fifty people marching down the street, some of them wearing colorful masks, many of them playing musical instruments, all of them carrying liquid refreshments. Not big, but enough to draw a brief crowd. The constant stream of movement around Mark finally enabled him to make his way slowly forward to the curb. He would have to cross Bourbon Street to get to his car. He looked out into the street, at the ragtag orchestra playing a crude but lively rendition of "Basin Street Blues," and at the dense, drunken crowd that watched and took photos, many of them dancing and singing along to the music on the opposite sidewalk.

That's when he saw him.

The man was standing directly across the street from him. He was unusually tall, taller than everyone around him. And there, before Mark's eyes, was all the rest of it: the now oddly familiar black hair and mustache, the black suit, and the long black coat that had been described by two witnesses. Mark had briefly glimpsed it himself. And, clearly visible through the crowds and the exploding flashbulbs and the dim light in the street, the scar: a long white slash down the right side of the man's ruggedly handsome face. But the single fact that proved his identity, even more than the scar, was the fact that he was looking not at the makeshift entertainment but at Mark. Not merely looking, but staring. He was staring directly into Mark's eyes. Into his soul.

The sudden materialization of his nemesis was the last thing in the world Mark had been expecting, and he did not react quickly. Not quickly enough, at any rate. By the time he moved, stepping off the

curb and shoving his way through the teeming mob to the other side
of the street, the man had vanished.

. He barged up onto the sidewalk to stand on the spot where the
man had stood only moments before. It was impossible to see very far
in either direction; there were too many people in the way. But he was
near a corner, just off to his right, whereas the sidewalk on his left was
a long, uninterrupted stretch. He glanced at the doorways to the bars
and restaurants that lined this block, dismissing them immediately.
The man who called himself Scavenger would never be so foolish as
to allow himself to be cornered inside a building. He would be on
the move.

Mark shoved his way rather violently to the corner and plunged
down the side street. There was no crowd here, they were all behind
him now, and he could see all the way to the next intersection.

A tall, dark-haired figure in a long black coat was at the far end
of the block, walking quickly, turning into the next street. He disappeared around the corner just as Mark caught sight of him.

Mark charged ahead, throwing himself down the length of the
block as swiftly as humanly possible. There was no time to think of
the obvious danger of what he was doing. Catching up with his opponent might be the worst thing that could happen to him, even deadly,
but it didn't occur to him in the panic of the moment, in his sudden,
overwhelming need to reach the man and confront him. He arrived at
the corner where the man had just been and spun around it into the
next block.

There were not many people or cars in this street, and one swift
glance told him that his quarry was nowhere in sight. In the space of
mere seconds he had simply vanished. Mark paused, panting, sweating, gazing wildly around him, and that was when he saw it.

The movement was so small as to be almost subliminal, the tiny
sound possibly imagined. On his immediate left, wide white steps led
up to huge double oak doors between columns. In that instant, Mark
thought he saw one of the doors swing shut, and perhaps he heard a
muffled thud as it did so.

Then he was rushing up the wide steps and pushing at the heavy,
brass-studded doors. He plunged forward into cool darkness and
stopped, gazing around at the cavernous place, blinking.

It was a church, a Catholic church, and the interior was so vast that
it might actually be a cathedral. Hundreds of polished wooden pews

stretched away toward the side walls, which were lined with big stained-glass windows depicting various Bible scenes. He had only fleeting impressions of Moses and Noah and what might have been the Tower of Babel. He blinked again, adjusting his vision to the gloom. The only light was supplied by what appeared to be a thousand candles before the altar a hundred feet in front of him. The dim light winked on gold and brass adornments and glowed softly on the rows of white columns at the sides, and on the endless rows of benches.

He stepped slowly, cautiously forward into the room, aware of the new fear that now suffused him. Despite the cavernous expanse before him, he felt a sudden constriction in his throat, a fresh beading of perspiration on his forehead. The walls, as far apart as they were, seemed to be pressing in on him, crushing him. He couldn't breathe, and it wasn't from the running. It was the old, familiar feeling from all his childhood years, the endless hours with his father, with his family, in similar settings. The rows of benches, the organ, the stained-glass windows, the inevitable cross with its dreadful burden. Now, as an adult, he knew that there was a name for it: claustrophobia.

There were only a few people in the place at this time; three or four elderly women, their heads covered with shawls, and a lone middle-aged man who knelt in a front pew, apparently praying. The evening service would have concluded by now, and anyone else who had been here was gone. Scavenger was nowhere in sight.

Mark stood at the top of the wide center aisle, peering into every corner, looking for movement of any kind. Just as he looked off toward the right of the front dais, he saw a tiny sliver of light, and a tall figure in long, flowing black slipping through what was obviously a side door.

And he was running again, down the center aisle, his pounding feet making no sound on the thick red carpet. He tore across the room between two long rows of pews and down the extreme right aisle toward the side door. The old-fashioned wooden confessionals were here, and he nearly collided with the first one in the dark, but he put up his hands to check himself and ran on.

When he found the door, he paused another moment, gasping for breath, and turned for one more look at the big room behind him. The scent of incense; the low whisper of prayer; the pinpricks of light from the votive candles; the enormous, gleaming gold cross suspended above the altar. With a shudder of distaste, he pulled the door open and barged outside into the cool, revivifying evening air.

He was now in a side alley, with the lit windows of a rectory on his left. On his right was the entrance to the alley, the street from which he had entered the church. He ran down the length of the alley and emerged into the street, gazing frantically in both directions. There was nothing, no one in the street to his left, so he turned right, toward the church, to the direction from which he had come.

He stopped short, frozen into inaction by the unexpected sight before him.

There, not twenty feet away, at the base of the wide steps to the church, the tall man in the long black coat was standing quite still, his back to Mark, embracing a pretty, laughing young woman. Mark stared, taking in the scene, the complete, abrupt surprise of it, feeling the rush of adrenaline as his feverish mind tried to decide what to do.

It never came to that. As he watched, the man kissed the woman's cheek. Then, joining her in her laughter as he threw his arm across her shoulders, the man turned around, and the couple began walking directly toward Mark.

He was not Scavenger. Not even close. He was off by at least twenty years. This tall, dark-haired man in the long black coat was not much more than thirty, and his handsome face was unscarred.

Mark stood quite still, rooted to the spot, staring at the attractive young couple. As they came abreast of him, the young woman pulled a black bandit's mask from her purse and handed it to her companion. As he slipped it over his head and down over his eyes, she produced a similar one, this one bright blue and edged with rhinestones, and put it on her face. Now they, along with the intoxicated throng in Bourbon Street a block away, were faceless, anonymous.

He stood there for a long time, long after the couple had passed him and gone to join the parade, staring blankly ahead of him into the darkness of this relatively quiet, relatively unpopulated street. The whole incident played through his mind in fast motion: the sighting in Bourbon Street, the headlong chase, the eerie cathedral with its sights and smells that reminded him of things long forgotten. And all for this. Again, as in New York two nights ago, he had been chasing a shadow. A phantom. Scavenger, whoever he was, was gone.

It was cool now, in this evening on this quiet street in New Orleans. A breeze wafted down the sidewalk, chilling him, bringing with it the faint music of the remote celebrants. Mark had no more choices, no more options. He knew what he must do now.

Once you have begun to play, you cannot stop for any reason until the game is over. With a little sigh, half of frustration and half of capitulation, he turned around and slowly made his way through the dark streets to his car.

25

Tracy got out of the taxi and walked quickly up the steps to the door of her building. She used the key on the first door, then paused in the entryway before the second locked door to check her mailbox. Bills, political announcements, a mail-order catalog, department store white sales, a literary newsletter to which she subscribed. There was only one piece of mail of a personal nature—an invitation, by the size of it. She carried everything in through the second door and up the stairs to her second-floor apartment.

She left everything but the invitation on the table beside her front door and went into the kitchen to make tea, shedding her coat as she walked. While she waited for the water to boil, she opened the envelope. Oh, yeah, she thought, the baby shower. A college buddy was expecting her first baby next month, a boy, and here was the information about the party. She would have to get a gift. She filed it away mentally as she made a mug of tea and went out into the living room. Thinking of her pregnant friend made her smile to herself, and she knew she was thinking of her own impending marriage to Mark.

Mark . . .

The smile faded as she went over to the telephone to check for messages. She hit the replay button and sat on the couch, sipping tea. The first voice was that of her friend Mona, who had also received the shower invitation, and what on *earth* were they going to get for the baby? Please call and advise. Then a frantic Richard Gaines, her author with the big medical thriller, who had just seen the proposed dust jacket copy of the book and was clearly not happy with it. Please call and advise. The third beep was followed by a few seconds of silence, then the click of a hang-up.

She called the author first, but he was out, so she left a message telling him not to panic; she'd call his editor in the morning. She couldn't remember Mona's number, and Mona had neglected to leave it in her message, which was typical of her. She was about to rise and go to the bedroom to check her Rolodex when she spotted the caller ID box beside the phone.

Oh, yes, she thought. She'd just begun the service with the phone company, and the little white box had arrived a few days ago. She still wasn't used to its presence. She pressed the button on the box to review the last few calls, and there on the electronic display was Mona's name and number, followed by Richard Gaines's name and number. The final display read, *Out of Area, 504-555-4723.*

Telemarketers, she supposed. She'd already gotten a couple of similar numbers in the few days she'd had the ID service, and she'd called the companies and had her name removed from their files. She left a message for Mona, who was also not answering. Then she dialed the third number, preparing to make a polite but firm demand of whichever magazine or time-share offerer answered. She was not prepared for what she heard.

"Mullins Guest House," said a woman's voice. An older woman, by the sound of it, with a distinct, musical Southern drawl.

Guest house? Tracy thought. Then she thought, Mark.

"Hello," she said. "My name is Tracy Morgan. Someone at this number called me about two hours ago, but they didn't leave a message. I'm returning the call."

There was a moment of silence on the other end of the line. Then the woman said, "Hmm. I didn't call you, so it must have been one of my guests. I'm afraid I don't really—"

"Do you have a Mark Stevenson staying there?" Tracy asked.

Now the woman sounded relieved. "Oh, yes, Mr. Stevenson. Well, he's out at the moment, but I can tell him you—"

"No, thank you," Tracy said quickly. He hadn't left a message, had changed his mind, and she didn't want him to think she was anxious, checking up on him. He'd only been gone two days. "No message. I—I'll call him later. I know he's busy there in Washington, and I don't want to disturb him." A lame excuse, but it would do. She was about to hang up when the woman surprised her.

"Excuse me, did you say Washington? My dear, we're in New Orleans. Mr. Stevenson is out to dinner, but—"

"New Orleans?" Tracy whispered, staring down at the number on the box. The area code, 504, stared back at her. "Oh. Oh, well, never mind. I'll just call him later. Thank—thank you." She hung up quickly.

She sat there for several minutes, wondering what Mark was doing in New Orleans. He'd said Washington. Well, he was now somewhere else, obviously, so his research must have taken him there. With a shrug, she stood up from the couch and went into the bedroom.

Once there, she proceeded directly to the desk by the window, where her computer terminal stood waiting for her. She dropped into her padded executive chair, wondering where to begin. Carol Grant's story over dinner had been a shock, but it was sketchy at best. Tracy was suddenly filled with an urgent need to know more, and that was where her job came in handy.

Because she was a representative of one of New York's biggest literary agencies, her computer was hooked up to the company's mainframe. She'd never used the excess information in the past, but she and everyone else at the agency had been instructed in how to do so. They had been told the services would be good for checking nationwide reviews of their clients' work. It took her only a few moments of scanning the various menus to find what she wanted. A few key entries, and she was in the newspaper morgue.

She decided on the *Chicago Tribune*. It was that city's newspaper of record, and it would presumably have the most extensive coverage of the Farmer tragedy. Summoning the window for subject requests, she paused, her hands poised above the keyboard. What exact subject did she want? Shrugging, she typed, FAMILY MAN.

After a few moments of blinking and whirring, a listing appeared. She scrolled down the list, staring. There were more than four hundred references under that heading.

She tried again. Erasing FAMILY MAN, she typed, FARMER, JACOB. Over three hundred references, nearly as bad. She wondered at that until she realized: Reverend Farmer would have been in the news a lot, long before his murder. He had been the local leader of a nationwide religious sect, and a celebrity on television.

Tracy erased the name and sank back in the chair, sipping her tea. The solution, when it occurred to her, was perfectly simple. She leaned forward again and typed, FARMER, MATTHEW.

Fifty-seven references.

She stared at the list of dates and page numbers for a long time.

Then she stood up and went over to the bedroom window. She gazed down into the dark street and the park across the way, thinking, FARMER, MATTHEW.

FARMER, MATTHEW was Mark. Mark Stevenson. The man she loved. The man she was going to marry. . . .

She stood there for a long time, staring down at Gramercy Park. She watched the occasional people straggling by on the opposite sidewalk in front of the park's decorative iron fence, and the occasional cars in the street directly below. A woman was walking a large dog. A couple, well dressed, apparently on their way to or from some function. Two young women, laughing as they dashed across the street. Then a tall, blond young man strolled into view, paused under a lamppost, and lit a cigarette. He glanced up at her building, and for one odd moment Tracy thought he was looking directly at her. Then he looked away and wandered off, out of sight. He seems vaguely familiar, she mused. Probably a neighbor.

She was aware of what she was doing. She was stalling, putting off the inevitable moment, and that wasn't like her, not at all. Taking a long, deep breath, she went back over to the desk and sat down again. In a moment her fingers were racing over the keyboard.

The first twenty-three references to FARMER, MATTHEW predated the tragedy. It was a mini-history of his childhood activities with the Church of the True Believers. She read slowly, getting a sense of his life. Revival meetings in Chicago, a local telethon, several appearances at nationally televised events involving the church. And on and on.

The newspaper pages were exactly reproduced, and there were occasional photographs of the family. Little Matthew, age seven, dark-haired and unsmiling, with a smaller boy and girl, his brother and sister, surrounding their parents. Reverend Farmer was a tall, stout, imposingly fierce-looking man with Mark's—or, rather, Matthew's—dark good looks, and Mrs. Farmer was a pretty woman with a big blond helmet of hair, obviously not her natural color. There were other family publicity pictures: Matthew at ten, twelve, fourteen; the reverend growing stouter and more fierce; the mother's false blond hair getting bigger; the family all in white, all in black. In one particularly obnoxious shot, the three children were dressed in choir gowns and carrying tambourines.

It was horrible, obscene, that these beautiful children should be used so by the obviously self-satisfied zealot and his creepy-looking wife. That the Church of the True Believers, whoever the hell they were, would fall for this artifice. But what Tracy couldn't help noticing, even as the bile rose in her throat, was that in every single photo, Matthew was the only member of the family who never smiled. He looked miserable. As well he should, she thought.

Then came the next group of stories, the Christmas morning massacre. Tracy stopped at the first Family Man story, scrolling back up the list, certain that she'd missed something. No, she hadn't. She was looking for references to Matthew specifically, not the rest of the family. But there was a gap in his reported history, a gap of nearly eight years, from when he would have been about fifteen until the Christmas morning when he had discovered the bodies of his family.

Of course. He'd run away, lived on the street, gotten into drugs. Then he'd cleaned himself up and gone back to school, putting himself through college with a job. Something about market research for consumers.

She scrolled quickly through the many entries about the murders, reading only snatches of stories and glancing briefly at the awful pictures. Stretchers being brought in a line out the front door of a big white house. A photo of the mercifully empty living room where they had been found, the garish Christmas tree and garlands providing a horrible counterpoint to the dark stains on carpets and furniture. Other, similar photos accompanying the story: a living room in New Orleans and a sundeck and swimming pool in Los Angeles, the sites of the first two assaults now linked to The Family Man.

"Dear God," she whispered as she clicked on the next newspaper entry.

She froze, staring at the bold headline:

SON QUESTIONED IN FARMER
FAMILY MASSACRE

Tracy blinked and read the words again. No, there was no mistake.

Here it was, the part Carol Grant had not told her. Carol obviously had not known. Mark hadn't told her about it.

She read slowly through the next few entries, feeling her anger rising again. It hadn't been enough that he'd stumbled on the scene that Christmas morning, found his entire family in that horrifying way. He'd then been taken into custody. Detained. Questioned by local police and an FBI agent named O'Hara. She read carefully: no, nowhere did it indicate that he had ever actually been arrested, charged with anything. He'd been taken to the police station for several hours, then released. After that, everyone apparently proceeded on the obviously correct assumption that it was the work of The Family Man.

They had questioned him, the paper reported, because of his absence, his fall from grace. His well-known antipathy for his parents, his family, the Church of the True Believers. His arrest record for shoplifting and drug activity. His "antisocial behavior," as the reporter called it.

What shocked her most about the shocking story was the photograph accompanying the penultimate entry, under the headline:

FARMER SON "NOT A SUSPECT" SAYS FBI

In the picture, Matthew—Mark, she reminded herself again—was walking down the snowy steps of what was apparently the police station. The face was familiar to her, if younger, but that was the only resemblance the scowling young man had to the man she knew as Mark Stevenson. The young man in the picture was rail-thin, with spiky blond hair and a dark beard. He wore small hoops in both ears, a down-filled coat, and carried a bunched-up knit hat sporting a Chicago Bears logo. But most unsettling were his eyes: big, wide, glazed with shock. With fear. And with unimaginable sorrow.

Tracy wondered that the market research people would allow this rather unkempt-looking young man to work for them. More than that, she wondered that he had gone home like that, to present himself, repentant, to his Fundamentalist Christian family. Most of all, she wondered how this rebel without a clue had ever, ever been transformed into Mark Stevenson, the award-winning author. Her lover, soon to be her husband.

She almost turned off the computer when she remembered that there was one more reference to Matthew Farmer in the *Chicago Tribune*. She clicked on the final entry and stared at the headline, a small surge of satisfaction growing within her.

FBI OFFERS FARMER SON A PUBLIC APOLOGY

FBI Special Agent Ronald O'Hara had called a press conference two days after the murders and exonerated Matthew Farmer of all suspicion in the matter of the Farmer murders. The agent went on to say that Judy Barlow had stated she was with Matthew at the crucial time, and that there was sufficient evidence at the scene to prove that the crime was the work of The Family Man. He apologized to Matthew Farmer for any distress he or his investigators might have caused. All of which meant one thing to Tracy: Matthew had obviously consulted legal counsel and been advised to press charges against the police and the FBI. The apology was their way of avoiding a lawsuit.

She turned off the computer, shaking her head in disgust. It took her several minutes and several more sips of the now-cold tea to realize that she was also relieved.

She was tremendously relieved.

Everything she had just learned about Matthew Farmer merely reinforced her love for him. He had rebelled against his obviously dreadful family, as she herself would have rebelled under the circumstances. His lost years on the streets and in the drug subculture were understandable, and his self-regeneration, education, and employment were admirable. His suffering at the hands of the bureaucrats was infuriating.

But the most wonderful thing about Matthew Farmer was his rebirth, in New York City, as Mark Stevenson.

Yes, Tracy decided. Now that she knew the whole story, all there was to know, she loved him even more than before. He was a strong man, brave and resourceful. Intelligent, too. And he was, to her, Mark Stevenson. Now and always.

Still, she wondered why he was now in New Orleans, and why he was apparently carrying a gun with him, and when he would come home to her.

26

The scent of river water was strong on the night air as Mark drove west out of the city. There was also a tinge of something else, something he could actually see reflected in the headlights, the first indications of a rising fog. The mist rolled in off the Mississippi, gleaming in the darkness on his left. He maneuvered the car over to the exit and left the highway.

He didn't know exactly where he was, wasn't even certain which parish he was in, but he found the riverside road with no difficulty. He drove on for several miles, crossing two bridges over the winding river and passing through a tiny, sleeping town. He glanced around at the dark buildings, thinking how different small towns were from cities. Here it was barely nine-thirty, and practically no lights remained on. As he left the town behind and drove on through the thick forest that gradually arrived on both sides of the road, he began to get the peculiar feeling that he was all alone in the world.

Two white pillars loomed up, ghostly apparitions in the mist before him. They marked the entrance to the turnoff on the left, the drive that would lead to the house. He made the turn easily, looking over at the corroded brass plaque on the right column as it was briefly caught in the light: TENNANT HOUSE. He drove silently up the long, curving driveway, flinching as the dark overhanging leaves and tendrils of gray moss materialized in the headlight beam lighting up the fog. The longer strands slapped against the windshield and whispered across the roof of the car.

The once-pristine asphalt drive had become rutted and potholed now from years of exposure and no maintenance, and he swerved several times to avoid the larger bumps. Sarah had said that nobody had lived here in a long time, and the drive was proof enough that this was true. Tennant House, like his own childhood home in the quiet North Shore suburb of Chicago, was haunted: a family had been slaughtered there, slaughtered by The Family Man. Who on earth would want to live there? People were now living in the townhouse in Brooklyn, but it was different in cities. A little renovation, a breakup into apartment units, and the history of a city building faded. New people constantly arrived, needing space, creating their own history. But for this isolated mansion and his family home in Evanston, the legend lived on.

He still owned his family's house, but he'd rarely been able to rent it. Adults shunned the pretty, three-story wooden house, and the neighborhood children dared each other to climb the steps to the front porch late at night and to throw rocks that smashed the windows. Then they would run away, laughing and screaming. Several years ago, after the third report from the surveillance company that guarded the property reached him in New York, Mark had hired a Chicago contractor to board up the place. He'd done this by phone: he had not gone back to Evanston, not once in twelve years.

A final curve, a final caressing hand of moss against the windshield, and the big, pillared plantation manor house appeared in the distance before him. He braked, cut the engine, and sat studying the facade of the house in the glow of the headlights. The fog was thickening, causing the beams to appear contained, suspended: two finite, horizontal cones of light stretching out before him in the gray mist. He switched off the lights and got out of the car.

As he walked the rest of the way up the drive, he noticed that the temperature had dropped sharply. It was chilly now in the late evening, and a breeze from the river beyond the house was moving the plumes of fog around, so that even the air around him seemed to be a shivering, animate presence. The rustling of the leaves in the trees created a low, steady background noise. Otherwise, all was silent. He came to the circle before the pillared veranda, where the drive curved off to the left toward the long, low building beside the mansion, now a garage but once a carriage house, and, still earlier, slave quarters. He wondered just how old this house was, and he wondered that the state had not offered to buy the place from Sarah Gammon and convert it into a tourist attraction, as so many other plantations in the area now were. Then again, perhaps they had. Perhaps Sarah simply refused all offers, holding on to the property in some misguided desire to keep others safe from her family's fate.

Mark stood in the fog at the base of the two steps to the veranda, gazing around as he pulled the big front-door key from his pants pocket. The windows were all boarded shut, as were his own windows in Evanston, and probably for the same reason. Malicious children would, no doubt, find this place hard to resist. *Lizzie Borden, with an axe, gave her father forty whacks. . . .*

Then he noticed that the front door was ajar.

The wind rustled the trees. The wet fog swirled silently behind him. A faint glow of light was visible beyond the crack of the door. And there was something else, a sound he now heard softly emanating from inside the house. Music: low, indistinct, at the very border of his threshold of hearing, he could just make out the tinny strains of a jazz band.

On that night, that Mardi Gras thirteen years ago, The Family Man had come here, moving silently, stealthily from room to room, finding the sleeping Tennant family and cutting their throats one by one. The father, the mother, the twenty-year-old son, the seventeen-year-old son, and a basset hound named Huckleberry. They had all been carried down the stairs to the living room, where they had been arranged, posed, on couches and chairs, the dog on the carpet at Mrs. Tennant's feet. Their dead faces had been covered with glittering holiday masks. Mr. Tennant's severed head, also masked, was placed on the floor beside the dog. Then the room had been meticulously decorated, festooned with balloons and confetti, and long red candles had been lit and placed on every available surface, even the floor. As a final flourish, when everything else was just as The Family Man had wanted it, the home entertainment center in one corner had been put to use. When Sarah and her friends had arrived on the scene many hours later, their discovery had been orchestrated by the music that played over and over in the otherwise silent room. It was the unofficial theme song of Mardi Gras, of New Orleans: "When the Saints Go Marching In." But the music that now emanated from beyond the open door was Jelly Roll Morton's "Dead Man Blues," the song Mark had put in his novel. Scavenger was following Mark's fictional blueprint, as he had done with the music in Brooklyn.

There was a moment then, in the cold, wet fog, when Mark very nearly decided to stop. It would be so easy, he realized, to simply get back in the car and drive away. He could return to the city, check out of the guest house, and go back to New York. To Bedford Street. To Tracy. He could find some other way to make this man, this Scavenger, come forward.

No. As if there were an actual human voice speaking from the mist behind him, the words of instruction came into his mind. *You must follow my scenario strictly, as it is presented to you.* This was his chance, his only opportunity to find out what Scavenger wanted him to know.

Mark did not leave. He didn't even turn around. Instead, he reached into his jacket and pulled out the Smith & Wesson .38. Then he walked resolutely up the two steps and across the brick-paved veranda to the open front door. Extending his left hand before him, he slowly pushed the door wide open. The creak of the unoiled hinges sounded like a shout.

The music was louder now, and the glow of light was coming through the archway that led to the living room on his left. The main hall before him and the other front room on his right were dark. He stood at the entrance of the house, listening intently. The music stopped, then began again. The rustling in the trees behind him continued. Otherwise, all was still silent.

Then, taking a long, deep breath to steady himself, Mark walked forward into the nightmare.

Beyond the archway, the enormous living room glowed in the light of a hundred candles. Long red candles, he noticed, everywhere, on every available surface, even the floor. The flickering lights made the white sheets that covered all the furniture seem to be alive, actually moving. Scattered evenly over the dust-rimed wood floor and the filthy Oriental carpets was a multicolored layer of confetti. The faded white ceiling was almost completely obscured by a riot of balloons in every color of the rainbow. The incongruous sounds of the Dixieland band emanated from a large portable compact disk player that stood on the sheet-covered coffee table in the center of the room, surrounded by tall red candles.

There was one other object on the coffee table, and Mark stood staring at it for several long seconds before he could will himself to move. He realized that he had been holding his breath ever since he'd entered the room, and the gun was clutched in his right hand, pointing rigidly out before him. When his breath returned, when the pounding in his chest and temples subsided, he walked across the carpet of confetti to the table.

It was a shiny black-lacquered cardboard box, somewhat larger than the boxes his shirts were in when they came back from the laundry, and it was carefully, festively decorated with black ribbon. A big black bow sat in the exact center of the lid. Mark stared down at the package, and several long seconds passed before he realized with a little shock of embarrassment that he was actually aiming the gun at it. Uttering a dry, mirthless chuckle, he put the gun down on the table and reached for the bow. The black ribbons fell away, and he slowly lifted the lid.

The box was filled with black tissue paper. Moving several crinkly layers aside, he discovered what he had suspected, had known, would be there: a big, ornately decorated papier-mâché Mardi Gras mask.

It was in the general shape of the face of some small animal, as well as Mark could determine. A wolf, perhaps, or a fox. A jackal? Yes, that was what it most resembled. The almond-shaped eyeholes, the tapering snout, the pointed ears, the tips of white lower teeth sticking up from the corners of the ferally grinning mouth. Nothing so noble, so elegant as a wolf: this animal, whatever it was, fed on the abandoned kills of other, braver creatures.

A scavenger.

Yes, Mark decided, a jackal. The lowest form of life.

But this was far from a realistic representation. It was closer to something Japanese, a garish Kabuki mask. The swirling lines of metallic red and yellow outlined, emphasized the cruel features. There was definitely something evil, something obscene about it.

Mark actually smiled to himself as he began to lower the object back into the box. Then he stopped, arrested by the sight of the black envelope that rested in the tissue.

He put the mask down on the table next to the gun, picked up the envelope, and tore it open. There was a folded sheet of black-edged white linen stationery inside. A funeral note, he thought as he opened the paper and stared down at the lines written in the now-familiar neat hand with a red felt-tipped pen.

The note read:

Four people and one animal died in this room. Can you feel them watching you? Masks were important to The Family Man because they let him be anyone he wanted to be. I have a very special gift for you. Check out the chair in the corner.

Silence. The music stopped temporarily, and there was an almost palpable, deathly silence in the house. Mark strained his ears to listen, but there was nothing anywhere. Then the Dixieland band started up again with its jaunty rendition of the old New Orleans song. His rational mind informed him that he was alone in the house, alone and far from any other humans. But he could feel the eyes. He was being scrutinized, silently assessed. *Can you feel them watching you?* Yes. Yes, he could feel them watching him. Four people and one animal. . . .

He turned slowly around in a circle, peering into every shadow, every dark corner of the room. The flickering candles caused the shadows and dark places to waver slightly, their boundaries constantly shifting. The empty doorway, the sheet-covered furniture, the confetti-strewn carpets. The chairs and carpets were new, presumably; the originals had been soaked with the Tennant family's blood. Sarah would have had them removed, destroyed. His survey ended when his gaze fell on the lone sheeted form in the farthest corner from where he was standing, in the darkest part of the room.

I have a very special gift for you.

Mark would later wonder why he didn't pick up the gun from the table. Instead, he picked up the nearest red candle. As he began to move, the music started up again, filling the place with its driving rhythm. Slowly, cautiously, his gaze riveted to the white sheet that glowed softly in the dark before him, he walked across the room.

Check out the chair in the corner.

He stood before it, looking down. It was one of those big, over-stuffed armchairs, from the shape of it, and the sheet hung loosely, tentlike, over the high, wide bulk. In one swift move, Mark reached out toward the top of it, grasped the dusty cover in his fingers, and yanked. With a soft whisper of sound, the sheet fluttered slowly to the floor.

The jolt of raw, electric shock welled up in him, exploding outward against his rib cage. His limbs went briefly numb, and he nearly lost his balance. The candle sputtered out as it fell to land at his feet. Uttering a little cry of surprise, he took an involuntary step backward and brought his hands up to cover his gaping mouth. He breathed heavily in and out, nearly hyperventilating, staring.

There was a man sitting in the chair. He was of medium height and build, as well as Mark could determine, with close-cropped, bright red hair. He was wearing black slacks and shoes, and his dress shirt was white—or rather, it had been white at one time. His entire face was obscured by the shiny, colorful Mardi Gras mask he wore, an exact duplicate of the one in the box on the table across the room. But even this, even the mask, was not the most remarkable thing about him. There was a deep, jagged brown slit across his throat just under his chin, and the blood, once red but now a dry rust color, had rained down onto the white shirt, saturating it. As Mark stared, a single fat black housefly materialized from somewhere to buzz around, and then to land on, the gaping wound on the man's neck. After a moment, the fly began to feed.

Mark couldn't think. Somewhere, in some deep recess, some fundamental part of him, there was an instinct to move, either toward or away from the thing in the chair that had very recently been a live human being. The man was not alive now; there was no question of it. The stench of dried blood and urine emanated outward from the body, permeating the room as it assaulted Mark's nostrils. Yet he did not, *could* not will himself to move. He merely continued to stand there, staring.

When the big, rough hand came around from behind him, clapping something soft and wet and sweet-smelling over his nose and mouth, it took him a full five seconds to react. But by then, of course, it was too late to do anything at all. He had drawn in his breath involuntarily, inhaling deeply of the odd perfume. His attempt to struggle against the iron grip over his face was almost instantly weakened as the chemical began to work. He tried to hold his breath, but after several long moments he inhaled again, sending a second dose into his lungs.

The gun, he thought. The gun is on the table behind me, next to the mask, some ten or twelve feet away. It might as well be a hundred miles.

And still the arms were holding him. He breathed in again, no longer able to fight it. An odd sense of euphoria overtook him now, and an overwhelming desire to go with the flow, to give himself over to the growing darkness. Perhaps this is death, he thought. Perhaps that was the goal all along, to isolate me and kill me. And yet . . .

It was his final coherent thought. Another slow, deep breath, and then the raucous Dixieland band exploded in his head in a white burst

27

He worked quickly and efficiently, because he didn't know how long Mark Stevenson would be out, and there was much to do before he regained consciousness. He moved around the room like a shadow, only occasionally illuminated as the flickering lights from the increasingly fewer candles caused his pale gray eyes or the shiny black buttons on his coat to sparkle. Manipulating the Dustbuster was not easy because the translucent rubber surgical gloves dulled the sensation in his fingers. But soon, after several hasty trips to his car behind the house, the job was done.

The fog was dissipating as he drove away down the drive, through the stone columns, and away down the road. He stopped once, at a remote section of a bayou, and opened the car's trunk. The soft splashes of the heavily weighted objects entering the murky water could not be heard even a few feet away. In a matter of minutes, he was back on the road. A bridge, and then the highway. The lights of the city soon appeared in the dark distance.

There was still much to do, and precious little time in which to do it. But he had memorized every action of his part in the game, assessed every brilliant detail. He knew everything he was supposed to accomplish, and why. This game had an irresistible reward. He wanted it as he had never wanted anything, not even his freedom. There would be no mistakes between now and midnight on Saturday.

Midnight, Saturday. The last scene of the game. The final dramatic flourish. The violent, bloody, screaming end of Mark Stevenson.

The end of Matthew Farmer.

In the chill silence of the speeding car, the man with the scar smiled as he reentered New Orleans. His first destination was Mullins Guest

House, but he was only there for a few minutes. Then he drove north through the dark streets toward the lake. He arrived in the parking lot of the Pontchartrain Clinic just before midnight, at the same moment when Mark Stevenson opened his eyes and stared up at the ceiling of the living room of Tennant House some twenty-five miles away.

WEDNESDAY

28

He had been dreaming about his family, about his father, and reality was slow in returning to him. He lay on his back on the floor, waiting for the dizziness to pass. His mouth was dry, and there was a throbbing in his temples. At first he wondered where he was, and why he was lying on the floor of an alien room.

Then he began to remember. He was in Tennant House, and there was a dead man sitting in a chair in this room. Hands—he had no doubt as to whose hands they were—had grabbed him from behind, and he had been drugged. Dr. Tilson with his slicked-back brown hair above his white lab coat: Mark had a sudden image of the veterinarian who took care of the Farmer family dog, Sam, and he wondered why that was until he remembered the distinctive smell. Chloroform. Scavenger had rendered him unconscious.

Scavenger. Was he still here, in this room with him? Mark rolled over onto his left side and tucked himself into a tight, fetal ball, bracing himself for whatever would come next out of the overwhelming darkness. A vicious kick, perhaps, or the sharp blade of a knife. The knife that had dispatched the red-haired man in the chair, whoever he was. The knife that could even now be moving forward in the darkness toward his jugular vein. . . .

Nothing happened. He remained there, still, silent, willing himself to breathe as quietly as possible, for several long minutes. After a time, he concentrated on listening. No sound emanated from any other part of the room. It was only then that he realized the music was gone. He peered through the darkness around him, and he began to make out the bulky forms of sheeted furniture nearby. There was a couch, and over there the table that had held the black-lacquered box. The mask and the note. *I have a very special gift for you.*

Now, at last, his panic and confusion receded, leaving him drained, heavy. He was possessed of a sudden, overwhelming urge to sleep. I mustn't do that, he thought. I have to get up from the floor and go back over to the chair. I have to remove that awful jackal's mask and see who is there. The red-haired corpse with the gash across his throat, the bloated housefly sucking his coagulated blood. . . .

When Mark opened his eyes again, he was aware that more time had passed, but he could not even guess how long he had been there. He had slept again, he was certain of that, but if he had dreamed this time, he didn't remember it. It had been the sleep of exhaustion brought on by the shock, the drug, the experience of being in this house, in this room. The carefully reproduced scene of the long-ago crime, and the dark mind that had conceived it. And the new victim, the body in the chair.

The body. This thought propelled him groggily, shakily to his feet. He wasn't later certain how he managed it, but he was standing upright, rubbing his eyes before peering through the darkness at the room. What he eventually saw in the gloom around him almost caused him to sink to the floor again.

It was gone. All of it. Everything. The candles, the balloons, the confetti. The box that had been on the table. The source of the music. He was standing in the center of the Tennant living room, slowly making out the shapes of sheet-covered furniture, empty surfaces, the immaculate rugs. All was as it had presumably been before last night, when Scavenger had arrived here to set the stage for Mark. He stumbled weakly forward across the open space to stand once more before the big armchair in the corner.

He remembered that it had been upholstered in a striped material, dark red alternating with deep purple, but the stripes looked gray to him now, as did the neatly folded sheet that rested on one overstuffed arm. Otherwise, the chair was empty. Slowly, trancelike, he leaned forward to inspect the upholstery, then he picked up the sheet and unfolded it, holding every section of it up before his face to study it. Nothing, anywhere. No drop of blood, not even the horrible smell of the dead man remained. It was as if Mark had hallucinated, as if the whole event had never occurred.

He wondered about that as he made his way through the archway and across the foyer to the front door. Was it possible that he had been somehow drugged, or hypnotized? That all of it, like the dreams about his family when he was unconscious, had simply happened in his *mind*? He arrived at the big front door and opened it, startled by the bright sunlight that immediately assailed him. He was now able to see the watch on his wrist: nearly eight o'clock. In the *morning*. He had been inside the house for some ten hours.

As he stared down at the face of his watch, all thoughts of drugs or hypnosis left him for good. A single, bright red flake of confetti detached itself from the sleeve of his leather jacket and fluttered down to land, a scarlet drop of blood, on the doorsill at his feet.

So, he thought. It was not a dream. It happened. The dead man in the chair had been real. Still, he knew that he could not go to the police with his story, even if he wanted to do so. Why would anyone, looking at the empty living room, believe the ravings of a man, famous for his crime stories, with his current bestseller based partially on the events in this very house? A stunt, they'd say. Publicity for his writing career. For the book he was planning to write, the actual nonfiction account. Especially as there was no physical evidence: no balloons, no candles, no confetti. And no dead body. Just a famous writer, a man with a bizarre story about a sick game he was playing with a phantom. A famous writer armed with a—

Mark's hands flew up to slap against the inside pocket of his jacket. The empty inside pocket. His gun was gone.

He turned around and plunged back into the dark interior of the house. Of course, he remembered as he ran, I left it on the table beside the box. He paused to flick the light switch just inside the living room archway. Nothing happened; the electricity had been turned off years ago. But there was now enough sunlight coming in through the open front door behind him to illuminate the downstairs rooms. And to illuminate the table.

It was empty. His gun was definitely gone.

Frantically, he inspected his pockets. His change, his key ring, his wallet with credit cards and cash. But no gun.

And no key. The big, old-fashioned key to Tennant House was gone, too, along with the gun. And the dead body. And all the rest of it.

Now he was running, out of the house and across the veranda, into the bright sunlight and down the drive to his car. Yes, at least *that* was still there, waiting where he had parked it last night. He got in the car and started the engine, glancing briefly over at the cell phone on the seat beside him before tearing off down the curving, moss-framed drive to the main road, trying to reverse his route in his mind so he would not get lost. Time, he knew, was precious. Scavenger was out there somewhere, waiting for him. Making plans. And somewhere out there, too—with Scavenger, perhaps—was a dead body. The body was an unknown man with bright red hair.

Traffic became heavier as he neared the city. Of course: it was eight-thirty, the start of another business day. Wednesday. He maneuvered the red Taurus through the streets as best he could, arriving at last in the lane off Decatur near Jackson Square. He parked in a space reserved for patrons of Mullins Guest House, snatched up the cellular phone, and ran inside and up the stairs to his room, the room he had rented but had not slept in. He switched on the overhead light and stood in the doorway of the guest room, staring.

There, on the blue chenille bedspread, was the black-lacquered box.

He moved warily forward, regarding the box, noting its height, breadth, and depth, and the shiny black ribbons and bow that had so carefully, so lovingly been replaced. He was reaching out for it, wondering. . . .

At that moment, the cell phone in his other hand began to ring. He didn't even pause long enough to allow the second thrill of apprehension to register on his brain. He flicked the instrument on and raised it to his ear.

"*What?*" he cried.

There was a sound on the other end of the line, a harsh intake of breath, followed by a little grunt that sounded like a laugh.

"And good morning to you, too, Mr. Stevenson!" Scavenger said. "Did you get up on the wrong side of the bed—or should I say, the *floor?*" Another chuckle.

"*Fuck you!*"

A pause now, and then the mellifluous, gratingly controlled voice continued. "Now, now, what did I tell you about being rude to me? Have you forgotten, Mark? I certainly hope not. Oh, indeed I do. Otherwise, you'll spend the rest of your life, however long that turns out to be, wondering. Aren't you the least bit curious? I mean, I thought Tennant House would just have you *fainting* with curiosity."

As upset as he was, Mark somehow remembered not to shout; there were Mrs. Mullins and the other guests to consider. His voice was low but sharp, a furious whisper. "Who was he, you sick son of a bitch? Who was the man in the chair? Who did you murder *now*?"

Another agonizing pause, another sharp laugh. Then the voice again, smooth as honey. "All in good time, Mark—though why your incivility should be rewarded, I simply cannot say. Listen carefully. You have until midnight tomorrow night. Your next destination is chronological, if you remember your Family Man lore, and who remembers it better than you? Eh, Mr. *Farmer*? You wrote the book, didn't you? You are looking for a word. That should be a cinch for a wordsmith such as yourself. A word, Mr. Mark-Matthew-Stevenson-Farmer. Just—a word."

Mark was staring at the bed in front of him. "What's in the box?"

Another chuckle. "Oh, I think you should look for yourse—"

"What's in the *box*, asshole?"

Now a long, pained sigh. "Oh, dear, your manners! Honestly! The *mask* is in the box! The mask of the scavenger. A souvenir of your sojourn to New Orleans. Midnight tomorrow night. You'd better get a move on. But have some breakfast first, before you go. I understand Mrs. Mullins is rather famous for her strawberry pancakes. She also provides each of her guests with a complimentary copy of the morning newspaper. *Bon appétit*, Mark." A final chuckle, and then the line went dead.

Mark uttered a low growl of equal parts frustration and disgust. Then he dropped the cell phone on the bed beside the box, tore off his clothes, and went into the little bathroom. A long, hot shower helped to make him feel slightly better, but he knew he wouldn't feel completely well again until the game was over.

The game. He thought about that as he put on fresh clothes and packed everything else in the suitcase. Almost as an afterthought, he tore open the black box, removed the Mardi Gras mask, and tossed it in the bag. The box with its macabre trimmings went into the wastepaper basket. He picked up the bag and made his way downstairs to the dining room.

It was late morning, and any other guests there were had apparently already eaten and gone. Mrs. Mullins seated him at a little table by the french doors, and she smiled and asked him if he'd enjoyed his stay in the room. Not having the heart to disabuse her, Mark lied that he'd slept well. He ordered the strawberry pancakes and gratefully accepted the little pot of coffee her assistant, a young woman in a waitress's uniform, brought from the kitchen. In minutes, the proprietress returned with the food. She lowered the heaping plate before him and placed a crisply folded morning newspaper beside it before leaving him alone in the room. He could hear clattering and running water from the kitchen as he began to eat.

He didn't get very far. He'd taken only four bites of the delicious pancakes before he idly picked up the newspaper and unfolded it. He placed it on the table and glanced down at the front page.

He stared, and the little coffee cup in his right hand nearly fell. He put the cup down and snatched up the paper. On the top half of the front page was a large photograph of a familiar-looking African-American woman, smiling under her snowy white cap. The big headline above the picture read:

NURSE SLAIN

It couldn't be, he thought. And yet it was. He knew it, even before he read the accompanying story, saw the name: *Millicent Call, 32, a nurse at Pontchartrain Clinic* . . .

Millie, the other nurse had called her yesterday. Nurse Call.

She had come off her shift at midnight. Twelve-oh-four a.m., according to her time card. She had said good night to two colleagues and left through the front door of the hospital, headed for her car. At approximately one-thirty a.m., a night watchman patrolling the grounds of the clinic had found her body in the farthest, darkest part of the nearly empty parking lot. She had been shot once through the heart, dead at least an hour, and a bullet had been retrieved. Preliminary investigators believed the shell to be from—

Mark lowered the paper to the table, staring blankly out the window at Decatur Street, frantically arranging a crude time line in his mind. He had arrived at Tennant House just before ten o'clock, and he had been drugged some fifteen minutes later. Ten-fifteen, plenty of time. The man with the scar had taken two things from him, the front door key and . . .

—a Smith & Wesson .38 revolver.

Scavenger had used his gun—his registered weapon—to murder the only witness to the scene in the dayroom of the clinic yesterday. Which meant . . .

No. Sarah Gammon was safe: he knew it. There was no way the

man with the scar could reach her, not on the fourth floor of Pontchartrain Clinic. Nurse Call had been message enough. Nurse Call and the red-haired man in the Mardi Gras mask, whoever he was. The game had taken a turn, and the only way Mark could ensure Sarah Gammon's continued safety was—

From nowhere, from everywhere around him, he heard the little chuckle, and the words: *I understand Mrs. Mullins is rather famous for her strawberry pancakes. She also provides each of her guests with a complimentary copy of the morning newspaper.* Bon appétit, *Mark.*

—to continue following instructions. If he did so now, Scavenger would follow him. It was the safest recourse, for Sarah Gammon as well as himself. He had received the new instruction—*Your next destination is chronological, if you remember your Family Man lore*—and he had understood.

Play the game, Mark, he told himself. Just play the fucking game.

Or more people will die.

And *I* will be one of them.

One hour later, Mark was at the airport. He turned in his rental Taurus at the Hertz counter and purchased a one-way ticket on the next available American Airlines flight to Los Angeles.

ARTICLE #3

WORD

29

When her telephone rang, Tracy was sitting at the table in the dining area of her Gramercy Park apartment, picking listlessly at her Japanese takeout dinner while she plowed through the latest submission from one of her authors. Another Wednesday evening: indifferent sushi and polished, professional, but ultimately indifferent romantic suspense. With a sigh, she put aside the manuscript of *Passion Flowers* and went to answer the phone.

Her mood improved immediately.

"Howdy!" Mark's cheerful-sounding voice reached through the receiver to kiss her lightly on the cheek, and her living room seemed to brighten at the sound. She smiled wryly, thinking that her reaction—or, at least, her description of it—belonged not in the real world but in the heavy-breathing pages she'd just been reading. Still, she was delighted.

"Mark! Darling, how are you?"

"I'm just fine. I'm in L.A., if you can believe it. I just got here a couple of hours ago."

"L.A.? I thought you were in, um, Washington." She bit her lip; she'd almost said New Orleans.

"Well, I was. But I had to come out here today. I'm—I'm interviewing a couple of people here, and I wanted to meet them in person. So I'm here for a day or two."

She noticed the slight change in his voice from buoyant and assured to a lower, more sober hesitancy. She wondered if this had anything to do with his failure to mention New Orleans as his last stop. But she decided not to comment on it. She was thinking of all the new information she had on him, courtesy of his former wife and the newspaper reports. She would not tell him about that; she would continue the charade of normality until he was back in New York, and they were once again face-to-face.

"I miss you," she heard herself saying now.

"I miss you, too," he said. "What are you doing today?"

She managed a laugh. "It's 'tonight' in New York now. I'm eating sushi and reading Stella Verlaine's latest bodice-ripper. A titled English-woman and a pirate named Jack Blood, shipwrecked together on a desert island. Need I say more?"

His laugh echoed hers. "Even so, it sounds more interesting than what I'm doing. I can't see my contacts until tomorrow, so I'm currently deciding between room service and one of the restaurants downstairs."

"Ah," she said. "Decisions, decisions." She cringed inwardly, hating this vapid conversation but uncertain how to change the subject. What could she say? *So, Matthew Farmer, tell me all about your dead family* . . . She closed her eyes, took a deep breath, and said, "When do you think you'll be coming home?"

There was a slight pause, and she could almost hear him thinking. At last he said, "Sunday. Monday at the latest. But you can do me a favor in the meantime, if you would. Could you sort of check on Jared, maybe give him a call? I don't know that he eats regularly if someone isn't making him do so."

Jared, she thought. Of course. . . .

"Sure," she said immediately. "I was thinking of calling him. Maybe I'll take him out to dinner one night."

"Good idea. Make sure he gets some solid food with his booze."

"I will."

"Thanks," Mark said. "Well, I guess I'd better—"

"Mark?"

"Yeah?"

"Mark, I love you. I really do. Come home soon, okay?"

Another pause. Then she heard him say, "I will. I love you, too, Tracy. I'll see you Sunday or—"

"Monday at the latest," she finished for him, unable to suppress the nervous little giggle that came after it.

"Yeah," he said. "Well, say hello to your mom, and get a square meal in Jared. And take care of yourself. 'Bye."

She opened her mouth, trying to form words, to ask him what he meant by that last remark, but then she heard the little click as he hung up. With a sigh, she replaced her own receiver.

Neither of them was still on the line to hear the third click.

Tracy had to consult her Rolodex to get Jared McKinley's number. Then she called him, fully expecting the answering machine. She knew he never answered the phone when he was writing, just like Mark. Or when he was drinking. Or when he was with a woman. Which, now that she thought about it, pretty much accounted for all of Jared's waking hours. She was therefore surprised when the phone was answered on the second ring.

"McKinley," the familiar, gruff voice said.

"Hi, Jared, it's Tracy Morgan."

"Tracy! What's shakin', babe?"

"Well, Mark just called, and he—he asked me to say hello to you."

"And hello to him, too. Where is the lucky stiff?"

"L.A., doing research or something. He'll be back in a few days. Uh, Jared, how'd you like to have dinner with me tomorrow night? I— I'd like to see you, and I want to talk to you about something."

"Nothin' serious, I hope."

Tracy blinked. "Why do you say that?"

"I don't know. You just sounded kind of . . . funny."

She wasn't going to get into this now. "How about Dave's Tavern, say, eight o'clock?"

"You're on, babe. I'll even put on a clean shirt."

"You do that. I'm buying."

"The *hell* you are!" His big laugh boomed through the phone.

Tracy smiled at the sound. "Oh, yes, I am. I'll see you at eight tomorrow."

"Forget the clean shirt," he said. "If you're buying, I'll be *naked!*"

Now she was laughing. "Just *dinner,* Jared!"

"Oh, all right. I've never stolen a friend's girl, so I'll be a perfect gentleman—though you *do* make it difficult. I hope Mark appreciates you. See you tomorrow."

"'Bye, Jared." Tracy was still laughing as they both hung up.

Again, she didn't hear the third click.

She made her way back to the table and sat down. Another bite of sushi. Another sip of diet Coke. She was reaching for the manuscript pages when she paused, thinking.

He'd been in Washington, then New Orleans, and now he was in

Los Angeles, and she didn't know why. Research for a new novel, he'd said, and she'd accepted that. But he was in the final phases of another novel, a work in progress, that was due at his publisher soon. So why was he doing this research now, of all times, when he had something much more pressing to do? He hadn't explained that, and she hadn't asked.

It occurred to her that she took everything people told her at face value: she was probably entirely too trusting. That would account for what had happened with Alan, her ex-husband. She was honest, always had been, and some fundamental, naive part of her automatically assumed that everyone else was honest, too. But they weren't.

She thought back over the two phone calls. The first had been stilted, strained, and the second had been charming and friendly. What on earth is Mark doing? she wondered. And why was I unable to ask him? Why was it so much easier to talk to a casual friend than to the man I'm about to marry? Why was he in New Orleans and—

Los Angeles. . . .

Then she realized. She had been hearing about his past, his personal involvement in the Family Man tragedy, the involvement that had prompted him to write his novel *Dark Desire*. Now she made the other connection: New Orleans and Los Angeles. They were the first two places where The Family Man had struck. Mark was going to the scenes of the crimes.

And he had a gun.

Tracy did not finish Stella Verlaine's novel that night, nor did she sleep. She sat in her living room, unaware of the darkness giving way to dawn outside her windows, thinking about Mark. She thought about his apparent preoccupation with the unsolved case. Most of all, she wondered whether she could accept his obsession and still be his partner in life.

"Do you love him?"

"Yes."

"And are you going to marry him, no matter what you may learn about him?"

"Yes."

Her replies had come so easily, so blithely, in the bar last night. She had been talking to his former wife, a very nice woman who had made the obviously painful decision to divorce him rather than live with his demons. Tracy had not yet married him, and now, for the first time, she truly wondered if she should.

She came to no conclusion, made no decision that night. She would wait until he was home and they were face-to-face. He would have to talk about it. He would have to be honest with her. If he was unwilling to do that, she would make new plans for her future.

THURSDAY

$$\boxed{30}$$

An empty lot. He had traveled nearly three thousand miles to stand here, staring at an empty lot.

Well, not quite empty. The broad hilltop had recently been flattened by bulldozers, and the cement block foundation of what would soon be a basement had been laid. It was going to be a complex of twelve one- and two-bedroom condominium apartments when the work was done. That would be sometime next year, according to the big billboard that faced the road in front of the property. There was a painting on the board, an artist's rendering of the finished product: a sleek, elegant structure surrounded by fountains and lawns and lush foliage, none of which presently existed. It would be very nice, he supposed, a pleasant place to live.

But it was not what he'd been expecting. He'd been expecting a murder scene.

Mark had arrived in Los Angeles late yesterday afternoon, and the activities of the previous night and morning in New Orleans had at last taken their toll on him. Throughout the flight, he'd felt himself growing increasingly exhausted as he'd gone over every detail in his mind, from the moment Saturday when he'd received the mysterious computer diskette that had started the whole thing. Now, three cities and two dead bodies later, he was no closer to understanding this than before.

The man, Scavenger, had killed the Banes family in Brooklyn; Mark was certain. Yet he had insisted that Mark go there and retrieve the first article, the newspaper announcing his handiwork. Why? What was the point? If he wanted to reveal his identity, why do it in such an obscure, roundabout way?

Then, on the plane somewhere over Texas, Mark reread the electronic letter. *I have always been a lover of games, Mr. Stevenson. . . .*

Yes, Mark thought. Indeed he *is* a lover of games.

By the time the plane landed, Mark had actually dozed off. A flight attendant gently woke him, and he stumbled into the terminal. He'd wisely decided to take a cab to the big chain hotel on Sunset where he'd stayed the only other time he'd been in L.A., more than ten years ago. He was too tired to drive; he would rent a car later. He'd looked around the airport, as he'd searched the entire length of the plane, but the tall man with the scar was nowhere to be seen.

During the cab ride, Mark had decided to register as Jared McKinley, and to pay cash, and that is what he did. He got a single room for two nights. He'd called Tracy and spoken to her, but he couldn't remember one word of the conversation now except the part where she'd suddenly told him she loved him. That had been wonderful. Then he'd eaten in one of the restaurants off the lobby, made his way back to his room on the tenth floor, and fallen, fully clothed, across the bed. He'd slept for nearly twelve hours.

Now, gazing at the construction site before him, Mark remembered the events of this morning. It was now ten-thirty. He'd risen at eight, showered, and gone back to the lobby restaurant for breakfast. As he emerged from the restaurant, Mark was stopped by a bellman who told him there was a message for him at the front desk. He wondered at that for a brief moment. As far as the hotel was concerned, he was Jared McKinley, and nobody could possibly know—

He cast the thought aside. Scavenger. Of course. Scavenger was omnipotent, omnipresent. Like God, only evil. Like Satan. He was here, of course. He was everywhere.

Aware that he was being watched, Mark had gone to the desk and accepted the note addressed to Jared McKinley. It was in a little black envelope with an adhesive label on the front. Neatly printed on the label were the words, *Mr. Jared McKinley, Room 1014.* The black-bordered note inside read:

Hello, Mark. The WORD you seek is closer than you think. In fact, it's in your room right now. But first, you must visit the Websters. Have a nice day.

  S.

He'd thanked the desk clerk, slipped the note into his jacket pocket, and headed for the elevator.

A quick search of his hotel room revealed nothing out of the ordinary. His suitcase was exactly where he'd placed it in the otherwise empty closet, and it contained nothing new: clothing, the newspaper from Brooklyn, and the Mardi Gras mask. He'd thrown away the now-useless box of .38-caliber bullets in New Orleans, before he'd gone to the airport. In the bathroom were his razor and toothbrush along with the hotel-provided soap, shampoo, conditioner, towels, and washcloths. The desk drawer of the dresser contained the hotel's complimentary stationery kit, a room-service menu, a pamphlet delineating and extolling the many hotel services available, a Bible placed by the Gideons, and a magazine called *L.A. Now,* courtesy of the Chamber of Commerce. He flipped through the magazine, the Bible, and the service manual, and he even riffled through the stationery folder, but there was no hidden slip of paper or message of any kind. Everything, as well as Mark could determine, was as it should be.

Then, as abruptly as he had begun the search, he stopped, remembering Scavenger's original instructions: *You must follow my scenario strictly, as it is presented to you. You may not at any time deviate from the order in which the clues arrive and the articles are retrieved.*

Of course, he thought. I have to proceed with the steps of this mad game as they arrive. *But first, you must visit the Websters.*

He'd taken a cab from the hotel to the nearest Hertz outlet and rented a Mustang convertible. This had been risky, because he'd had to do it as Mark Stevenson, and to use a credit card. Car rental companies did not accept cash: you couldn't steal a hotel room, but you could steal a car. Welcome to the modern world. Then he had driven here, to this empty, or nearly empty, lot.

This site in the Hollywood Hills, with its panoramic view of the city, had once been the address of the big, two-story stucco-and-glass residence of the Webster family, the second group of victims of The Family Man. Ian Webster, the head of the family, was a British-born American television star of long standing, having appeared in not one but two successful series over a quarter of a century, in addition to many plays and films. Mrs. Webster, the former Melinda Logan, had given up her modestly successful acting career to marry the television star and raise their three children, two boys and a girl.

In the early hours of July fourth, thirteen years ago, Ian and Melinda Webster and their three teenage children had been killed in their beds by The Family Man. They had been carried from their beds to the kidney-shaped swimming pool's redwood sundeck on the cliff overlooking the city. All five of them had been dressed in their bathing suits, over which had been placed matching T-shirts with an American flag pattern. The bodies were arranged on chaises at one end of the deck, their poodle and Siamese cat at their feet. Melinda, the three children, and the animals had their throats cut, and Ian Webster had been decapitated. His head was found floating on an inflatable raft in the center of the pool.

The cleaning woman, a Mrs. Ruiz, had found them at nine o'clock the next morning, July fifth. They had been sitting there, frozen in their bizarre family tableau, for more than twenty-four hours. Everywhere around them, on the deck and floating in the pool, were hundreds of little American flags and firecrackers. Washing over the awful scene was the music that emanated from the home entertainment center in the living room just beyond the open glass doors to the sundeck, a rousing recording of Sousa's "Stars and Stripes Forever." After fainting, regaining consciousness, and being violently sick, Mrs. Ruiz had called the police.

It was with this crime that the legend of The Family Man was born. The Tennant murders four months earlier had been investigated by the New Orleans police, but the Webster murders brought the killer to the attention of everyone in America. The LAPD called in the FBI when it became clear that the same modus operandi had been utilized in two states, presumably by the same person or persons. The bizarre nature of the crimes put it on the front pages, and Mr. Webster's star status helped to keep it there for weeks. It was generally believed that the crimes were committed by a lone killer, presumably male, and one reporter dubbed him "The Family Man." The nickname immediately spread throughout America.

Even with the added federal help—and the first appearance of Special Agent Ronald O'Hara—the investigators were stymied in their meticulous search for leads. There were no unusual fingerprints or footprints, and no fibers, blood, semen, or other indications of a human presence that couldn't be explained. The little flags and firecrackers were so common as to be generic, and the T-shirts were sold in every department store, gift shop, and mall in America. Even so, O'Hara's team slavishly tracked down every outlet of every store that sold that particular lot of that particular brand of T-shirt. Hundreds of hours were spent in this endeavor, with no positive result. Whoever had bought the shirts had presumably bought them one at a time in various locations, paying cash. A virtual army of salespersons was interviewed, but not one of them could remember anything remotely helpful.

This eventually proved to be the pattern in all five cases. The Mardi Gras masks were purchased separately, from various New Orleans stores. The Christmas decorations at the Chicago scene, the Halloween trimmings in upstate New York, and the Easter things in Brooklyn were always the biggest, most widely available brands, and no amount of searching could trace them to a specific store, to say nothing of a specific customer. The federal agents couldn't even pin them down to a specific state. The main weapon in all five cases was apparently a hunting knife of some kind, with a sharp blade that was somewhere between six and nine inches long. A thin, serrated, sawlike implement was used to decapitate the men in the first three cases, but something thicker and smoother was used in the final two. The inference here was that The Family Man was improving with practice.

As for any possible eyewitnesses, or witnesses of any kind, there were none. The first four murder sites were remote, so much so that it was determined that The Family Man had chosen them mainly for this reason. Only the fifth place, the townhouse on Kane Street in Brooklyn, was near the rest of humanity, in a row of identical townhouses. Still, none of the immediate neighbors had seen or heard anything on that Easter morning.

Everyone who had known the five families—however intimately or slightly—was investigated, and many were interviewed. In the cases of the L.A. star, the Brooklyn doctor, the musicians in upstate New York, and Mark's own father, this ran to hundreds, even thousands of people in show business, the New York medical community, the international classical music scene, and the widespread network of religious evangelism.

There was the usual assortment of jealous actors, former lovers, and one particularly unpleasant television executive connected to Ian Webster, but everyone was accounted for on that Fourth of July. Similarly, a couple of rival surgeons of Dr. Banes in New York were inspected, along with a rival conductor of Michael Carlin and several rival evangelical ministers of Jacob Farmer and their minions. There were even a few horrified families of runaways who had joined Jacob Farmer's church. But with the brief exception of Mark himself, no one connected to the five families had proved to be suspicious in any way. It was, for O'Hara and his people, the biggest dead end of all. The Family Man had apparently had no contact with his victims before the crimes.

Later, when Mark had been able to bring himself to write about these things, even though he couched them in the guise of fiction, he dutifully recorded every detail of the unsuccessful investigation. He mentioned every detail of the crime scenes: the garish holiday trimmings, the music, the positioning of the bodies in an obvious attempt to create harmonious domestic pictures. Everything.

And now, in Los Angeles, he was standing on a cliff overlooking the city under a darkening sky, staring at an empty lot. A flash of light in the distance was quickly followed by a low rumble of thunder: yes, it was going to rain soon. There was nothing here for him. He would have to search elsewhere.

He was in the act of turning around to go back to the rental car when he heard the sudden burst of music, the familiar flourish followed by the familiar, stirring anthem. He had used it in *Dark Desire,* as opposed to the Sousa march that had actually been playing at the Webster house.

"The Star-Spangled Banner."

He froze, glancing around, trying to determine the source of the recording. It was coming from the billboard. He walked over to it and looked down. There was a portable cassette recorder in the grass at the base of the sign. He looked around the lot and up and down the road, searching for a car or a human figure: the recorder must have been activated by some remote means, so the person activating it would have to be nearby. But there was no one, anywhere, as far as he could see.

He looked up at the big billboard sign again, and that was when he noticed the little slip of black-bordered white paper taped to the lower left corner. He knew what it was, even before he went over to the sign and ripped it down. The big red Magic Marker capitals were unmistakably the work of his opponent. The note read:

WRONG!!
TRY AGAIN.

Mark stared at the note, thinking, Yes. Of course. I knew that. But where on earth am I supposed to . . .

But first, you must visit the Websters.

Visit.

The Websters . . .

That was when he figured it out.

He stood staring at the empty lot, nodding to himself, when the first big, heavy drops of rain began to pelt him. He turned around immediately and headed for the car at the side of the road a few yards away.

Visit the Websters. . . .

He would have to find out how to visit them, but for that he would need information. He didn't know anyone on the *L.A. Times* any-more, and he'd never known anyone on the other local newspapers. His best bet was a library. Yes. . . .

He looked back down at the recorder. In a sudden, swift move, he pulled back his right leg and kicked it. It cracked and broke apart against the wood column, and the anthem abruptly stopped. Silence. Mark looked down at the broken plastic, a smile slowly forming on his lips.

By the time he got in the car, put the top up, and drove away down the hillside road, the skies had opened up in earnest. The heavy torrent smashed down on the windshield as he moved inexorably toward his next destination.

31

He stood in a doorway across from the Central Library on West Fifth Street, waiting for Mark Stevenson to come out. The writer had been in the library for nearly an hour now, but there was no reason to observe him inside and risk being seen by him; he knew what the man was doing in there. He smiled. Yes, the former journalist would certainly be able to figure out the next move, visiting the Webster family.

And he had done so.

Two women with shopping bags and a man in a gray suit stood near him under the awning, waiting out the rain, so there was no fear of his being conspicuous, of anyone wondering if he was loitering. The weather had, oddly enough, given him a quite legitimate reason to be standing here. Even so, he had bought a large container of coffee from a nearby shop, and he sipped it as he listened to the heavy barrage pelting the canvas above his head and peered through the rain at the library entrance. In his mind's eye, he saw Mark—harried and dripping wet, but galvanized by a sense of purpose—approaching the front desk and inquiring, then marching off to find the appropriate section of the appropriate floor. He saw him waiting, patiently or impatiently, for a free terminal before sitting down before it and reading the instructions. Then would come the requests, the typing in of key words that would result in the information he sought.

Ian Webster had been a star, and his wife had briefly been a starlet. These facts, coupled with the sensational nature of their deaths, would result in mountains of print, all meticulously recorded in the library's electronic data banks. It was the third largest library in America, and the periodical morgue would be comprehensive. Every word about every film and every television show; every review; every premiere, publicity junket, talk show, and charity appearance; the award ceremonies; the births of the three children—all of it would be there, with thousands of pictures.

And then there would be the murders. The Family Man. The bloody Fourth of July thirteen years ago, with the flags and the firecrackers and the star's head floating on the raft in the swimming pool. There would be no mention of the Sousa march, "The Stars and Stripes Forever." The music was the only detail withheld from the press, as it was at the other scenes where it had been playing. It was the single thing only The Family Man could know about, the noose with which the police and the FBI had hoped to hang him when he was apprehended. But The Family Man had never been caught.

He smiled now, under the awning, as he imagined Mark Stevenson confronting the photographs, many of them quite graphic, on the computer screen before him. He was beginning to feel exquisite pleasure at the other man's discomfort, and he would have given much to be able to be there, beside Mark Stevenson, watching him. He tried to picture the expression on the man's face. . . .

No. That would have to wait for later. He would see that expression, or something very like it, and soon. Later this afternoon, if all went well. And all *would* go well: he would see to that. He would presently see Mark Stevenson's look of utter shock and fear. Of horror. It would crown the next sequence, the next move in the game. And that sequence would begin as soon as Mark came out of the library.

But first . . .

With a quick, surreptitious glance over at his fellow refugees under the awning, the big man with the scar on his face reached inside his duster coat and produced his portable telephone. He punched in the appropriate speed-dial sequence and raised the instrument to his face, turning slightly away from the man and the two women so as not to be overheard. Not that they could possibly hear anything, he mused, with the pounding rain a few feet above their heads, but better safe than sorry. Almost immediately, the ring was answered.

"Yes?"

"He's in the library."

"Good. Is everything in place?"

"It will be."

"The hotel?"

"No problem."

"How about Barton?"

"Ready. All systems are go."

"Good."

The big man under the awning smiled at the compliment. Then he said, "How's New York?"

"Ready."

"Okay. It's raining here at the moment, but that may actually be good for us."

"Yes. Slow him down a little."

"Uh-huh." He reached up absently and ran a finger down the length of the white scar on his face before adding, "When does New York happen?"

"Tonight."

"Okay." He watched through the downpour as the door of the library across the street opened and Mark Stevenson emerged. "Here he comes. Gotta go. I'll call you when it's done."

"You do that." This comment was followed by the sound of a low, throaty giggle.

The tall man smiled. "You sound happy."

"Well, this is fun, isn't it? The suspense is killing me."

He nodded. "As long as it kills *him*. 'Bye."

He returned the cell phone to the inside pocket, looking over once more to be sure the others were not noticing. No fear of that: the two women were chatting animatedly and the businessman was already gone, hurrying off down the wet street. No one was paying the slightest attention to the tall man in black.

But Mark Stevenson was also hurrying through the rain across the street, presumably toward his car and the next destination. Smiling to himself, the man in black glided off through the downpour toward his own car. He would arrive at the next place before Mark Stevenson, and everything would be ready.

And he would see that look on Mark's face, the expression of horror he had been dreaming about all these long years.

32

Rain. Pounding into the windshield and hissing under the tires on the freeway. Obliterating everything but the car in front of him and the car behind. Falling from dark gunmetal clouds to drench the city and the sere deserts nearby. Obscuring the sun: twilight at three o'clock in the afternoon. Rain, everywhere.

The interior of the Mustang seemed to him to be a cocoon. He was aware of feeling alone, isolated, cut off from the rest of humanity. From his life. The quiet, polite, successful novelist who was about to marry the beautiful literary agent in New York was still there, in a way, three thousand miles away from him across the vast expanse of America. That is some other person, he thought as he drove up into the hills for the second time that day. Some other man. I am now the object of a demented creature who controls me, and until this game is over I must do his bidding. Then I can be Mark Stevenson again.

At last he came to the turnoff, and a few minutes later the gray stone wall arrived on his right, just as the librarian had told him. He followed the long stretch of wall to the inevitable big black wrought-iron gates. He turned in through these and continued up the drive to the main building of the compound. There was a parking lot off to the right of the building, so he parked the car there, picked up the little wreath from the passenger seat, and ran through the rain to the arched entrance doors.

The huge, ornately columned structure was apparently a combination of greeting center and business office, but it looked like a mausoleum, which he supposed was intentional. The lobby he entered was large and austere, all cool blue-veined white marble and plush red velvet. The scent from the many vases of lilies about the place hung in the air, as did the soft classical music piped in from concealed speakers. He was briefly reminded of the Pontchartrain Clinic two days—a hundred years—ago. Forcing the thought from his mind, he went quickly, purposefully over to the desk in the center of the room.

The attractive, fiftyish woman behind the desk had looked up and smiled at him as soon as he had come in, so he produced a smile of his own as he came up to her. She was wearing a Chanel-style suit of pearl gray, he noticed; not mourning, exactly, but a concession to the mourners with whom she dealt. A discreet gold badge above her left breast informed him that her name was Arlene Wolcott. Still smiling, she stood up and came around the desk, extending her hand.

"Good afternoon," she murmured in a low, clear voice. "Are you with the Fitzgerald party? Everyone's assembling in the Blue Room just down that hall over there—"

"Uh, no, Ms. Wolcott," Mark said. "I'm not with them. I'm—I'm here to pay my respects to Ian Webster and his family." He held up the dripping wreath. "Mr. Webster worked with my father in the theater years ago. When Dad heard I was coming to L.A., he asked me to . . ." He trailed off, letting Ms. Wolcott fill in the rest for herself.

She did. "Of course. Have you been here before?"

"Uh, no, I haven't."

"Well, then," she said, smiling sympathetically, "you'll need directions."

She bustled back around the desk and opened a drawer, and it was as simple as that. In moments he was holding a detailed map of the cemetery with the Webster graves clearly marked for him. Ms. Wolcott even handed him a black umbrella from a stand beside the desk, which she told him to keep with the cemetery's compliments. He thanked her profusely and went back out into the rain.

It seemed to have intensified, and he was grateful for the gift of the umbrella. He moved as swiftly as possible across the parking lot and through a small border garden to the first rows of markers. He now saw that the cemetery stretched out in all directions over hilly green land, with sidewalks crisscrossing the terrain. Glancing again at the map, he moved off down the appropriate walkway. In just under ten minutes, he came to the correct section, and he counted off the rows of headstones until he arrived at the one he sought.

The five headstones stood in a somber line in the center of the row, under a big, leafy tree. The name WEBSTER seemed to jump out at him from all of them, and the final date, identical on each one. The largest pink marble monument in the center of the cluster belonged to Ian Webster, with a quote from Shakespeare's *Antony and Cleopatra,* a play in which Webster had scored one of his biggest stage hits, the queen's lament for her dead lover:

> "THE ODDS IS GONE,
> AND THERE IS NOTHING LEFT REMARKABLE
> BENEATH THE VISITING MOON."

Mark knelt before the center grave, grateful for the limbs and leaves above his head that somewhat protected him from the downpour. There was another black umbrella, opened, stuck in the ground before Ian's headstone, and under this, leaning against the pink stone, was a small plastic bag. He laid down his wreath, picked up the bag and opened it, and pulled out a little black envelope. He tore it open and removed the black-bordered white card with the red Magic Marker message.

> *Study these graves carefully. There are more victims here.*
> *Can you feel their pain? The WORD is in your hotel room . . .*
> *Matthew.*

He knelt there in the rain, staring down at the final word of the note. *Matthew.* It was his original name, of course, and Scavenger certainly knew that. But it kept arresting his attention, and he tried to figure what it was about the use of his name that was somehow significant. *Matthew.*

WORD. Capitalized in both notes, this one and the one at the hotel this morning. *WORD. Matthew . . .*

Then he got it. He slipped the note back in the envelope and put it in his coat pocket, then rose slowly to his feet. *WORD* was the Word of God: the Gideon Bible. The Book of Matthew. He had to get back to the hotel.

On a hill in the distance, off to his left, he saw a slow procession of perhaps fifty black-clad people with black umbrellas, following a hearse. The group came to a stop and began to assemble in a circle around a tall minister or priest—he couldn't tell with the rain and the distance—as the hearse was opened. The Fitzgerald party, he presumed, burying their dead on this awful, wet day, this gray afternoon. He stared at the tableau on the hill, remembering the gray, rainy morning his family died, and the brilliant, snowy day he buried them: the sunlight glinting on the ice in the cemetery, hurting his eyes, as some zealous minion of the Church of the True Believers ranted on and on about God and Jesus and Judgment Day. He wondered what the weather would be like when he died. Not that it would matter to him, of course. But he wondered if it would rain. . . .

A tall man was standing on the brow of the hill, a little apart from the others. Even through the rain, even at this distance, Mark knew immediately who it was. The long black coat was unmistakable, and, as on the street in New Orleans two nights before, he was looking directly at Mark, this time through binoculars.

Then, as on the street in New Orleans two nights before, Mark began to run. Uttering a small cry of anger, he dropped the courtesy umbrella and charged out across the sodden field, through row after row of headstones, toward the figure in the distance. The tall man melted away into the rain, circling around the crowd of mourners and disappearing over the rim of the hill. Mark ran up the hill to the crest and stopped short, unaware of the astonished faces of the Fitzgerald party as they turned to stare. He could just make out the tall black figure among the stones a hundred yards or so ahead of him, gliding swiftly toward the main building and the parking lot.

He was already breathless, but he propelled himself forward as fast as he could, half running, half staggering down the hill. The rain pelted his face, blinding him, and suddenly his knee smashed into a gravestone and he went down, landing in the muddy grass. A sharp pain ran up his side to his brain, and he gasped as he pulled himself up and started to run again. By the time he reached the parking lot, he could just make out the red taillights of a car as it moved quickly away down the drive toward the front gates.

He ran to his car and took off after the taillights. It occurred to him that history was repeating itself: as in New Orleans, he had no plan. He didn't have any idea exactly what he would do to the big man in the unlikely event that he actually caught up with him. He only knew that he must try. The Mustang fishtailed as he swung out through the wrought-iron gates onto the road that would eventually lead back to the highway, but then it righted itself and plunged forward. The red taillights were far ahead of him, nearly invisible in the downpour. Mark pressed his foot more firmly down on the accelerator, determined to close the gap.

He had managed to get within fifty yards of the other car, and they were very close to the entrance ramp to the freeway, when Mark heard the shrill siren right behind him. In the rearview mirror he saw an approaching motorcycle. The man on the bike, obviously a police officer, was gesturing for Mark to pull over to the side of the road.

Oh, great! he thought as he slowed and reluctantly moved the car over to the shoulder. Just as I was about to . . .

The thought vanished as he came to a full stop, glancing ruefully forward at what he presumed would be the vanishing car. He stared in wonder as he saw the car he'd been pursuing slow and pull over to the shoulder, as well. What on earth was Scavenger doing?

The rain beat on the cloth roof and poured down the windshield in rivulets as the officer dismounted and came up to stand beside the driver's door. He was a young man, about twenty-five, with a mustache. That was about all Mark could determine: he wore a helmet and a blue poncho, and he was soaked. He didn't look remotely friendly. Mark rolled down the window.

"License, please," the officer said.

Mark nodded nervously and produced his wallet, pulling the card from its plastic sheath at the center. Without a word, he handed it over. He wondered vaguely what the fine was for a speeding ticket in L.A. as he watched the young officer read the information on his driver's license.

Then the officer did a strange thing. With a small but audible exhalation, he looked up at Mark's face, then back down at the card. Slowly, his right hand was lowered to his side, hovering above a suspicious bulge beneath the poncho.

"Mr. Mark Stevenson?"

"Yes."

"Step out of the car, please."

Mark didn't get it. "Look, Officer, I know I was speeding, but I don't see—"

"Step out of the car, please," the man repeated, this time more firmly. He took a step backward, never for a moment removing his gaze from Mark's startled face.

Mark got out of the car. Leaving the door open, he stood before the policeman. "What is this all about?"

The man was still peering at his face. "You're the writer?"

"Yes."

"From New York."

"Yes."

The officer nodded, more to himself than to Mark. Then he reached under the poncho. Mark lowered his own gaze, fascinated. What on earth . . . ?

From under the poncho came a clip-on transmitter. Mark stared, confused, as the man slowly raised the instrument toward his lips.

The explosion seemed to come from all directions at once. One moment there was only the steady sound of falling rain, but in the next the world was full of a sharp, earsplitting noise. The reverberation from it continued in the following seconds as everything shifted into slow motion. Mark stood riveted, uncomprehending, watching the black walkie-talkie sail out into the empty road. Then he saw the officer moving toward him. Before his brain could process the information, the man's wet poncho and heavy bulk slammed into his chest. He heard the officer utter a soft, burbling sound, and saw his blue eyes, widened in surprise, staring into his own. Instinctively, he grabbed at the man, but it was too late. The two of them went down hard, Mark onto his back on the wet asphalt and the officer on top of him. The breath left his body as the man crashed into him. He blinked, dazed, pinned down by the heavy weight. And still the echo of the explosion continued to rage in his ears.

Then everything was once more silent. He was lying on his back on a wet road, and there was a man lying on top of him.

A police officer.

When he could breathe again, when he could move again, Mark reached slowly up and pushed the heavy weight aside. The young man rolled off of him to land on his back, blue eyes staring up into the rain, on the asphalt beside him. Mark tried to sit up, but the first wave of shock overcame him and he fell, gasping, onto his back. Then his vision cleared, and he pushed down with his arms and managed to rise to a sitting position. He stared at the still figure beside him for a long moment, then lifted his gaze to the scene beyond his open car door.

The big man, Scavenger, was standing beside his own car, arm still extended. As Mark stared at him, he actually smiled; Mark would later convince himself of that. The mustache rose up a little, and the white scar on the ruddy right cheek seemed to twitch. Through the downpour,

Mark was certain he even saw a twinkle in the man's pale eyes as he slowly raised the extended arm above him. He was holding it up for Mark to see clearly. And Mark saw: in his big hand he was clutching what was unmistakably Mark's Smith & Wesson .38 revolver.

There was a moment, then, of perfect clarity, perfect understanding. Mark lay in the muddy road, the rain lashing down at him, the dead or dying policeman mere inches away from him, looking into the eyes of his tormentor. Scavenger: one who preys upon the dead. Eater of carrion. This man, this creature before him would not stop until Mark had completed his game. And he would do whatever he wanted, whenever he wanted, to achieve that purpose. Mark was his pawn, a mere playing piece on a huge, elaborate game board. And Mark was something else as well: he was the chosen one, the appointed scribe. The recorder of the exploits of Scavenger, and of The Family Man. One and the same, or so this man would have Mark believe. So he would have the world believe. The man was insane; Mark knew it, and he knew Mark knew it. And they both knew that Mark was his captive, in his thrall.

As if Mark had spoken his thoughts aloud, as if to underscore Mark's epiphany, the big man nodded once. Then he turned around, got in his car, and glided away through the rain in the direction of the freeway.

33

The second round of drinks was served, and Tracy was already apprehensive. She was sipping white wine, as usual, but Jared McKinley was knocking back huge tankards of stout. Jared's soft gaze and slurred speech informed her that he'd had a few before he'd arrived at the restaurant. Any minute now, she thought, he's going to be loaded.

But he wasn't loaded yet. Taking a hefty swallow of his new drink, he said, "So, what's on your mind?"

Tracy blinked. She briefly wondered if he had noticed her involuntary reaction to his drinking. Then she remembered his similar question on the phone the night before.

She had already decided to tell this man, Mark's friend, the whole story of Mark's past, his childhood as Matthew Farmer, so now she did. By the time she was finished, Jared had consumed another beer and their entrées had finally arrived.

"Wow!"

Jared's one-word summation said it all, and they ate for a while in silence. She studied him across the table as she ate, realizing how much they had in common. She was Mark's girlfriend, lover, fiancée, and he was his closest friend, perhaps his only friend. Yet Mark had shared nothing of his shocking past with either of them. It had taken his former wife the better part of three years to find it out, and even Carol hadn't known everything.

Well, they knew now, and she still wondered what to do with the knowledge. As if reading her mind, Jared chose that moment to put down his fork, lean forward, and speak.

"You know, maybe you shouldn't mention any of this to him. I think he might be peeved if he finds out you went and talked to Carol behind his back. I know *I* would be. Maybe you should just wait and see if he wants to tell you about it on his own."

Tracy had already decided otherwise, but she wasn't going to tell Jared that. Still, she did want his advice, so she pressed on.

"I'm actually grateful to Carol," she said, "but you're right. Mark might see the whole thing differently. I mean, it probably isn't the best way to start out a permanent relationship, going behind someone's back for information about them."

"Yeah," Jared said. "My ex did that, and I hated it. Of course, she had every reason to be suspicious. I was a louse with her. I deserved what I got."

Tracy hadn't known this. "What did you get?"

He laughed and downed more beer. "I got to pay alimony. *Lots* of alimony."

She nodded, wondering what, exactly, had disappointed the former Mrs. McKinley, whether it was the drinking or other women. Both, probably. Well, then, he *did* deserve it. But Mark's problem was nothing of that nature. She'd told Jared about Mark's past, but not about his present: New Orleans and Los Angeles, and the gun. She wondered how to do that.

She was still wondering when the waitress brought the dessert and coffee. She dug into her fruit salad, wincing as Jared ordered yet another beer. She would not tell him any more—not tonight, at any rate. Maybe later. Now she would just have dessert and go home.

She was beginning to truly dread the day Mark would come home.

34

When Mark staggered from his car in the hotel's parking lot, he had only vague impressions of how he had arrived there. It had been perhaps twenty-five minutes since the incident on the road near the cemetery, but he was barely aware of the passage of time.

He remembered moving the officer as gently as possible to the side of the road beside his motorcycle. Then he was in his car again, driving furiously onto the freeway toward downtown L.A. He remembered wondering that nobody else seemed to be around, that the winding hillside road from the cemetery had been so deserted. He was trying to take it all in, trying to formulate some sort of plan as he drove, instinctively putting as much distance as possible between himself and the fallen policeman.

He was just beginning to convince himself that he must get to a phone as quickly as he could, dial 911, and report the incident anonymously, when he saw an ambulance and three police squad cars racing by him in the opposite direction, four swift blurs in the heavy rain. So someone had happened upon the scene on the lonely stretch of road, perhaps people leaving the Fitzgerald funeral. But the officer was dead, he was certain of it. There was no help for him now.

Scavenger. Scavenger had done this.

And he had done it with Mark's gun.

Mark stumbled across the lobby and into the dark, nearly empty bar. He ordered a glass of brandy that he quickly drained, then a second one that sat on the bar before him while he willed himself to calm down, ignored by the few other customers in the place and the bored bartender. The liquor soon worked its way through him, restoring and reviving. He willed himself to breathe slowly and evenly as he sipped the second drink and wondered what he should do.

His gun. Scavenger had his gun, and he was killing people with it. Mark had purchased the weapon shortly after moving to New York from Chicago, a few months after the slaughter of his family, when he realized that even in a new city with a new identity he did not feel safe. He'd bought it new at a store on Canal Street, and he had the appropriate license and registration, but he had only fired it at the private range where he went for instruction. As far as he knew, the police had no way of tracing the weapon through ballistics. On the other hand, they had records of everyone who legitimately owned Smith & Wesson .38 revolvers, and his name would be there. But would the police assume that the nurse in New Orleans and the policeman in Los Angeles—even if the two crimes were ballistically linked—were killed by a legitimate, licensed owner?

He took another long sip of the soothing amber liquid. No, he thought, there was no reason for the police in two cities to link the crimes; not immediately, at any rate. That could take weeks, even months. And by then, the game would be over.

The game.

The cemetery. He had been to visit the Websters, and he had received Scavenger's new instructions. *The WORD is in your hotel room . . . Matthew.*

He thought about the house outside New Orleans. The dead man in the armchair, his throat slashed, the horrible mask obscuring his face.

The pretty, friendly young nurse, shot, lying in the darkness at the edge of a deserted hospital parking lot.

And now, in Los Angeles, not one hour ago, a young police officer's lifeless body had crashed into him. The vacant eyes staring up at the rain. . . .

The WORD is in your hotel room . . . Matthew.

Mark finished the second brandy and got up from the barstool. He paid the bartender and went out into the brightly lit lobby. He blinked around at the well-dressed men and women who strolled about the place, smiling and laughing together, talking animatedly. Normal people with normal lives. He had rarely felt so removed from them as he did at this moment. So isolated. So alone.

With a quickening step and cold resolve, he moved through the milling throng of warm humanity and entered the elevator. When he arrived in his room a few minutes later, he went directly over to the desk and opened the top drawer.

The Gideon Bible was still there, but it was not as he had last seen it. Now it was wrapped in the familiar black paper and ribbon, with a black bow on the front. Shaking his head in disgust, he tore the wrapping away. He opened the book to the second half and thumbed through the pages until he came to the beginning of the New Testament, the Book of Matthew.

A little sheet of paper, three inches by five, had been inserted between the second and third pages of the section, with a message scrawled on it in red Magic Marker. On the two-column page that now faced up, a passage had been highlighted in yellow. He read the passage first. It was Matthew 7:1–2:

> Judge not, that ye be not judged.
> For with what judgment ye judge, ye shall be judged; and
> with what measure ye mete, it shall be measured to you again.

He read the passage twice. He already knew it by heart, as he knew so much of the Bible by heart. His father had seen to that. How many times had he heard his father bellow these very words, his stentorian voice booming out from a variety of pulpits, many of them televised? Of course, the late reverend and the rest of Mark's family had all but disowned him, proving that the words had merely been mouthed, never taken to heart. Grim irony: they had been judged. On the Christmas morning that the prodigal had returned to them, they had met their gruesome fate at the hands of The Family Man.

Then Mark read the message on the slip of paper. It was only one sentence:

The Family Man had his own religion.

He stood there staring down at the words, gradually becoming aware that somewhere nearby a telephone was ringing. It was the portable phone, which he hadn't taken with him on his travels today. When he'd arrived in L.A. last night, he'd attached it to its battery pack and plugged it into the wall socket near the bed. This morning, before leaving the hotel, he'd unplugged it and tossed it on the bedside table next to the hotel room phone. A breach of the rules, but he was beginning not to care. Now, with what had happened since this morning, he marched over to the table, snatched up the instrument, and snapped it on.

The familiar voice was there, as ever: low, melodious, full of implied good humor. "Good evening, Mark."

"Fuck you."

"Did you have a nice time today?"

"Fuck you!"

"I'm glad to hear that. I thought you might be . . . amused."

"*Fuck you!*"

"Oh, I'm fine, thank you. A little damp, I suppose, but this weather is frightful, is it not?"

Realizing the futility of continuing to scream at a madman, Mark capitulated. He drew in a deep, ragged breath and slowly let it out. When he spoke again, his voice was controlled. "What do you want?"

A giggle. "Lower taxes. A better insurance plan. Sharon Stone in a bikini. World peace."

Mark almost began to shout again, but he caught himself, merely repeating as reasonably as he possibly could, "What do you want?"

There was a pause, and another soft giggle. Then the voice continued. "It's nearly six o'clock, time for the news. I think you should turn on the set in the cabinet beside your dresser with the remote on the table near the phone. May I recommend Channel Six? They have the most excellent coverage in the City of Angels. That Sandra Chan is a marvelous anchorwoman, always so thorough. And I think tonight you'll want to hear *all* the news. It should be most . . . revealing. I'll talk to you later, Mark."

The line went dead. With a moan of frustration, Mark dropped the phone on the bed, picked up the remote from the bedside table, and went across the room to the cabinet. He threw open the doors to reveal a big television set. Aiming the remote, he turned it on and punched in Channel Six. He sank wearily onto the foot of the bed, aware of how cold he was. He was still damp from the rain, and the room's air conditioner was on full blast. A hot shower, he thought, but first the news.

He glanced at his watch: five fifty-eight. A shampoo commercial, followed by a car commercial. Then the fanfare of trumpets and drums, the announcer's voice, and the screen was filled with the image of a pretty Asian woman with glistening hair.

"Good evening, I'm Sandra Chan. More fighting has broken out in Bosnia, and at least forty-three people are . . ."

Mark drew the bedspread up around his shoulders, staring at the screen. The civil war footage was followed by an airline disaster off the coast of Georgia, then a local fire that had gutted a popular delicatessen in the Valley. Another United Nations ultimatum to a Middle Eastern dictator. A scandal in the Los Angeles government. Then a fast-food commercial. Mark was beginning to wonder why Scavenger wanted him to watch this when the program came back on.

Sandra Chan said, "Police in New Orleans and Washington, D.C., are puzzled by a series of incidents in their cities in the last two days, and concern is growing that the notorious Family Man may have struck again. As you no doubt recall . . ."

The television screen was suddenly filled with images. The five murder scenes, including the Farmer home in Evanston. The victims, including Reverend Farmer and Mark's mother, brother, and sister. Then came more recent footage, the parking lot of the Pontchartrain Clinic with paramedics wheeling a sheet-covered body on a gurney. The anchorwoman's voice faded in and out of his consciousness.

". . . local nurse Millicent Call, who attended Sarah Gammon, formerly Sarah Tennant . . ."

Now came new images, and Mark felt the first shudder of fear. An exterior shot of Tennant House, the front drive swarming with police cars and news vans. The footage was followed by a still photograph of an attractive, smiling man with bright red hair.

". . . the discovery today of the body of lawyer Robert Gammon, thirty-nine, of New Orleans. An anonymous phone call led police to Tennant House, the scene of the first Family Man incident. Gammon was the husband of Sarah Gammon, and his murder is reminiscent of the Tennant murders thirteen years ago. He was found sitting in a chair in the living room of the mansion, his throat slashed, and the room had been decorated with balloons, candles, and confetti, exactly as it was on the night . . ."

Robert Gammon, Mark thought. The man in the chair was Robert Gammon. They found him where I found him. But no, that can't be. He took Robert Gammon away while I was unconscious. The body and the decorations were gone the next morning, when I—

His thought was interrupted by new images on the screen.

Washington. The street in Georgetown. More police cars. A stretcher being placed in an ambulance. Mark blinked, then stared.

". . . approximately two hours ago when a neighbor heard a single gunshot from the house in the quiet residential area. Former Federal Bureau of Investigation Special Agent Ronald O'Hara, fifty-six, had been shot once in the temple with his own gun, which was found clutched in his hand. Police are calling this death a suicide, but they are cooperating with authorities in New Orleans due to the coincidental nature of the deaths. O'Hara was the special agent in charge of the multistate FBI investigation into the Family Man murders. His former wife, Grammy-winning and Oscar-nominated actress/singer Wanda Morris, was unavailable for comment. Lieutenant William Alton of the Washington police said, and I quote, 'We do not want to speculate at this time as to whether there is a connection between this unfortunate . . .' "

Mark closed his eyes tightly and flung the bedspread away from him. The room, so cold only moments ago, seemed to be growing increasingly close, stifling. Warm perspiration began to mingle with the cold rainwater that had soaked his clothes.

Then someone, a woman, uttered his name. He opened his eyes and looked once more at the television screen, and the warm perspiration turned to cold sweat.

He was looking at himself.

There, on the huge monitor behind Ms. Chan's glossy hair, was the publicity still from the dust jacket of his latest book. His own face filled the screen behind the woman as her voice once more crashed into his consciousness.

". . . bestselling author Mark Stevenson, who visited Mrs. Gammon in the Pontchartrain Clinic, where she has been a patient for several weeks, just two days ago. Robert Gammon's secretary has informed the New Orleans police that Stevenson spoke to Mr. Gammon on the phone, as well. Stevenson's latest novel, *Dark Desire,* is a thinly veiled fictional account of the Family Man murders. Though Stevenson is not a suspect, the NOPD would like to question him, as he might have information relevant to their investigation. He is believed to be in or near Los Angeles, as he purchased an airline ticket from New Orleans to Los Angeles International Airport early yesterday morning. The all-points bulletin was issued today by New Orleans authorities, and anyone with knowledge of Stevenson's whereabouts is asked to contact them at the following toll-free number. . . ."

Mark couldn't breathe. The room now seemed to be getting smaller, closing in on him. The officer on the motorcycle had seen his name on his driver's license, recognized it from the APB that had obviously extended to L.A., where they very correctly believed Mark to be. That was why he'd told Mark to get out of the car. . . .

The toll-free number of the NOPD appeared on the screen, followed abruptly by another legend: BREAKING STORY. Ms. Chan leaned forward slightly, apparently reading something unfamiliar that had just been fed into the TelePrompTer. Mark gaped: it was as if the television itself had read his thoughts.

"This just in: the body of a Los Angeles police officer has been found on a hillside road outside the city limits. He was shot once in the back. Emergency personnel arriving at the scene attempted to revive him, but were unsuccessful. The officer's identity is being withheld pending notification of relatives. Once again, a Los Angeles police officer has been found dead of a gunshot wound. We'll bring you more of this story as soon as it becomes available. . . ."

The phone on the bed beside him rang again. Mark stared at it a moment, then picked it up.

"You can turn it off now, Mark. That's all the news."

Mark aimed the remote and switched the television off. In the silence that followed, he was aware of his own heavy breathing. He licked his lips and said, "You killed Robert Gammon."

The giggle again. "Oh, come now, Mark! *You're* the one who got him involved. You shouldn't have spoken to him."

"Shouldn't have . . . ? How the hell was I supposed to find Sarah, much less get in to see her?"

"Oh, Mark, don't whine. It's *so* unattractive. A journalist like you, unable to find a prominent woman in a little city like that? Please!"

Mark tried a different tack. "The New Orleans police are looking for me."

"Yes, I believe they are. What are you going to do about that?"

"I'm going to call them. I'm going to tell them everything I know about you, you sick bastard!"

"Oh, you are, are you?" Another giggle. "I don't think so, Mark. I have something that belongs to you. Have you forgotten that? I think the medical examiners in New Orleans and Los Angeles would be very interested in it—if it were to, shall we say, fall into their possession?"

Mark shut his eyes tightly. The gun. The Smith & Wesson .38 that had killed Millicent Call and the as-yet-unidentified cop. *His* gun. Rage welled up inside him, the acute rage of complete impotence.

"Why did you kill O'Hara?" he cried. "I didn't break your rules with him. I didn't talk to him without your precious permission! You *sent* me to him! Why kill him?"

Now there was a pause on the line, and for a moment Mark thought Scavenger might have hung up. Then the low voice came again.

"Think, Mark. Think like a writer, like a journalist. O'Hara died two hours ago, at approximately seven o'clock p.m., eastern standard time. *Four* o'clock, Pacific. Where were you at four o'clock this afternoon?"

Mark actually had to think a minute, clear the fog of all the events of the last few hours. "Four o'clock? I—I was in the cemetery."

"And what were you doing there?"

"You know what I was doing there. *You* were there, watching me through—binoculars. . . ." He trailed off, realizing the import of what he was saying.

"Ahhhh," said the voice on the other end of the line.

Mark licked his dry lips again. An image had come into his mind now, a memory from Washington three days ago. A sad, lonely man in a big, empty townhouse in Georgetown. His wife and children gone. His illustrious, exciting career gone. Everything he'd ever wanted, gone. All gone.

"So," he finally managed to whisper, "O'Hara really *did* kill himself . . . ?"

Now Scavenger's tone was eminently reasonable. "You know, Mark, it's like they say: Sometimes a cigar is just a cigar. I assure you, I was just as surprised as you to hear that particular news. Oh, well. You've learned everything you can learn in L.A., and I must congratulate you. You managed it with six hours to spare! Not bad! You're beginning to get the hang of this! And about time, too, because the game is nearly over. I think it's time you got your second wind, don't you? Your *second wind*, Mark. Be there at exactly midnight tomorrow night. You're looking for a photograph. Cheerio!"

"*Wait!*" Mark cried, but the line was already dead.

Mark dropped the cell phone and lay back on the bed, absorbing the various slings and arrows that had assaulted him in the last few hours, to say nothing of the last few days. How much of this could he take? he wondered, absently fingering the bunched-up bedspread. How much could anyone take?

Well, he had taken a lot in his life, more than most. He had lived through the massacre of his family, drug addiction, life on the streets, a new identity in a new city. He had worked his way through college. He'd been a market researcher and a journalist, and now he was a novelist with a growing reputation. An award-winning writer. He had accomplished a great deal, and he had survived even more—more than anyone he'd ever met, certainly.

And he would survive this.

He dragged himself up off the bed and shed his damp clothing. The clothes he'd worn here from New Orleans—jeans, work shirt, briefs, and socks—had been cleaned by the hotel's laundry service and were now neatly piled on the dresser. He went into the bathroom and turned on the shower, waiting until the water was hot enough to steam the mirror. Then he got in and stood under the spray, washing his hair and body repeatedly. He inspected the darkening bruise on his right shin just below the knee where he had collided with the gravestone. It was tender, but the damage was minimal. It would be gone in a week or so.

He emerged from the tub and dried himself with a big, soft towel. It was Thursday now, and the scavenger hunt was supposed to be over Saturday at midnight. What had Scavenger just said on the phone? Oh, yes . . .

"The game is nearly over."

Would that it were, he thought as he came out of the bathroom. He stopped, looking down at the cell phone on the bed, then over at the hotel telephone on the night table, thinking, Tracy.

The New Orleans police had issued an APB on him, which had extended to Los Angeles. But what about his home, New York? What about Tracy? Had the police contacted her? His agent? His publishers?

He was all the way around the bed, reaching down for the hotel phone, when he stopped abruptly. No, he told himself, Tracy knew nothing of this. He'd spoken to her when he'd arrived here yesterday. Although he could barely remember their conversation now, he was certain he'd told her where he was, what hotel he was in. If anyone from the police had called her looking for him, she would have called him here immediately. He looked down at the elaborate console of buttons on the instrument, noting that one of them was for messages received. The little red light that indicated messages was unlit: no one had tried to reach him here today.

He would not call Tracy now, he decided. He wouldn't share any of this mad game with her. He would keep it as far away from her as possible. He'd spoken with her yesterday, and he'd call her tomorrow from the next location.

Still naked, he lay on the bed again, facedown, resting his head on the cool, soft pillow. He had to close his eyes for a few minutes; it was an overwhelming need. Then he would get up, dress in his clean clothes, check out of the hotel, and head for the airport, for the next city. Scavenger had conveyed his cryptic instructions. *Second wind.*

Second wind, he thought, and he shuddered. He knew what that meant, and he wondered what the big, scarred sociopath had in store for him there.

No, he wouldn't think about it. Not now. Later. Now he would just lie here and rest for a few minutes. He thought about his wallet: he still had nearly seven hundred in cash, and he would risk using his ATM card for more cash at the airport. Now that he couldn't use his name, he couldn't use his credit cards. He would need lots of cash. He doubted that the police would put an alarm on his checking account. He was wanted for questioning, nothing more. He was not a suspect; he was an innocent bystander. He would close his eyes for a minute, then he would go. . . .

In seconds, he was asleep.

35

"Good night, Jared."

"G'night, Tracy. Thanks for the grub. Let's do this again just as soon as Mark gets back to town."

"It's a date," she said, leaning down to peck his cheek. He was already in the backseat of a cab outside the tavern, and that had taken some manipulating and maneuvering on her part. He'd stumbled twice in the short trip from the table to the front door. Outside, she'd flagged down the taxi, given the driver Jared's address in Greenwich Village, and pressed some money into Jared's hand, closing his fingers around it. She'd actually had to steady him as he shimmied down and sideways into the car. But now he was in, and she sighed in relief as the cab pulled away and turned south at the next corner.

She turned around and headed off in the direction of her own home three blocks away, instinctively clutching her shoulder bag more tightly against her. She would have preferred a sober Jared who could have walked her to her door now, at nearly ten o'clock on a Thursday night, but it was not to be. Too bad: the streets around Gramercy Park were nearly deserted at this hour on a weeknight, and the bag was a target for thieves. She herself was the bigger target, she knew, but she also knew about the Mace canister in the purse. Another reason she clutched it so tightly against her hip.

She came out of the side street into the one that ran along the east side of the park. Glancing over at the black wrought-iron fence that ringed the square, she could see no suspicious types loitering anywhere. She saw no one at all. The lights in the townhouses and apartment buildings around the park provided reassuring proof that others were nearby, all around her. This was, after all, the largest city in

America, and Gramercy Park was hardly a remote part of it. Her apartment building was just around the corner, on the north side of the square, and she would be there in a few minutes.

She reached up and clutched the collar of her light coat more tightly around her throat. The temperature had dropped while they had dined, and a strong breeze rustled the leaves and branches in the park. The weather report on the six o'clock news had not mentioned rain, yet it felt like an imminent possibility. The wind that whipped through her hair and against her cheeks was moist and heavy. If I were a farm woman, she mused, I'd get the horses into the barn and the chickens into the henhouse, or whatever it was they did when a storm was brewing. This wind was a precursor of rain, and even she, a Noo Yawker, knew that. She actually smiled at her whimsy.

Her smile faded as she remembered the expression on Jared's face, and her own growing trepidation, as she had repeated to him what Carol Grant and the *Chicago Tribune* had told her about Mark.

Matthew Farmer.

No. She couldn't, *wouldn't* think of him by any name but Mark Stevenson. That was his name now—his legal name, she presumed—and she would honor it. He was Mark Stevenson, and that was all there was to that. After all, it was Mark Stevenson, not Matthew Farmer, with whom she'd fallen in love.

Love . . .

Oh, stop it! she chided herself as she turned the final corner onto the north side of Twenty-first Street. She increased her pace, glancing once more about her. No one, anywhere.

Well, not quite no one, she noticed as she turned into her building's doorway and reached in her bag for her keys. A large black van, a minibus, was parked at the curb before her building, its sliding rear door open. Someone—a big man in a long, dark coat, judging from what she could see of him—was standing on the sidewalk, leaning into the open door. She could only see him from the waist down: the rest of him was inside the van.

A new neighbor? she wondered as she turned and fit the key into the lock of the first of two lobby doors. Perhaps, but it seemed like an odd time to be moving in or, at least, unloading a van. Oh, well. She hadn't checked her mail earlier. She should do that before she went upstairs. . . .

When she heard the two swift footfalls behind her, she assumed it was the man from the van. The new neighbor, or whatever he was, and he was probably carrying something. She could hold the door for him. She formed a smile on her lips and prepared to turn around.

She never made it. A huge, strong hand grabbed her left shoulder from behind and shoved her against the glass of the door. In the same instant, another huge hand shot over her right shoulder and clamped down over her mouth and nose. The hand was clad in a thick leather glove, and it was holding something, actually pressing it against her face. Something soft and white and . . .

Wet. The sickly sweet chemical odor assaulted her nostrils, burning them. She drew in a deep breath, preparing to scream, but now the fumes were in her mouth, as well. She pulled the key from the lock and reached behind her, stabbing with it as best she could. It sank into a hard torso, and she heard a harsh grunt against her ear. Then her hand went limp. Everything seemed to be going limp, and getting darker. She tried to take in another breath, but the burning, sweet wetness was overwhelming her. The Mace was in her purse, but her right hand refused to take orders. It hung at her side against the cold glass of the door, utterly useless.

This isn't happening! her mind shrieked as she was pulled roughly away from the door and lifted up, up, up into the air. This *can't* be happening on my own doorstep, in the middle of the largest city in Amer . . .

Then her mind began to shut down, to retract as a telescope is retracted after use. She couldn't breathe, couldn't move, couldn't think. She was going to die. She was floating through the air, borne up by massive arms, and then she was being set down on something soft, a carpet. She heard metallic sliding and the slamming of a car door. The van! was her final coherent thought. And she heard a deep, gruff voice beside her ear shouting *"Go! Go! Go!"* A grinding of gears, the roar of a powerful engine, and she and the entire dark, sweet-smelling world lurched violently forward into black oblivion.

36

He was in the cemetery again, and he was running. The rain was pounding into him, lashing his face and soaking his clothes, but still he ran as fast as he could. Gravestones, markers, and mausoleums flew by him, threatening to trip him up and send him sprawling in the muddy grass. His breath was coming in sharp, painful gasps that he concentrated on trying to control lest he hyperventilate. That would not be good, he knew; it would force him to stop, to pause in his flight, and then Scavenger would get away.

But where was Scavenger? He searched the hazy, rain-soaked landscape before him, peering among the monuments for the familiar, tall figure in the long black coat. A fog seemed to be settling down among the graves, and the rain was increasingly colder. It felt like ice. It *was* ice, he realized. Hailstones, tiny and sharp, stinging his exposed skin. He knew without looking up that the sky above him was black, ragged with clouds, and the gathering darkness was punctuated by the distant rumble of thunder.

Still he ran. He threw himself forward through the black, wet graveyard, possessed of an overwhelming sense of panic such as he had never felt before. Fear—sharp, naked, all-consuming. Why was he so afraid? What was this compulsion, this need to propel his body on through the storm? If there were some haven, some sort of shelter . . . No. He knew, even as this thought occurred to him, that he must go on. He couldn't stop, not for a moment. If he did, all would be lost.

Lost? he wondered, reaching up with his wet hands to clutch his aching chest. *What* would be lost? Scavenger?

No. His life. If he stopped running, he would die. It was as simple as that. He knew now what had been eluding him as he ran. He was not chasing Scavenger.

Scavenger was chasing him.

And now he heard it through the rain and the hail and the thunder and the closer, louder sounds of his own gasping breath and thudding heart: footsteps. Behind him. Getting closer. Closer. . . .

Oh, God, he had to run! The big man with the scar was gaining on him, closing the gap between them. Any moment now, Mark would feel the hot breath on the back of his neck, and the powerful hands clutching at him as they had come out of the darkness in Tennant House to clap the chloroform-soaked rag over his mouth and nose. He mustn't let that happen, because this time Mark would not get away. This time Scavenger would finish it, kill him. Run! his mind screamed. *Run!*

But there were too many gravestones. They were much larger than Mark remembered, and much closer together. He noticed now that the biggest ones in his path were mere inches apart, that he had been snaking through them, actually twisting his flying body sideways more than once to pass between them. They rose up before him more and more, faster and faster, bigger and bigger. How can that be? he wondered as he blinked to clear the rain and hail from his eyes, and the inevitable finally happened.

The huge pink marble stone arrived out of the fog and rain—massive, impenetrable, final. The oversized letters chiseled into the wet surface were lit by a sudden, brilliant flash of lightning: FARMER. He collided with it at great speed, his legs and groin and stomach smashing against it, causing a wrenching, numbing pain. He doubled over, sprawled across the stone, then slid sideways to land facedown in the mud beside it. He lay still on his stomach, stunned, winded, aware of the wet dirt pressing into his face and his clothes and his outstretched hands. He gasped for air, wincing at the pain in his legs and his testicles, scrabbling with his hands for some purchase in the sodden earth. He had to get up now, *now,* or he would die.

Then he realized.

FARMER.

Oh, God! he thought as he struggled to rise from the mud. I'm not in the cemetery above Los Angeles where I was this afternoon. I'm in the other place, the one near Evanston, where my own family is buried! How did I get here . . . ?

Before any logical answer could make its way into his frantic mind, the black figure was upon him. There was no time to shout, to breathe, to do anything. The sharp, clawlike fingers dug into his shoulders and yanked him roughly up from the ground. He was raised up into the wet, freezing air and slammed against the gravestone. Then the hands whirled him around, smashing his back into the stone, and he at last stood face-to-face with the monster.

The pale white face loomed before him, huge, bigger than a face could possibly be. The bright red eyes bored into him, and the hot, fetid breath of the cemetery assaulted his nostrils. The great mouth was open, agape, yawning wide mere inches before him, the huge, jagged white slabs of teeth resembling nothing so much as the rows of tombstones that surrounded him. There was a sound coming from the monster's throat, a strangled cry of desire, of hunger. Blood hunger. As Mark stared, frozen, powerless against the irresistible force that pinned him to the grave, the massive jaws came forward, toward his neck. In a second, he knew, those rank, dripping headstones would clamp down on his shoulder, piercing, sucking the lifeblood out of him.

Then there was another flash of lightning, and in that moment Mark saw it, just below the hot red eyes and jutting mouth of the specter, above the black duster coat. The detail of the man he had not noticed before: the open red wound that slashed across his throat, separating his head from his torso, spilling bright red blood down onto his starched white clerical collar. The creature before him, the thing that had pursued him through the cemetery was not, had never been, Scavenger. It was Reverend Jacob Farmer.

His father.

Mark screamed. Pinned back against his family's monument, with the hailstones whipping against his hot cheeks and the foul stench of death exploding into his startled face, he opened his mouth and cried out. He pressed himself back, back against the freezing, wet stone, using every ounce of strength he had left to recoil, to get away from this man, this vampire, this thing that had once been his father. But something was wrong, very wrong. His voice rose up, sharp, piercing, filling the landscape of death with his cry, but the grave behind him was no longer cold, no longer even stone. It was soft and warm and pliable. It was . . . it was . . .

A bed. The big bed in the hotel room in Los Angeles. He was sitting on the floor of the room, naked, drenched in sweat, leaning back against the side of the bed. The pillows and most of the bedspread lay nearby on the burnt-orange carpet. He was making a low, strangled sound deep in his throat, and his arms were stretched out rigidly in front of him to ward off the biting, hungry mouth. But there was no longer anything holding him, mere empty space where the red-eyed Reverend Farmer had been a moment ago. The bedside lamp cast a friendly, reassuring glow, enough to clearly illuminate the empty, warm, dry, safe hotel bedroom.

He leaned back against the bed, gasping, willing his heart to slow down, and his aching arms fell limply to his sides. He sat there, blinking several times to clear the final echoes, the last vestiges of the dream from his eyes. But the feverish feeling continued, and at last he began to think. Logic and reason crept slowly into his hot brain, and he concentrated on trying to move, to get up from the floor and go into the bathroom. There was a bottle of aspirin in his bag, and all he had to do was stand up and find it. . . .

Then he was up on his feet, shivering as the conditioned air attacked his gleaming skin, drying his perspiration, causing a thrill of goose bumps everywhere on him. He brought up a clammy hand to push the damp hair out of his eyes and looked around for the bag. He rummaged through it until he found the little plastic bottle, then walked unsteadily, drunkenly into the bathroom and switched on the light.

The aspirin was extra-strength, but he swallowed four of them anyway, followed by a glass of cool water from the tap. He turned on the shower, aware that he had taken one just before he'd lain down on the bed. No matter: once inside, the warm spray washing over him, he began to feel better, almost normal. Whatever normal was.

He used a fresh towel from the ample supply on the rack to dry himself before the bathroom mirror, gazing into it. He was struck by how normal—that word again—he appeared. Eyes, hair, skin: all just as before. The nightmare had taken no physical toll, which seemed odd. He'd fully expected to look different: wild, sick, haunted. But the eyes he'd regarded every day of his life gazed steadily back at him, clear and shining. The dream was over.

And now he had to leave. He dried his hair with the hotel's blow-dryer and went out into the bedroom for his clean clothes. It was just after nine o'clock; he'd been asleep for more than two hours. He had to get to the airport. There would be late flights, he was certain, and he would be on one. If not, he would sleep in the terminal waiting area and take the first available flight out tomorrow. But he had to go, had to be moving.

Ten minutes later he was in the hotel lobby, paying cash to settle his bill. Then he went quickly outside to his rented Mustang. The pain of the afternoon had ceased, he noticed. He drove away from the hotel and headed through the late evening traffic on the wet streets toward the airport. As he traveled, he tried to sort everything out in his mind.

Robert Gammon, Millicent Call, the LAPD officer. Three murders. Ron O'Hara was dead as well, but that had been suicide. Why would Scavenger lie, decline to take credit for one kill, when he was so obviously proud of his handiwork? Mark remembered the odd little smile, the expression of triumph on the tall man's face as he stood in the rain beside the hillside road, holding up Mark's revolver like a trophy, a winning lottery ticket. No, such a person would never hide his light under a bushel. It was not in his nature.

Besides, how could Scavenger possibly have murdered the FBI agent in Georgetown this afternoon, when he was at the cemetery watching Mark at the moment in question? Unless . . .

What had Ron O'Hara said the other night? *"This tall man with the scar could be legs."* Mark thought about that. Was it possible? Was it *logical*? Was Scavenger working with someone else? Working *for* someone else? How could that be? More to the point, *who* could it be?

No. He would not entertain that line of thinking. He would go mad if he did. He would accept that this man, Scavenger, was in charge, as he so obviously was, and proceed accordingly. He would go on to the next destination, the next phase of the game, but it was time to establish rules of his own. Rule number one: be prepared. He could do that as soon as he got off the plane. He would find some insurance, some weapon, now that he no longer had the gun. But first, rule number two.

He looked around him. He had left the highway and entered the airport grounds. Now he was turning into the road that would lead to the terminal. Off on the left, dimly illuminated by yellow sodium-vapor lights, was a big, crowded parking lot. The sight of it gave him an idea.

He turned into the parking lot. Then he stopped the car, got out, and began to walk, moving quickly between the long rows of cars, remembering the cemetery and its rows of headstones. He walked until he came to a relatively uncrowded section at the farthest part of the lot from the terminal. There was a field beyond it, and runways beyond that. Off in the distance, the lights of a 747 winked in the night as it taxied slowly down the long runway and turned around, preparing for takeoff.

Mark stopped when he reached the edge of the lot, gazing out across the grassy field. It was a wide space, perhaps a hundred yards of grass before the fences separating it from the runways. Yes, he decided, this field would do. It was as good a place as any.

He dropped the bag, unzipped it, and reached inside, rummaging. When he found what he wanted, he walked out into the wet field. There was a rumbling in the distance, growing louder as the 747's powerful engines revved to full capacity and the airliner began to move, gaining in speed as it went. The roar was deafening as the plane rose majestically up from the earth and sailed off into the night sky. Mark raised his arm, reared back, and threw.

The black cellular telephone took off, sailing up and out in a wide arc, as the plane had just done. The lights of the parking lot allowed him to watch it fly away across the field before plummeting down to land near the far fences. Even with the roar of the jet, Mark could hear the faint, profoundly satisfying sound as the phone, the instrument symbolic of Scavenger's domination of him, smashed to pieces.

Then Mark picked up his bag, walked back across the parking lot to his car, and drove away. He parked in the Hertz lot and went into the terminal, moving purposefully, carefully surveying every person and knot of people before him as he went. No police, as far as he could see. He would avoid anyone in a uniform who might be airport security, and he would avoid any newsstands. He had not seen a newspaper since the one in New Orleans yesterday, and he had no way of knowing whether there were pictures of him in any of them.

No way of knowing, he mused as he approached the Hertz counter in the corner of the big main concourse: that was precisely the problem. He had no way of knowing the extent of police interest in him. The newscaster had merely said that he was wanted for questioning. He didn't know how much manpower that would entail, how carefully or thoroughly they would be looking for him. But he was taking no chances.

The Hertz agent took no unusual notice of him as he turned in his

keys and settled his bill. Then he moved on to the nearest bank of automated teller machines. He used his bank card to remove the maximum amount of cash allowed, hoping again that his checking account
had not been flagged. He glanced nervously around the terminal as the
machine produced his money. Three hundreds, the rest in twenties and
tens. When he added it to the cash already in his wallet, he could buy a
one-way ticket and still have several hundred left. Good. But first, another precaution.

He walked quickly away from the ATM, found a big chain drug-
store in the row of shops on the mezzanine, and went inside. A quick
stop in the men's grooming section, then a pair of reflective mirrored
sunglasses. Almost as an afterthought, he added a pair of scissors and
a battery-operated electric shaver. What the hell? he decided as he paid
in cash and went on to his next destination.

There was no security guard in the men's room, he noted with relief. Nearly eleven at night: off hours. He went to a sink, removed his
leather jacket, wet his hair, and went quickly to work. A few tired
travelers came and went from the bathroom as he stood before the
mirror, allowing the shampoolike substance to sink in, but no one
took the slightest interest in him. Then he rinsed and started in with
the scissors and the razor. The electric hand dryer did the rest. He
gazed in the mirror, thinking, Not bad for an amateur.

Minutes later, the tall man with short, dark blond hair got in line at
the airline's ticket purchase counter. When it was his turn, he went up
to the smiling young woman, producing an expression of sorrow on
his face. He told her where he wanted to go, and she said there were
seats available on the one o'clock flight. He pulled out several hundreds, which gave her pause. He explained in a low, sad voice that
there was a family emergency. His father was ill, probably dying, and
he would have to pay cash because his credit cards were maxed out.
He even managed a couple of tears as he gazed sadly at the woman.
Nodding sympathetically, she began to process the ticket.

"Name?' she asked as she typed information on her computer
keyboard.

Mark stared at the woman, not seeing her. He was lying in a wet
road above this city, a dead police office beside him, staring into the
eyes of madness. And now, as then, came on epiphany.

He took out his new sunglasses and put them on. Then he reached
absently up to touch his short blond hair. He hadn't uttered it in so

long, he was wondering if he could, if it would be possible. But he surprised himself. He was going home, after all, home to his family. His voice, when it came, was clear and strong.

"My name is Matthew Farmer."

ARTICLE #4

PHOTOGRAPH

F R I D A Y

$$\boxed{37}$$

At first there was darkness, followed by a glimmer of light. No, not a glimmer; merely the sensation, the knowledge that there was light against her closed eyelids. It was her first thought as she swam slowly back to consciousness. Her second thought was that she was bound. She knew before she opened her eyes that her hands and feet had been restrained, were tied to something, and that there was tape over her mouth. Somewhere very close by, someone was playing a piano.

Wood. She felt cold, smooth, polished wood at her wrists and under her forearms. She was sitting in a chair with wooden arms, and there was upholstery, soft cushions under her and at her back. A big, sturdy, mahogany dining room chair, perhaps. She wriggled her left hand slightly: tape. She was not tied, but taped to the chair. Duct tape.

She did not open her eyes, not yet. Some instinct, some primeval rule of survival instructed her to stay very still in the chair. She listened: there were at least two other people in the room with her. The music was in front of her, and she heard the scrape of a chair and the rustling of paper—a newspaper?—behind her. She drew in a breath through her nose: smoke. The person somewhere behind her was seated, reading a newspaper and smoking a cigarette, or maybe a cigar.

Because her forearms were bare, she deduced that they had removed her coat. She was wearing the dark blue, short-sleeved wool dress from dinner with Jared. When had that been? she wondered. Yesterday? The day before? How long had she been unconscious?

Still without opening her eyes, Tracy tried to apply reason. The sweet chemical smell had to have been chloroform, or something very like it. It would only affect a human for—what? Three hours? Six? Not much more than that. The light against her closed eyelids seemed to be bright, brighter than artificial light. Conclusion: daylight. She'd been assaulted at ten o'clock at night, and the drug and her own shock would have kept her out for mere hours. It was the next morning, Friday. Had to be.

Now she concentrated on relaxing back into the chair and listening to the music. What could that tell her? She recognized the melody, an elegy by Mendelssohn. No, Massenet. Massenet wrote elegies. Her mind was working better now, getting up to speed. That would be important, she knew, after she opened her eyes and the people in the room with her knew she was awake. If there was going to be any opportunity for escape, she would have to be ready for it. She would probably be given only one chance, if that. As soon as she was unbound, she would run for her life. Or fight for it.

A sudden image came into her mind, of her mother preparing dinner in the house she'd grown up in, the house in Garden City, Long Island. And her father at the kitchen table, reading stock reports while her mother chopped vegetables. She'd stood in the kitchen doorway, just home from cheerleading practice, watching them, filled with a delicious feeling of warmth and security. Then the image faded, and she was in Paris with Alan, on their honeymoon, wandering along the left bank of the Seine, tossing breadcrumbs to the—

Birds. She banished the reverie and brought her frantic mind back to the present, to this unknown danger she was in. There was a bird nearby, somewhere outside the room, chattering. After a moment, another bird replied. And there was a different, more distant sound, nearly indistinguishable. Like a lawn mower, only deeper, more powerful. A tractor? Yes, a tractor. She was not in New York City, not in any city. She was in a house near trees, which explained the birds, and an open field, which would account for the tractor. The country. But where?

She inhaled deeply and took a risk. Slowly, carefully, she opened her eyes a little, just a slit, and peered into the gloom before her. The thin vertical line of harsh light came from between the drawn curtains of a very large window. No, French doors. The curtains were dark red and of some heavy material, velvet or damask. A wall, with pictures— framed photographs. A table by the wall, just at the perimeter of her vision, was crowded with gleaming white and black objects: a chessboard set for a game. Near the windows, in front of her and to her right, was a huge black grand piano with a silver candelabrum on it.

The candles were lit, and whoever was playing the instrument was on the other side of them, blocked from her view. She dared not risk moving, attempting to twist around in the chair to see who was behind her. She closed her eyes again and waited.

While she waited, she allowed herself one more brief indulgence. She thought of Mark, of his eyes and his hair and his smile and his hard, lean body. They had made love that night, Sunday, the last time she had seen him. She thought of kissing him, laughing with him, grasping him, taking him inside her. His way of smiling across the pillows afterward, and of pulling her close before sleeping. Oh, God, she thought. Mark, will I ever see you again? Will we ever—

A harsh, discordant chord. Silence. A low, muttered profanity. Then the music began again, from the top of the piece. She strained slightly forward in the imprisoning chair, listening to the elegy more carefully because there was definitely something wrong with it. It was being played with a remarkable lack of skill, with frequent sour notes and fumbled chords, as if the pianist's hands were unformed, too small to reach the required fingering. As if they were the hands of a child.

No, she reasoned. That is not possible. No one, not even a madman, would have a child in a room with a woman bound to a chair. She shook her head from side to side, dismissing the thought.

And the music stopped again.

"Good morning, Ms. Morgan."

It was a man's voice, low and clear. Amused? Her heart lurched against her chest, and then she shivered. In the silence of the moment that followed, she realized that she had been moving about, shaking her head, and that the pianist had seen it. He knew she was awake. It was no use pretending that she wasn't. The scrape of a chair, the rustle of paper, and the person in the room behind her apparently stood up. Then the scrape of the piano bench, and the pianist, the one who had spoken, was on his feet as well. She took a long, deep breath through her nose and opened her eyes.

It was probably a good thing that her mouth was taped shut, she decided. When she saw, when she looked at the figure who now stood beside the piano, her first impulse was to scream. Bound as she was, she could only stare, her eyes widening in terror, in revulsion, in panic, as the figure grinned and came slowly toward her.

38

Thirteen years, Mark thought. Twelve years and four months, to be precise. He would be confronting the past, facing his demons here. Here, as never before.

He was home.

He remained in his seat until the plane had arrived at the gate and the seat belt sign was turned off. He listened as the engines' roar subsided, stopped. A flight attendant was welcoming them to Chicago, thanking them for flying the airline, and reminding them to take all personal possessions. Please fly with us again, and have a nice day.

A nice day, he thought, glancing out through the porthole. Hardly that. Gray clouds were gathering here, as they had in Los Angeles. The bad weather seemed to be following him, tracking him across the continent. It was six in the morning here: he'd lost two hours flying east. The sun had presumably risen, but you wouldn't know it looking out over the vast runways of America's busiest airport. The clouds obscured everything, turning day to night.

He stood up and retrieved his bag from the overhead compartment, and he helped the pretty young blond woman who'd been sitting across the aisle from him to get down her overnight case. She smiled and thanked him. Mark smiled back, thinking briefly of Tracy. Then he followed the stream of passengers out of the plane into O'Hare International Airport.

Home, he thought again. I am here again, in the city where I spent the first twenty-three years of my life. Where my family lived, and where they died. I am in this place I vowed never to return to, and Scavenger has brought me here.

Scavenger. He began the now-familiar routine, scanning the crowds all around him for the tall, dark figure who was constantly there, constantly watching. He was not at all surprised to see that the man with the scar was nowhere in evidence. But he was here somewhere, Mark reasoned. He had to be.

Mark continued his surreptitious search as he made his way through the terminal to the Avis desk. He rented another Chevy, this one a Cavalier that turned out to be dark blue, watching the salesman nervously as the credit card sale was processed. No, Chicago wasn't looking for him—yet. He went out to find the car in the lot, smiling once more at the pretty blond woman from the plane who was now getting into the rental car beside his. She smiled back, and he again thought, Tracy.

During the drive from the airport to Evanston, he went over it in his mind again. *Second wind.* That was what Scavenger had said, and his meaning was patently clear. Chicago, known variously as the Second City and the Windy City. *Second wind.* Very clever. But he already knew that his opponent was clever. It came as no surprise now.

Now it was up to Mark to be just as clever.

He had decided where to stay, hoping that the guest house within walking distance of his family home in Evanston was still in business and not full. No matter: there were other guest houses and hotels, and one would do as well as another. But he would start at the Red Rose Inn. He would book a room for two nights as Jared McKinley. He couldn't use the name Matthew Farmer here, so close to the scene of the Farmer family tragedy. People might remember, particularly the British couple who owned the inn. He didn't know them personally, but he remembered that their guest house was a favorite of the many visitors to nearby Northwestern University, designed along the lines of a small British hotel. He would drop off his bag in his room and proceed to the next move. *His* move, not Scavenger's. The thought filled him with grim amusement.

The big, gabled white mansion was still there on the corner four blocks from his home, the pretty swinging sign still proclaiming it to be a guest house. He parked in the little lot behind the building, got his bag, and went inside, looking around him as he went up the walk to the front door. Still no sign of Scavenger, not that there would be. But Mark was being watched; he was certain of it.

The desk was in the front hall, with a cozy sitting room to his left and a cozy dining room with four or five tables on his right. The young woman who appeared when he rang the bell on the counter was American, not British, and Mark was sure he'd never seen her before. She introduced herself as Mrs. Baker, the proprietor, and Mark remembered that was the name of the old couple. This woman would be their daughter-in-law, he decided. They must have retired, leaving the business to their son and his wife. Mark smiled, paid cash for two nights, and signed the register as Jared McKinley.

"Welcome, Mr. McKinley," she said as she led him upstairs to a cozy, immaculately clean little bedroom on the second floor. "We only have two guests at the moment, you and an elderly lady across the hall from you, so you should find the place quiet. Enjoy your stay with us."

Mark thanked her again, and with another smile she left him alone.

He looked at his watch: eight o'clock. He hadn't been able to sleep on the plane, using the three-hour flight to formulate what he now thought of as his countermeasures, his defense against Scavenger. And he had only slept for a couple of hours last night, and fitfully at that. So his first order of business was a nap. He knew that Scavenger would show up eventually, later today, and he wanted to be alert when that happened.

He unpacked his toothbrush and other toiletries, and put them on the sink in the bathroom. Then he took off his shoes and socks and lay down on the big, firm bed. He was thinking about Ron O'Hara again. The agent was dead, a suicide, and Mark regretted it for several reasons. He had seemed like a nice man, but it was more than that. Mark knew that he could now use the man's help. He needed the expertise of someone who was used to dealing with people like Scavenger. Someone who understood the twisted minds of sociopaths.

Just before he drifted off, he sat up on the bed, remembering his promise to himself. He reached for the bedside telephone, read the instructions for an outside line, and followed them. Tracy would not be home, as it would now be nine o'clock in New York, but he didn't want to bother her in her office. He dialed her home number and waited while her recorded voice went through the familiar litany.

"Hi, babe," he said after the beep. "I'm thinking about you, and I'll see you in a couple of days. I'm now in Chicago, believe it or not. This is the last of my research, I think." He read the phone number of his room. "Give me a call if you've got a minute. I can't wait to see you. You take care of yourself. I love you."

He hung up and lay back down on the bed, remembering their last night together, just four days ago. They had made love, and now he wanted her here with him. It was yet another inconvenience, another pebble in his shoe, courtesy of Scavenger. The man owed him dearly, and Mark was determined that he would eventually pay.

He was nervous about going to sleep. He wondered if he would have the dream again, the nightmare in which his father appeared to him in the cemetery. He knew what the dream signified without having to consult a psychiatrist. It was obvious to him that Reverend Farmer was transformed into a monster, something unspeakably evil, by Mark's own guilty conscience. He would have to suffer through the dream if it came again. He didn't know what he could do to assuage his guilt and make the dream go away. He was here again, in Evanston, where his family had met their fate, and the guilt was palpable. He could taste it in the back of his throat.

It took a long time for Mark to finally get to sleep. He slept for nearly eight hours, and the dream did not come. His sleep, at least for now, was undisturbed.

39

"The Red Rose Inn. It's in Evanston, just a few blocks from the house."

"I see. And what is he doing now?"

"Asleep, as far as I can tell. He checked into the room a couple of hours ago, and he's been in there ever since."

"Okay. Stay there. If he goes anywhere, you know what to do. I'll be there shortly."

"Right."

The man with the scar put away the cell phone inside his coat, smiling to himself. Matthew Farmer was making the game infinitely more challenging for himself. That business at the L.A. airport, hair coloring and reflective sunglasses. He now had short blond hair. Not that he could hide from *me,* he thought, but that obviously wasn't his intention. He's thinking about the New Orleans police, the APB. He must continue on the assumption that at any moment someone might recognize him, turn him in to the authorities. So, a disguise. Very good, Mr. Farmer. One point for you.

He wondered what else Matthew Farmer was thinking, what other surprises he had in store. Not that anything would surprise him: concessions had been made for just about every possible eventuality. It had been decided early in the planning stages that Mark Stevenson/Matthew Farmer was an unusually intelligent specimen, and that the notion of his altering the rules, going maverick, was not out of the question. He had changed his appearance, but that wasn't his biggest act of defiance. Not by a wide mile.

He was still smiling as he glided out of the motel to his new rental car, a green Oldsmobile Intrigue, trying to imagine the scene in the airport grounds last night as it had been described to him. His quarry had been doing the expected, driving from the hotel on Sunset to the airport, when he had suddenly done something unexpected. He'd stopped the car in a parking lot and walked away toward the runways. It had taken some fancy driving and a quick sprint through the lot in the darkness for his assistant to witness what happened next.

He had destroyed the cell phone. But it was more than that, the man with the scar knew. It was the act of throwing it as far as he could that explained Matthew Farmer's state of mind. He was obviously desperate now, desperate to reclaim some modicum of authority over his own life, his own fate. He was no longer meekly accepting his opponent's autocracy. Whether or not this was a good thing remained to be seen, but it certainly made the game more interesting.

He drove out of the motel lot and turned north toward Evanston. He had missed the incidents in the L.A. airport last night because he had already left for Chicago by then. He had come here last evening, rented a car, checked into the motel, and gone to get his materials for tonight. They were in the trunk of the car now, waiting for their eventual placement in the next location.

Tomorrow, Saturday, would be the last day. Tomorrow at midnight, it would all come to an end. The final locale, the final retrieved article. Then would come the part Matthew Farmer did not know about, *must* not know about.

Tomorrow at midnight, Matthew Farmer was going to die.

It was that simple, really. He would watch Matthew Farmer die, slowly and painfully, and it would all be over. Complete. Perfect.

He crossed Howard Street and entered the suburb of Evanston a few minutes later. It took him a while to find the right street. And there it was, the Red Rose Inn, just as he had been told. He parked in the lot of a church across the street from the guest house and relaxed back in his seat, waiting. In moments, his assistant materialized at the driver's window.

"He's still in his room, second floor on the left. He's driving a blue Cavalier that's parked in back."

"Good." He glanced up at the appropriate windows. The curtains there were closed. "I'll take over now. Did you leave the message for him?"

"Yes. When do I get the rest of my money?"

"When it's over."

"Right. See to it." And the assistant was gone.

He sighed and shook his head. Then he reached inside his black coat and pulled out a pack of cigarettes. He lit one and sat back again, staring up at the curtained windows, thinking about how he would kill Matthew Farmer.

He thought about the first man he'd killed, when he was fifteen years old. The two men when he was seventeen. And the three other men, all in one day when he was eighteen, who had felt his eight-inch blade enter their hearts.

He thought about the five families: Tennant, Webster, Farmer, Carlin, Banes.

He thought about the man and woman in New Orleans and the man in Los Angeles, and he smiled.

At last, he thought about his wife, dead these many years, and the smile disappeared.

He sat there for several hours, smoking cigarettes in the green Oldsmobile Intrigue across the street from Matthew Farmer's hotel, waiting for the next move in the game.

40

Scavenger was sitting in a green Oldsmobile Intrigue in the parking lot across the street from the hotel, smoking a cigarette. Mark spotted him immediately, as soon as he woke up and went over to the window to peer through the curtains. He looked as if he'd been sitting there for several hours.

Good. Mark had planned the next few hours carefully, and the fact that the man was here watching him was good. More than good: essential. While he dressed, he went over his itinerary in his mind. His only other stop after this afternoon's business was his family home, a mere four blocks from here. But first . . .

He left the inn through the front door, walking slowly around to the lot at the back, careful not to so much as glance over at the green car. When he had driven a fair distance down the block, he saw the green Olds pull out into the street behind him. Fine.

Now he was in charge. He knew something Scavenger didn't know: he knew where they were going. He glanced up at the sky as he drove. It would rain soon, he knew. The dark clouds hovered above the city, as if biding their time.

He was heading in the opposite direction from his home, and he wondered what Scavenger would make of that. His first stop was at a florist's shop in Evanston, where he purchased two dozen roses, again with cash. The man wrapped them in green paper, and Mark thanked him, went back to his car, and continued on his way. Scavenger followed.

As he drove west through Evanston, Mark passed a women's clothing shop where his mother had bought many of her dresses. He thought about her, and about Josh and Mary. He had vivid memories of them: what they looked like, the sounds of their voices, the way they laughed. Mary, especially. He hadn't been close to them at the end, had not seen them in years at the time of their murders, but he still remembered. He made a conscious effort not to think about his father. The graveyard dream was still too fresh.

The graveyard . . .

He turned left off Dempster Street and drove to his next stop. Yes, there it was, up ahead on the right, surrounded by high stone walls. The entrance gate reminded him of the similar one in Los Angeles. He drove inside, aware of the other presence down the road behind him. He parked in the big main lot and proceeded on foot down a series of crisscrossing sidewalks, gazing around at the expanse of green lawns dotted with hundreds of graves. His second cemetery in as many days. And now, as then, he was being monitored.

The four white headstones were similar to those of the Webster family, perhaps a little smaller. But the name FARMER was prominent on them. Jacob, Charlene, Joshua, Mary. The housekeeper was buried elsewhere, and the dog, Sam, had been cremated.

Jacob, Charlene, Joshua, Mary. He stood before them, aware of their presence, of the feeling that they were here with him now. It was the familiar feeling of haunting, the one he'd assimilated, carried with him everywhere. He looked up from the graves at the dark sky. Yes, rain soon. He remembered the icy rain that Christmas morning, rain that had turned once more to snow in the following days. He remembered the bitter cold of the funeral, the snow everywhere around him in this place. The big crowd from the Church of the True Believers, singing and praying. The cameras and journalists. And over there, at a discreet distance, the lone FBI special agent, watching the proceedings. Ronald O'Hara. Ron. Respectful but vigilant. He was probably expecting The Family Man to show his hand, but nothing out of the ordinary had occurred. The snow had fallen, the hymns had been sung, the words spoken. Mark—Matthew—had stood closest to the graves, surrounded by more than a hundred people. Yet alone; acutely, finally alone. And so cold.

He knelt now and placed the roses between the two center graves, his father and mother. He wanted to weep, felt that he really should weep, but no tears would come. He stared down at the stones, dry-eyed, imagining himself as Scavenger must be seeing him from wherever he was. Somewhere behind him, no doubt. He tried to imagine what the tall man must be thinking as he watched him, but he hadn't the slightest idea. The man was insane, and the insane could not be predicted.

He sighed. It was nearly five o'clock now, and it was time for the next move. He stood up, brushing the dirt from his pants. Just before he left the graves, he uttered a small prayer, or part of one, half remembered words about the lambs of God coming together in Paradise. He wasn't even aware of the meaning of the words, only of his need to say them, to say something over these people after all this time. It had been a long time since he had seen these graves, and much longer since he had last prayed to a deity in which he did not believe. But his family deserved a prayer from him, so he went through the motions.

Now he had all the time in the world. He wandered slowly through the cemetery, stopping to read random stones as they appeared before him, deliberately taking his time. He, too, could be manipulative, and it felt good to have some measure of control back after the last few days. Scavenger would have to wait for him.

He left the cemetery at last, walking slowly back to his car. The green Olds was stopped on the other side of the lot, its engine idling. Mark got in his car and led their odd little procession down Sheridan Road to Lake Shore Drive, into downtown Chicago. His new destination was Water Tower Place, the huge vertical shopping mall on Michigan Avenue. There were restaurants there, and he would find a likely one and enjoy a leisurely meal. Then he would go into the multiplex cinema and purchase a ticket for any one of the films on view. But he wouldn't stay there. Theaters always had back doors, fire exits, and he would utilize one.

When he was out of the theater, when he was certain that he had eluded Scavenger, he would be on his own. He knew where Scavenger would go, must eventually go, and he would prepare himself. After all, Mark now had one distinct advantage.

They were now on his turf. This was his city, and Evanston was his hometown.

And it would be his house.

Smiling to himself, Mark continued on his way.

41

Damn Matthew Farmer, he thought. I've lost him.

Or, to be more precise, Matthew Farmer had managed to lose *him.* It had happened at the crowded movie theater in the mall near the restaurant, and he cursed himself for his inattention. He had let the man get out of his sight for a mere ten minutes, but that had been enough.

He had waited outside the restaurant while his quarry was inside. He watched as the man slowly, deliberately enjoyed everything from soup to nuts, obviously making a mockery of him. Then he had shadowed him to the multiplex and allowed him to go inside. He noted the man's selection, then followed. He bought his own ticket for the same film and waited in the lobby for ten minutes.

Ten minutes. In that short time, Matthew Farmer had disappeared.

He'd waited until the lights were off and the movie had begun before entering the theater. He swiftly, efficiently scanned the room, walking down the side aisle to the screen and back. No Matthew Farmer. He'd dashed from the dark cinema back into the bright, crowded mall, but it was too late. He knew it even as he ran. He stood there, shaking his head in wonder and grudging admiration; admiration for Matthew Farmer's success, wonder that he would even try such a thing. He had been so passive, so cooperative thus far, but now he was obviously taking the initiative. The blond hair, the wrecked cell phone, and now this. Matthew Farmer had led him into a bustling shopping center and lost himself in the crowds. The man was not merely following the game, but playing it.

He had used his cell phone to place a brief call, and the result had been what he had expected. His employer was furious. He'd stood in front of the theater in the mall in Chicago, wincing at the hissed words, but there was no help for it. Finally, the new instructions were given, and he quickly, gratefully broke the connection. He was to let Farmer go temporarily, leave the mall, and prepare for tonight. He hated it when his employer was angry. He felt as if he had failed, as if he had let down the one person in the world to whom he owed everything, including his life and his freedom.

Well, not his employer, really. His employer's parents. But they were gone these many years, and for their sake he remained loyal to their child.

He truly did owe them his freedom: that was no exaggeration. They had made it possible for him to stay in America. And Anna, his wife, his only love. They had taken both of them in when there was nowhere else to go, except back to Russia.

Their international fame and frequent trips to the Soviet Union had made everything possible. Anna, at sixteen, had been assigned to the wife as a lady's maid, while he—with the help of a family friend—had become the husband's assistant. He had been sixteen, too, and the job had lasted a mere month, during which time a friendship developed between the two Russian teenagers and their glamorous charges in Moscow. And he and Anna had fallen in love.

Then had come his father's arrest, and his own, and the mining camp in the gulag prison system.

His father had been training him and an ever-growing band of other men in guerrilla warfare. This had been almost forty years ago, of course, long before the sweeping changes in his country, and his father was preparing them for rebellion. A rebellion that never took place, as it turned out. Instead, he and his father had been sent to Siberia, and he had never seen his mother or his sister again.

His father lasted only a few weeks in the grueling place, succumbing to pneumonia brought on by exhaustion in the mines and close proximity to too many dying workers. But he himself had survived for two long years, steeling himself for the day when he would make the long trek, or die. After two years in the mines, he almost didn't care which. But he was bolstered in his survival by one dream: Anna.

The American conductor and his Russian-born pianist wife had taken her with them. It had required much cajoling of bureaucrats to get the girl permanently employed, and to get her out of the country. Their celebrity had made all that possible. But even they could not get him and his father out of Siberia. He and his father were traitors, that much was certainly true, and their fate was sealed.

Now, as he made his way back to the car in the Water Tower Place garage and drove north toward Evanston, he remembered the work in the mines, and his illnesses, and the hunger. He remembered the beatings, and the humiliation at the hands of the guards. The fight in which he had killed two men with his bare hands, a guard and a fellow prisoner. The resulting solitary confinement that had lasted six months.

And he remembered his escape: the fences; the endless, bleak expanses of snow that almost permanently blinded him; the friendly but frightened farmers and townspeople along the way who concealed him and kept him alive; and his eventual arrival, weeks later, at a border manned by several soldiers, three of whom had spotted him, chased him, and caught him. They were responsible for the scar on his face. Three men in one day, with the blade that even now was strapped to his chest. And then a new expanse of snow, and a new life with Anna.

He had found their benefactors in Vienna, performing, and Anna was with them. More red tape, more outright bribery, and the two young people, now eighteen, were on their way to America. They married soon after, and eventually became full American citizens, thanks to their famous friends.

And now, nearly forty years later, he worked for their son. He had remained loyal to him all these years for their sake. He was bound to him: the man could not survive without him. So he stayed. Even after the murders. Even now, with one more killing to go.

One more killing. Yes. . . .

He drove through the quiet evening in the university town, arriving at last in the short, dead-end street that ended at the Farmer house. It was time to go to work again. He hadn't truly lost Matthew Farmer, he knew. Matthew Farmer would show up again eventually. He'd simply had to go off on his own for a while, to give himself the illusion of being in control of the game. That was ridiculous, of course, and he was certain that Matthew Farmer knew it.

They both knew who was in control of this game.

42

The bartender was getting suspicious, and Mark decided it was time to leave. He'd slipped into the dimly lit restaurant after his sprint down the stairs to the mall level just below the movie theater. He'd ordered a beer, which he had barely touched, glancing constantly out the window for any sign of Scavenger. The barman, a big, burly, middle-aged type straight out of central casting for bartenders, had noted his uneasiness. Now he was openly watching Mark, sensing potential trouble of some kind. The last thing Mark wanted was to draw attention to himself.

Mark paid for the beer and left the man a dollar. He got up from his stool and went over to the door, checking once more out the window before opening it. He looked both ways, scanning the crowded mall, but there was no sign of Scavenger anywhere. Then he walked out onto the concourse and proceeded in the direction of the escalators.

There was no way he could get a new gun, or if there was, he didn't know how, so he had dismissed the idea in favor of another. The store he was headed for would have what he wanted. He had been told to be at his house at midnight tonight, and he was going to be prepared.

He was also going to be early. This was the real reason for the ruse in the movie theater: he didn't want Scavenger to know what he was doing. Let *him* worry, for a change. It was about time the shoe was on the other foot, even if it was only temporary.

Mark was remembering the house outside New Orleans and the cemetery in Los Angeles. If Scavenger was running true to form, he would be at the Farmer house hours before the appointment, setting up some sort of surprise. He could even be on his way there now, for all Mark knew, so time was of the essence. He had to hurry.

He scanned the crowds and shop doorways surreptitiously, carefully keeping his head down and avoiding eye contact with anyone. He had no idea when he might run into Scavenger, and no way of knowing whether or not his picture had yet made the newspapers and local telecasts in Chicago. He doubted it, but he wasn't taking any chances. He couldn't risk the sunglasses in the mall, though. It was night now, and dark shades would attract more attention than the lack of them. He'd noticed the odd looks in the L.A. airport last night while he waited for his flight, and he'd soon figured it out and taken them off. Sunglasses at night meant you had a black eye or you were a drug addict.

Or someone wanted by the police.

The store he wanted was on the top floor, according to the mall directory. He afforded the crowd waiting at the bank of elevators a mere glance before stepping onto the first of several escalators. People packed together in an elevator fall into two categories: those who carefully ignore everyone and those who carefully study everyone. Even with his short blond hair, he wouldn't take a chance that some perceptive type might recognize him.

He finally arrived on the appropriate floor. He walked down the corridor and entered the store he wanted. He began looking around, politely shrugging off the friendly, avid salesman who almost immediately materialized beside him. It took him mere moments to find exactly what he had in mind. He took it over to the register and paid cash, marveling at the high prices for such things. Then he made his way quickly back to the escalators.

As he descended, he found himself thinking about Judy Barlow, the girl he'd lived with for most of the time he was estranged from his family. They'd spent their first two years together partying, then the next two in Narcotics Anonymous. They'd gotten jobs, and he'd gone to college, which he'd ultimately finished in New York, after the move. After the murders. Judy had, to all appearances, been on her way out of her self-inflicted hell, as he had been. But then had come the murders, and his decision to leave Chicago. Judy had died just before he left for New York, of an overdose.

Poor Judy, he thought now. But I am different: I am a survivor. And what I have just done here, in this mall, proves it. I am going to survive this.

I am ready for Scavenger.

He arrived at the parking level, pausing to glance at his watch.

Eight-twenty. He would leave the car at the Red Rose Inn and walk the four blocks to his former home. He got in the blue Cavalier and drove away from Water Tower Place with somewhat more confidence than he had felt before.

He was now in possession of a good, solid, heavy Louisville Slugger baseball bat.

43

This man is insane, she thought.

Tracy sat back in the chair, trying not to look at him. She was in the same chair as this morning, but at least they had untaped her. Not that it mattered: there was no escaping them. The other one, the big one from this morning, had left during the afternoon, gone off somewhere and not yet returned, but he had been replaced. Another man now stood by the doorway, a tall young blond man she vaguely recognized but couldn't quite place. He was armed, she knew. She'd seen the holster under his jacket. But the blond man wasn't her greatest fear. He wasn't the crazy one.

The crazy one sat across from her now, in an armchair, sipping red wine. There was a glass of it on the table at her elbow as well, but she was afraid to touch it. More drugs, no doubt. He sat there, smiling politely and speaking in a low, clear voice, but nothing he was saying to her made any sense. It was some sort of sick fantasy of his, as far as she could tell, but it involved Mark. His name had been mentioned several times. Something about a game, a scavenger hunt, if she'd heard him properly. But Mark was in Los Angeles. She didn't understand anything anymore.

And she couldn't bear to look at this man.

They had offered to feed her, but she had refused, as she refused to touch the wine. She just wanted to go home. But she couldn't; they'd made that, if nothing else, very clear to her. She was a prize, the crazy one had told her. The grand prize in the treasure hunt. They were all going to wait here tonight—wherever *here* was—and Mark would arrive tomorrow. That was what he'd said, anyway.

Tracy could only pray it wasn't true. Why would Mark come here? How could he possibly know these awful people?

And what would they do to him if he *did* arrive?

What were they going to do to *her*?

Well, they apparently weren't going to rape her. That had been her first thought, as it is every woman's first thought when violence from strangers is suddenly, inexplicably visited upon her. The crazy one had been polite, even solicitous, and the other two men she had seen so far did not seem to be interested in her in that way, either. She had been kidnapped, but now, as it was turning out, the reason for it was apparently Mark. They were playing this game with him. But why? Why Mark, of all people? Just because he'd written that book about those old murders? Was this some sort of bizarre *fan club*?

The murders . . .

She thought about that, about everything she'd learned from Carol Grant and the *Chicago Tribune*. The Farmer family had been killed, slaughtered by—

Now she shrank back in the chair, gripping its arms tightly in her hands. Was that it? she asked herself. Could this demented creature possibly be . . .

No. *No,* she assured herself. He's dead, has been dead for years. Everybody knows that. The Family Man is *dead.*

So, a fan club. A pack of crazy true-crime groupies with way too much time on their hands. Now, she decided, I should concentrate on getting away from them, finding my way back to Planet Earth.

They were in a big house somewhere in the country, but they were apparently near a town; she'd heard one of them mention that. The big man from this morning had departed, and she'd heard the sound of a car pulling away. Perhaps there were other cars. There had to be; the black van must be around. If she could somehow get to it, or, barring that, simply get out of the house. Then she could run, find the town, get help. Get someone to do something about these people. But how was she to do that? There were at least two of them here, perhaps more. And she was alone. She had no weapon, no recourse. No hope, unless . . .

Mark. He had told her he was going to Washington to do research. But the research was unnecessary, as far as she could tell; he was supposed to be finishing another novel entirely. Besides, he had also gone to New Orleans and Los Angeles.

And he was armed.

The odd facts had already occurred to her before this. Before these people had drugged her and bundled her into the van. What if he really *was* doing what this creature said he was doing? What if he really was on his way here? But *why*? The whole thing was . . .

Insane. Like this man before her.

As she continued to stare at the carpet at her feet in an attempt to avert her gaze from him, the insane man smiled, took another sip of the blood-red wine, and started his bizarre story again from the beginning. She tried to block out his voice, feeling the horrible combination of terror and frustration once more welling up within her. A single tear made its way slowly down her cheek.

Oh, Mark, she thought. *Mark.* . . .

44

The black clouds hung in the sky over the Great Lakes region, obscuring the moon. There was a chill, a dampness in the air that made Mark think the rain would come very soon. Only the street lamps and an occasional porch light illuminated his way as he walked.

And here was the street at last, where he had once lived with his family. A dead end: there were only five houses, two on each side and the Farmer house on the lot where the street actually ended. Big trees lined the walks, and there were more around the handsome, well-appointed homes, each set well back from the street on a two-acre lot. Lights shone from the porches and curtained front windows of three of the other houses. The last house on the right and the Farmer house at the end were the only two that were completely dark. Behind the Farmers' big backyard was a wooden fence, and on the other side of it was public property, the edge of the grounds of an elementary school. The entrance to the school was on another street, and a virtual forest of oak and elm hid the distant buildings from view. Now, at nine o'clock, the cul-de-sac was silent.

He didn't want to be here. Here, he was Matthew Farmer, not Mark Stevenson. And Matthew Farmer was dead. Buried with the rest of his family in the cemetery he'd visited this afternoon. He felt like a ghost, a dead man standing on this sidewalk, looking down the road at that dead house.

Scavenger was not here yet.

Mark made his way down the sidewalk to the empty lot of the house on the right and walked up onto its front lawn. There were two huge oak trees, one on each side of the walk leading up to the now-deserted house. There was a FOR SALE sign near the porch. The family that had lived here when he was growing up were the Friedmans. They'd had two sons about his age, but he and his brother and sister were not allowed to play with them because they were Jewish. Reverend and Mrs. Farmer had grudgingly allowed them to play with the Methodist children down the street—at least they were Christians, however misguided—but Jews were to be avoided. Reverend Farmer had even looked into possible ways to get the Friedmans to sell their property to his church, but they had refused. Mark—Matthew—had secretly admired them for that.

The Farmer children had not been allowed to play much, in any case, as their church duties were fairly constant. When they reached their teens, they were rarely allowed out of the house at all.

Now, all these years later, the forbidden property of the forbidden people would serve him well. The oak tree on the right nearly abutted the Farmer lot, and he could conceal himself behind it and wait.

And wait he did, for nearly an hour in the cold, damp, pitch-black night, peering through the darkness at the house next door, his house. He set the baseball bat down on the grass at his feet and leaned against the rough bark of the oak, watching. The wind rustled the leaves above his head, filling the air with a constant, low sound. This place was not dead, after all: it was whispering to him.

It certainly gave the appearance, the illusion of death. The windows of all three stories of the elaborate wooden Victorian mansion had been boarded up by expensive professionals, and the front and back doors were locked, padlocked, and rigged with a delicate, costly alarm system.

He knew about the cost: he'd had the boarding-up done and the electronic alarms installed himself. But even the realtor who had occasionally rented the place, like the surveillance company, didn't know his new identity. She had merely been given a box number in New York City, and she addressed all correspondence to "Owner #43," as per his instructions. Forty-three was the street number of the house. He had a messenger service check the box once a week and forward any correspondence from the realtor to a second box number, which he checked from time to time. It—this house—was his only remaining connection to Matthew Farmer. But no one had sought to rent it in years. The last tenants, some five years ago, had stayed a mere six months before fleeing, claiming the house was haunted.

Well, perhaps it was. If anyone could convince the Almighty to let him stay and guard his own house on earth, it was Reverend Jacob Farmer. But Mark did not believe in God—and even if there *was* a God, Mark doubted He had much use for the Church of the True Believers. A truly perfect God would let that charlatan and all his followers rot in hell.

When he felt he couldn't stare at it anymore, he turned his attention from his former home to the corner down the street. He watched the intersection for some time, waiting for the green rental car to appear. After a while, he slid down to sit at the base of the tree, and he nearly dozed off. He was suddenly tired, numbed by the memories of that house next door, the house he'd grown up in, run away from, returned to on that rainy Christmas morning. . . .

He checked his watch again: it was a few minutes before ten. Where was Scavenger?

This question brought with it an idea, and he acted on it instantly. He'd been intrigued, wondering exactly how the man with the scar was going to get into the house, now a veritable fortress of boarded windows and alarm systems. But now he had a better idea. He would go inside and wait for Scavenger. It didn't matter how Scavenger got into the house: he'd already proved to Mark's satisfaction that he could do anything he wanted, go anywhere he wanted. Locks and alarms were nothing to him. Scavenger would get in somehow.

And Mark would be waiting for him.

Then he was up from the base of the tree and running, sprinting across the Friedman lawn to his own, the bat clutched firmly in his hands. He circled the house to the back, heading for the one entry he knew would be easiest.

There was a cellar entrance to the left of the kitchen door at the back of the house, and Mark remembered the combination to the padlock. It was the only access to the building that was not rigged for an alarm. He could enter here, go down the stairs to the cellar, and up the inside stairs to the kitchen.

He did so, locking the slanting door behind him: no sense making things easier for his opponent. Let him find his own way in. He descended the stone steps into the pitch-black cellar, wishing he had a flashlight, or even a book of matches. No matter; he knew his way by heart. Across the empty, dank room, through a door, and up the narrow wooden staircase to the kitchen door. It creaked as he swung it open and stepped into the kitchen. He paused in the middle of the empty room, getting his bearings in the dark.

There was no need to bother with the light switches, although the electricity in the house was still active because of the alarms; he knew every square inch of this house by heart. Now, in the dark, he imagined this room as it had been years ago, brightly lit and filled with the aromas of cooking. It had always been the domain of Mrs. Tornquist, their widowed, live-in housekeeper, who was a devout member of his father's congregation. Despite her strict piety, she had been a cheerful woman, even warm, and she had always treated him and his brother and sister kindly. His mother rarely entered the kitchen, leaving all the household chores and decisions to the other woman, and his father was far too busy to ever come here. It had been, he thought now, the most cheerful room in the house. The *only* cheerful room, he amended.

He was here again, in the house, and the rest of it was around and above him, cloaked in darkness and silence. The living room and dining room where the children were rarely allowed, his father's home office where the children were *never* allowed, the six bedrooms, the attic. It had always been a quiet place, this house of strict rules and strict religious devotion where the sound of laughter so infrequently rang out. But now, all these years later, with all the other occupants so long gone, it was quiet as the grave. And yet . . .

It was then that he heard it. He held his breath, straining his ears to listen. It was very faint, almost a whisper, and at first he thought he was imagining it, remembering it. But after a moment he knew that what he was hearing was real, and that it emanated from somewhere in front of him, at the front of the house. It was coming from . . .

The living room, he realized. Of course.

"Jingle Bells."

He froze: everything inside him seemed to turn to ice. It was the same music, the same recording, that had been playing in this house on that cold, rainy Christmas morning. He'd used it in *Dark Desire*, the only scene-of-the-crime music he hadn't been able to bring himself to fictionalize. He stood in the dark kitchen, unable to move, to think, to breathe. He almost dropped the baseball bat on the linoleum, grasping it firmly at the last possible moment before it fell.

It was this action that galvanized him. Raising the bat up before him with both hands, he moved slowly forward through the swinging

door into the dining room. He was aware that the hands clutching the
bat were trembling, and there was a roar, a rush of blood throughout
him, pounding in his temples and his chest. He crossed the empty
room to the opposite door, the entrance to the living room. Unwrap-
ping the shaking fingers of one hand from the bat, he turned the knob
and pulled the door open.

After the darkness of the rest of the house, the sudden, brilliant
light assaulted him. He sagged against the doorframe, trying to blink
the red spots away from in front of his eyes. When they dispersed, he
opened his eyes and stared around the room.

It was Christmas morning thirteen years ago, all over again. There
were the couches and chairs, and the blue carpet and drapes, the bookshelves crammed with religious tomes, and the home entertainment
center in the corner dominated by the enormous television screen. And
they had been augmented: the twinkling Christmas tree, the shimmer-
ing garlands around the walls and fireplace, the red and green candles
shining on the coffee table, even the little sprig of mistletoe hanging in
the archway to the foyer. And the music, emanating from a portable
CD player on the end table nearest to the tree, washing over the scene:
the Boston Pops recording of "Jingle Bells," over and over. Only the
people were missing: the bodies of his family, and the housekeeper,
and the dog, Sam.

But not quite completely missing.

He took it all in, every sparkling detail. Then, because he could not
resist it, as if drawn to it by some overwhelming magnetic force, his
gaze moved slowly back over to the Christmas tree and down. And
there, in a black-lacquered box that had been red all those years ago,
nestled in soaking wet red tissue, staring up at him through glassy, vacant eyes, was his father's severed head.

The baseball bat was the first thing to go. It sailed slowly down
from his numb, useless hands to land with a soft thud on the blue carpet at his feet. His body followed it, suddenly limp, rubbery, sagging,
sinking, blind. He landed hard on his knees, sending a jolt of pain up
his legs and spine to his neck. His head snapped forward, then lolled,
nearly touching the carpet as he doubled over, gagging. The first hot,
acid torrent of vomit spewed out of him onto the carpet, but the second heave caught in his throat, burning, choking him, cutting off his
respiration. He knelt there, coughing and spitting, forcing the vomitus
from his mouth to dribble down his chin onto his clothes as he gasped

for oxygen. He pressed his forehead down into the soft carpet, gradually becoming aware of the warmth spreading outward between his legs, and he realized that he had wet himself. He stayed in that position mortified, terrified, breathing in the smells of his vomit and urine, waiting for the room to stop spinning around him.

Only when his vision cleared did he notice the odd silence. The song had stopped, but it had not begun again, as if . . .

As if someone had turned it off.

He shuddered, processing the information. When he was finally able to move again, he pressed his hands down into the carpet and pushed himself slowly, painfully up from the floor. He immediately noticed two things.

The baseball bat was no longer lying on the carpet in front of him.

It had been replaced by a big pair of black boots.

Still nauseated, still disoriented, he rose to his knees, raising his gaze as he went. The black boots became a pair of black pants, the edges of the long black coat swirling around them. The massive thighs, the sparkling silver belt buckle, the black shirt. And then, at long last, the pale gray eyes in the face with the long white scar down one side. Scavenger: all six feet eight inches of him, towering over him, glaring down at him, holding something up above his head in both hands.

What happened next seemed to be in slow motion. The baseball bat whispered down toward him, coming closer, closer, finally smashing into his forehead just above his left eye. The room exploded in a burst of dazzling white. Somewhere very close by, a woman cried out. He sagged over sideways to the floor, landing hard on the carpet. A jolt of excruciating pain tore through his head, and he briefly lost consciousness. When he was aware of his surroundings again, he felt a warm, sticky wetness cascading down the side of his face. He opened his eyes, but he could barely see the figure leaning over him through a curtain of red. The woman's voice came to him again, much nearer now, reverberating as if in an echo chamber.

"You you didn't have to hit hit him so hard hard."

And then the man's voice replying, deep, cold, thickly accented:

"Sorry sorry I I couldn't resist resist."

Scavenger. But . . .

Mark blinked, and the red curtain fell away. He moaned, trying to roll away from them, to reach up with his arms and protect his head from the inevitable second blow, the one that would kill him, but he was too weak to move. He stared up at the figure above him as it loomed nearer, his aching brain suddenly filled with the image of the beautiful face and blond hair of Tracy Morgan.

Good-bye, Tracy, he thought. Good-bye. . . .

But it wasn't a dream. It *was* Tracy! Tracy was here, now, leaning down over him, her blond hair shining, her grave face mere inches from his own. But—but . . .

But it wasn't Tracy. It was—it was . . .

It was the woman from the plane this morning, the woman he had helped to get her bag from the overhead luggage compartment. The woman who had smiled at him as she got into her rental car beside his.

And now the woman was reaching for him. She turned her head and said something over her shoulder, to someone else farther back in the room, out of his line of vision, but he couldn't make out the words, only the sound. The deep, accented voice replied with something equally unintelligible, a monosyllabic grunt.

Scavenger. But . . .

Mark felt the tug as the left sleeve of his coat was pulled down and off of him. Then his left shirtsleeve was being rolled up. He felt a dab of something freezing cold against the flesh just below his shoulder, followed almost immediately by a sharp pinprick. He cried out, trying to push her away from him, but there was no strength left in him. His blurry gaze traveled down from her face to her hand. She was holding a needle, a hypodermic syringe, emptying its contents into his arm.

He was going to die now. Here, on the floor of the living room of his father's house. With his father's head staring up from a blood-soaked box not ten feet away from him.

He lay there blinking at the blond woman who was not Tracy, feeling the icy numbness as it crept slowly up his arm to his shoulder and over to his chest. He sank heavily down into the carpet, feeling every individual strand of the soft pile pressing into the side of his face. The numbness was descending into his stomach, his legs, his feet. Finally, inevitably, it rose up through his neck into his face and his head, filling his eyes and his brain with water. Cool blue water, the bluest water he had ever seen.

In his last moments of consciousness, he was thinking of his family in the cemetery this afternoon. No, *not* his family, not his family at all. It had been the Webster family in the other cemetery, yesterday in Los Angeles, in the rain. He had been watching a funeral nearby, a funeral for somebody named Fitzgerald. Rain. Umbrellas in the rain. Then, mere minutes later, a dead police officer, the sightless eyes in his startled young face staring up at the rain. Always rain, falling as it had fallen that Christmas morning when his family had died. And he had been wondering what the weather would be like when he died, if it would rain, if at the moment of his death—*this* moment, right now—there would come soft rains. . . .

45

"You didn't have to hit him so hard," the blond woman said again.

He looked over at her for a moment, affording her the briefest of glances, dismissing her opinion as he had dismissed the woman herself. She was a mere employee. As was her husband, or her partner, or whatever he was, back in New York. The less they knew about all this, the better. When their services were no longer required—well, there were plans for that.

Then he went over to stand above Matthew Farmer. He studied the unconscious man on the floor, checking to see that he was still breathing. Yes, his chest rose and fell at slow but regular intervals. He lay on his back, his arms flung straight out at his sides in a manner reminiscent of Christ on the cross. But there the similarity ended: Matthew Farmer had vomit on his upper clothing and a dark stain on the front of his pants. He grimaced as he gazed down at the writer, thinking, Hardly the stuff of martyrs.

He turned now to gaze slowly around the room, admiring his handiwork. Yes, it had been perfect. Just as it was in the photographs he'd spent so many hours studying, poring over, while he had been preparing. Everything, right down to the window curtains, had been carefully sought out and selected to be brought here. This was the room where this unconscious man's family had died, the exactly reproduced setting where he had found them that morning.

At last, he went over to stare admiringly down at the black-lacquered box.

Yes, he thought. Perfect. A true work of art.

Matthew Farmer had been sent to Brooklyn, and to Washington, and to New Orleans, and to Los Angeles. And then here, to his own home. For this. His reaction to this room had been all that could have been wished. And hitting him with his own weapon had been icing on the cake.

Looking back across the room at the inert form on the floor, the man smiled.

But it isn't over, he mused. Not yet. There is still one more setting, one more article to retrieve. One more shock to the writer's delicate system.

The biggest shock of all. . . .

And now they had to move, to get all this out of here and leave Evanston for the next phase. The final phase. He signaled to the blond woman, who nodded. Then he pulled his cellular phone from his black coat and raised it to his face.

"Yo," he heard.

"Done," he said into the receiver. "Bring the truck around to the driveway."

"You got it," came the reply.

He returned the phone to its inner pocket, reaching briefly up to finger the knife in its sheath under his left arm. He was looking over at Matthew Farmer again.

It would be *so* easy, he thought.

He shook his head, dismissing the fantasy. It would be easy, yes— but nowhere near as much fun as what was planned for tomorrow night.

Tomorrow night . . .

At that moment he heard the rumbling approach in the drive. He glanced over at his assistant, who was placing the black envelope—the only thing they would leave behind—where the unconscious man would be sure to find it. Then he unplugged the Christmas tree and reached carefully, reverently down to pick up the wet black box beneath it.

SATURDAY

46

From somewhere very far away he heard a man shouting. He came up from the void slowly, slowly, gradually becoming aware that he was lying on a floor. A carpet. There were rough hands on him, pressure on his shoulders, and he was being shaken. The shouting seemed to be coming closer, closer, and now he could just make out the words.

"... *up! Wake up! Come on, Mark!*"

The shaking was more violent now, and something hard was slapping his face, over and over. A hand. But why? And where was he?

"*Mark!*"

He could not identify the voice, although he thought it sounded familiar. All that registered was the obvious desperation in it.

"*Mark, wake up!*"

Mark? he wondered. Who is Mark? My name is Matthew Farmer. . . .

"*Mark!*"

Then, with a sudden rush of clarity, it all came back to him. Mark . . . Matthew . . . the house . . . the Christmas tree . . .

The head.

He burst up from the floor, a strangled cry escaping his lips. He was in a sitting position now, and strong arms were holding him, propping him up. There was a sticky wetness on his face, and a throbbing pain in his forehead. He remembered the baseball bat. There was a vile taste in his mouth, and he remembered that, too. He had been sick, vomited, and his bladder had failed, when he had seen the box under the tree.

His father's head.

He gasped, drawing air into his heavy lungs, trying to lift his heavy arms. He blinked his heavy eyelids several times, and the room around him slowly came into focus. The dark blue carpet, the light blue walls. Robin's-egg blue, his mother had called the color. The Farmer living room. But there was something wrong with it. He blinked again, and then he knew.

The room was empty. The furniture, the bookshelves, the Christmas decorations. The box. Gone, all gone. He was lying on the floor of an empty room, but he was not alone. The strong arms continued to hold him. When he slowly turned his heavy head to see who it was who knelt beside him, he nearly passed out again.

Former FBI Special Agent Ronald O'Hara.

Ron!

A dead man. Here, in this room in Evanston, holding him up in his massive arms. Calling his name.

"Thank God!" the specter cried. "Oh, thank God! I thought you were dead!"

Mark blinked again and took in another deep breath, staring up at him. He made an attempt at speaking, but all that emerged was a dry croak. He licked his lips and tried again, and this time he was successful. "That—that makes two of us."

Ron O'Hara—yes, it definitely *was* Ron O'Hara—stared down at him. Then he burst into laughter. It was the booming bass sound Mark remembered from Georgetown five thousand years ago. After a moment, Mark began to laugh, too. He raised his arms, which now responded to his command, and hugged the man.

"Whoa, there!" O'Hara bellowed, still laughing. "You're a mess, man! Don't get *too* close, okay?"

Then O'Hara stood up, and Mark felt himself being lifted to his feet. He slumped momentarily, almost falling to the floor again, but he was borne up by the huge man beside him, lifted up into his arms. He was carried across the room and through the archway to the front door. When they got there, the big man inclined his head toward the electronic alarm beside it. Mark peered over and saw the wires sticking out of the side, carefully cut. Scavenger.

"The door was wide open when I got here," O'Hara said.

Then the door was opened again, and Mark was carried out into dazzling brightness. It had apparently rained during the night, but now the rain clouds had gone, and the sun was—

Wait a minute, he thought. The *sun*?

"What—what time is it?" he slurred.

O'Hara chuckled as he carried him over to a gray sedan parked beside the house. "Eight o'clock. You must have had yourself quite a nap. When did you come here, anyway?"

"I—I think about nine last night. They—they drugged me. . . ."

"Yeah, you junkies are always blaming other people."

"No, Ron, they *really*—"

"Hush, now," O'Hara said. "You can tell me later, after we wake you up." He put Mark down, still keeping him firmly on his feet, and helped him into the passenger seat of his car. He went around, got in the driver's seat, and started the engine. "Where to?"

Mark thought a moment, getting his bearings, then pointed. "Four blocks . . . that way . . . Red . . . Rose . . . Inn. . . ."

And he was asleep again. The next thing he knew, he was standing, still firmly held up by O'Hara, in the lobby of the inn, and he heard snatches of conversation between the former agent and the proprietress.

". . . visiting us . . . old friend of his father's . . . too much to drink . . . fell and bumped his head . . . stayed at our house last night . . . room?"

"Upstairs, first door on the left."

". . . clean him up a little . . . breakfast?"

"Fifteen minutes."

"Thanks. Whatever's available—and coffee. *Lots* of coffee. Let's go, Mark." And then he was being helped up the stairs.

"Mark?" came the woman's voice from below. "That's Mr. McKinley. Mr. Jared McKinley."

"Well, of course it is!" he heard O'Hara bluff. "Mark is an old family nickname!" As he was all but dragged up the stairs and into his room, he heard O'Hara mutter, "Jared McKinley, eh? Is Jared McKinley a *blond*, by any chance? Nice dye job."

Then he was lying on the bed, and his clothes and shoes were being removed, and he heard the roar of rushing water, and he was being helped across the room into—

"*Yikes!*" he cried, coming fully awake. He was naked in the shower, under a torrent of freezing cold water. He lost his balance again, colliding with the tile wall, but he was still being held up. He turned around to see that O'Hara, also naked, was actually standing in the stall with him, handing him a bar of soap.

"Here, use this. A *lot*. Then give it to me."

Mark did as he was told, washing the blood and the vomit and the urine and the whole episode in the Farmer house from him. By the time he was finished rinsing, he could stand up unassisted. The moment he stepped out of the shower, he noticed that O'Hara immediately turned on the hot water for himself.

"That's better," O'Hara sighed. "Now brush your teeth, Mark. Several times."

He did, seeing in the mirror that there was a small cut on his forehead, surrounded by a large black bruise. Then he went out into the bedroom. By the time O'Hara emerged from the bathroom, fully dressed in a fresh suit, Mark had managed to put on clean clothes without any help. He frowned, realizing with embarrassment that O'Hara must have gotten his blood, vomit, and urine all over himself. Mark cleaned off his leather jacket, but he rolled everything else he'd been wearing last night up into a ball and stuffed it in his bag for later disposal. He never wanted to see those clothes again. He picked up the bag, and O'Hara picked up a folding suit bag he must have brought with them from the car, and they went downstairs.

"But you didn't even use your room the *first* night!" Mrs. Baker protested when he checked out, telling her to keep the money for the second night.

"It's okay," Mark told her, smiling. "It isn't my money, anyway. I'm on . . . an expense account. I insist."

"Well, thank you very much. Your breakfast is ready, gentlemen, just through there. I—I hope you're feeling better, Mr. McKinley."

"Yes, much better."

"Good. You certainly *look* better."

They thanked her and went into the little dining room off the lobby. An elderly lady was just emerging as they went in. The only other guest, Mark remembered. Good: they'd have the room to themselves. What he had to tell O'Hara—and what O'Hara presumably had to tell him—was not fit breakfast conversation for elderly ladies. Nor anyone else, for that matter.

A table had been laid for them next to a window facing the street and the church parking lot across the way, where Scavenger's green car had been. They sat down, and a friendly teenage girl immediately brought them huge plates of scrambled eggs, bacon, home-fried potatoes, and toast. There was a pitcher of orange juice as well, and two pots of coffee. Mark fell ravenously upon the food, washing it down with the juice and coffee. He could actually feel the energy returning to his body as the aftereffects of the drug dissolved.

O'Hara watched him silently, merely picking at his own food and keeping Mark's coffee cup constantly full. By the time the girl arrived to remove their plates, Mark remembered everything clearly, but he was also full of questions. The girl went away again, leaving the two men alone, and they settled back with the rest of the coffee.

"Okay," Mark said, "you first. What are you doing in Evanston? How did you know where to find me here? And, for that matter, how did you manage to survive a self-inflicted bullet in your temple?"

The big man, who had been so grave, so serious in his home in Georgetown a mere five days ago, burst into laughter again. He was positively beaming, and Mark soon realized why.

"Now, Mark," he admonished, chuckling, "don't believe everything you read in the newspapers." He leaned forward, resting his arms on the table. "It's pretty simple, really. You see, I heard on the news about Robert Gammon, Sarah's husband, being found in the Tennants' house, and about Sarah's nurse from the clinic. I figured out what your friend was doing, eliminating everyone as they came in contact with you. And I thought, What about *me*? *I* was part of it. What if he comes back for me? So I decided to trump him. I still have friends at the Bureau and in the Washington PD, so . . ."

"So you faked it," Mark said. "I see. But how did you know where to find me?"

"The news said you'd gone from New Orleans to L.A., and I figured out what Scavenger was doing, what the scavenger hunt was. He was sending you to the scenes. He started with the last one, in Brooklyn, but after that he was doing them in order, start to finish. New Orleans, L.A.—Evanston. Yesterday, I figured you must have come here, and I got to thinking. Why was he sending you to your own home? What did he have in mind for you there? And I got nervous. I know I told you I wouldn't interfere until you knew who he was, but then things changed. He didn't kill Sarah—she's locked up, for one thing, he can't get to her. But she's also, well, kind of dead, anyway, I guess. But he killed her husband. And the nurse. He must have: they couldn't be coincidences."

"No," Mark said, "they weren't. And someone else, a motorcycle cop in L.A., who stopped me for speeding and recognized me. He didn't want the cop fucking up the game, so he shot him. Right in front of me. With *my* gun!"

O'Hara's eyes widened. "How did he get your gun?"

Mark shook his head, remembering the house in Louisiana. "Long story. I'll tell you later. So you came to Chicago—when?"

"Just flew in this morning, about six. I wasn't sure where to find you, but I figured your old house would be part of the game, so I decided to start there. I rented a car at O'Hare and went there. The door was open, and you know the rest." He was studying Mark's face now. "So, what happened in your house last night?"

Mark took a deep breath and told him. The tree, the decorations, the music. The head in the box. O'Hara emitted a low whistle when he heard that part. The attack, the needle, the blond woman from the plane.

"So," O'Hara said, "he has an assistant."

Mark shrugged. "I guess . . ."

That was when it struck him. He stared at O'Hara for a moment, then turned to look out the window, at the parking lot of the church across the street where the green car had been parked yesterday. He remembered the face from the street in New Orleans, the cemetery in Los Angeles, the rainy road with the dead officer, the house last night. He remembered the words spoken over him as he lay on the floor:

"You didn't have to hit him so hard."

"Sorry, I couldn't resist."

Then he remembered the telephone calls. The first one in Washington, the second in New Orleans, the two calls in Los Angeles:

"This game will not continue if you are rude to me again!"

". . . strawberry pancakes . . ."

"Sharon Stone in a bikini."

". . . second wind . . ."

He blinked, gasping. Then he slowly turned back to the former agent across the table from him. The words from last night returned, confirming it: *"Sorry, I couldn't resist."*

"Sorry . . ."

"Oh, my God!" Mark whispered. O'Hara leaned closer, watching him.

". . . I couldn't resist."

He'd almost noticed it last night, but he'd been too hurt, too disoriented, too terrified. Scavenger, *but . . .*

"It isn't him," Mark finally managed to say.

"What do you mean?" O'Hara asked.

Now Mark, too, leaned forward. Their faces were inches apart, and he was aware that he was whispering. "The man with the scar. The man on the phone. They're two different people! The man with the scar has some sort of thick accent—I don't know, maybe Europe somewhere. Last night was the first time I ever heard him. The guy on the phone is American, I'll swear to it! There are two of them!"

O'Hara leaned back in his chair, slowly nodding. "I was afraid of that. I've always been afraid of that. Even back then, when we were working on it, it was the big question everyone kept asking. How does one person kill an entire house full of people and arrange them with all those props and things? I suppose one person *could*, but two people makes more sense, doesn't it?"

Mark nodded, too. "So The Family Man is actually The Family *Men?*"

"Looks that way." O'Hara leaned forward again. "And we want *both* of them. Sorry, Mark, but you're not on your own anymore. I'm coming with you."

"But—"

"No buts. I'm with you, period. So what's next? What are your new instructions?"

Mark opened his mouth, then snapped it shut. He stared at the man across the table, feeling the icy prickles of fear again. "Oh, God! I didn't find it!"

"Find what?"

"The photograph! He said I was looking for a photograph. The other things were there: the newspaper in Brooklyn, a mask in the Tennant house, a Bible in my hotel room—that was the 'word' I was looking for, the Word of God. Cute, huh? But there wasn't any photograph at my house."

"Are you sure?"

"Of course I'm sure. It would have been there for me to find, in a black frame or something. The newspaper and the mask and the Bible were all done up in black. Even the cell phone he gave me was wrapped in black. So I should have been looking for a photograph in a black frame. . . ."

O'Hara leaned forward again. "Or a black . . . *envelope?* Look in your jacket, Mark. Right pocket."

Mark blinked, then turned to take his leather jacket off the back of his chair. He reached into the pocket and pulled out a small black envelope. He stared at it for a long moment. "What the hell . . . ?"

"It fell out when I was undressing you, and I put it back. I didn't know what it was. They must have planted it on you after they knocked you out."

The two men studied the envelope in silence. Then Mark took a deep breath and tore it open. There was a photograph inside, a Polaroid. He held it up to the light, peering at it. It took him a few moments to recognize the subject. It was a woman with blond hair sitting in a chair, taken from several feet away in a dark, shadowy room. She appeared to be asleep, but that was not the most arresting thing about her. She was bound and gagged. There were wide strips of silver duct tape at her wrists and ankles, and a strip across her mouth. Because of the poor lighting in the room where the photo had been taken, Mark had to squint at the face before realizing. When he did, the picture fell from his hand. He reached swiftly out to grasp the corners of the table to keep himself upright. The breath left his body and everything before his eyes disappeared.

"No," he whispered. "Please, God, no. . . ."

When his breathing and his vision returned, he looked up at O'Hara, who had picked up the photograph and was now studying it. "Who is this woman?"

Mark raised a hand to his mouth. "It's—it's Tracy. My fiancée. Tracy Morgan. Oh, God." He could taste his breakfast in the back of his throat. He reached swiftly out for his cup and drained it before he could be sick again. "Oh, God. . . ."

O'Hara closed his eyes a moment, then opened them. He turned the photo over. "There's writing on the back." He read it in silence, then slowly handed it across the table, standing up as he did so. "Let's go."

Mark looked up at him, then down at the object in his hand. It was the familiar red Magic Marker scrawl. As he read the message, he felt everything in his body once more turn to ice.

Hello, Mark. Welcome to the final round. Photographs were important to The Family Man because they always recorded his work. Come join us for the end of the game. Midnight tonight—and don't be early this time, please. I hate surprises. Ms. Morgan is looking a little GREEN, if you catch my drift. You know where we are. You are looking for—

ARTICLE #5

THE FAMILY MAN

47

It was a woman's bedroom, and it was probably very beautiful. Under any other circumstances, Tracy thought, I might actually be comfortable here. But not under these circumstances. Feeling as I feel now, I wouldn't be comfortable in Buckingham Palace.

She wondered whose room it was, what sort of woman would live here with—with—with that person downstairs. Well, she supposed he was downstairs: she had no reason to think he wasn't. Downstairs with his henchman, or whatever the blond man called himself—the blond man from the hotel bar and restaurant two days ago, who'd walked by her house, looked up at her window shortly afterward. She'd finally placed his face, and she wondered who the blond woman with him in the restaurant had been. And there was the other one, too, the big man from yesterday morning, if he was back from wherever he'd gone. She'd finally placed his face, too.

The bedroom door was locked, of course, and there was no other way out. She'd already checked. There was only one other door, and it led to a lovely bathroom with pink marble walls and gold fixtures. There were two windows on the far wall and a window in the bathroom, but they were out of the question. She'd noticed the high ceiling in the living room yesterday, and last night she had been led up many stairs from the ground story to this, the second floor. She'd had the idea that she was in one of those old Victorian painted-lady things where the second-story windows would be some thirty feet above the ground. Now, in the daylight, a glance out the window had confirmed her theory. She was at least that high, too high to jump without killing herself or at least breaking her legs, either of which would preclude escape.

She nearly laughed at that: jumping out of windows, running

through the night, screaming for help, perhaps with a pack of dogs snapping at her heels. It seemed like something out of *The Perils of Pauline*. But it wasn't funny. It was really happening to her. There was nothing she could do about it at the moment. Now all she could do was wait.

To distract herself, she began to make a study of the room, to see what she could surmise about its owner. A rich woman, certainly. Impeccable taste in clothes and makeup. Her scent was Chanel No. 5. Tracy wondered if the woman who occupied this room was the beautiful woman in the painting in the living room, the pianist with the incredible necklace. Probably. But where was she now?

Because she had no answers to any of it, Tracy pushed it from her mind. She had actually managed to sleep here last night, which had surprised her. This morning, the blond man had brought her food, eggs and toast and coffee, and she had eaten it with no ill effects. The other one, the crazy one, had mentioned something about dinner in the dining room tonight. She decided she could try some of that as well.

She went into the bathroom, took a long, hot shower, and put on her clothes again. The woman, whoever she was, had everything she needed; shampoo, towels, blow-dryer. She even sprayed herself with Chanel from the crystal atomizer on the dresser, wondering why she felt so odd about it. Then she realized: these things in this room had apparently not been used, not even been touched, in a long time. Tracy was certain of it. Perhaps the woman was dead. . . .

The thought made her shudder, and the reality of her situation returned full force, filling her with dread. She sat at the strange woman's dresser, gazing at her face in the mirror, wondering what was going to happen when Mark arrived here tonight. *If* he arrived.

She was thinking about that when she heard a soft knock on the bedroom door. It was the blond man again, telling her that her host would like her to join him for lunch.

With a sigh, she followed him out of the room and down the stairs.

48

Ms. Morgan is looking a little GREEN, if you catch my drift.

Well, Mark thought, at least we know where we're going. *GREEN.* Very funny. Green Hills, New York, home of the Carlin family.

Ron O'Hara had taken charge of everything. They had flown from O'Hare to La Guardia in New York, and O'Hara had rented a car at the airport. He drove through the gray, overcast afternoon in silence. Mark glanced frequently up at the sky over the Long Island Express-way, remembering his impression that the rain seemed to be following him from Los Angeles to Chicago. It was still following him. Several times during the ride, he heard the low, faraway rumble of thunder.

Their first stop had been a house in Queens, home of a friend and former colleague of O'Hara's, who had been expecting them. O'Hara had made several phone calls from the Chicago airport, but Mark had not heard what he'd set up. He had been offered only sketchy informa-tion during the plane trip, and he had decided to place his trust in the other man.

The house belonged to a couple who were introduced to him as Larry and Shira. No last name was mentioned. They were a fortyish couple, and she was small and attractive. Her husband was big, almost as big as O'Hara, and very capable-looking. While the woman gave Mark a cup of coffee and entertained him with pleasant small talk in her immaculate living room, Larry and O'Hara had gone off together to an-other part of the house. They were gone for some twenty minutes.

The woman informed him that her husband worked out of the New York office of the FBI, and that he had met O'Hara during the Banes murder investigation in Brooklyn. They'd been friends ever since. Mark, who could tell from her manner that she had no idea what was going on between the two men now, smiled and told her that her house was lovely and the coffee delicious. She smiled and thanked him, and they waited.

At last the two men rejoined them. O'Hara hugged the woman, shook the man's hand, promised to call soon, and led Mark back out to the car. It was dark outside now, dark and cold. O'Hara drove north out of the city, and it was more than an hour later when he pulled into a roadside diner in a small town north of Westchester. They had driven the entire way in relative silence. Mark knew that the former agent would fill him in when he was ready.

This occurred over dinner. They ordered sandwiches, and when they had finished eating, they ordered coffee. O'Hara, with a surreptitious glance around the relatively empty place, leaned forward and spoke in a low voice.

"We weren't at my friends' house this afternoon. You never met them. Got it?"

Mark nodded, waiting.

"Okay," the big man went on. "Larry gave me some things we're not supposed to have, but under the circumstances, I feel better about having them. One for me." He pulled open the left side of his jacket, and Mark glimpsed a shoulder holster and the butt of a silver weapon before the material fell back in place, concealing it. "And one for you. It's in my coat pocket in the car. It's just like your own, a Smith & Wesson .38 revolver. I figured you'd be more comfortable with something you know. They're both fully loaded and ready for action. I hope it won't come to that, but I have a feeling it might."

Mark felt his mouth go dry. He reached out shakily for his coffee cup, thought better of it, and sipped from his water glass instead. The cold water seemed to burn his throat.

"What did you tell Larry?" he finally managed to ask.

O'Hara shrugged. "Nothing. We go back more than ten years. He didn't ask and I didn't offer, just told him what I needed. I'd do the same for him."

Mark nodded again, marveling at the old boy network that was the result of working together in a dangerous job. Brothers and sisters, all of them. Cops, Feds, the Armed Forces. The CIA, too, probably. He glanced at his watch: it was nearly eight o'clock.

"We have four hours," he said. "What do we do in the meantime?"

O'Hara grimaced. "Recon."

And that was that. O'Hara paid for dinner, and they drove north again. As they rode in the now-familiar silence, Mark thought back over everything he'd learned about the Carlin family during his research.

On Halloween night twelve years ago, Michael and Raina Carlin and two of their three children, a young man and a young woman, and their housekeeper, Mrs. Kolnikov, had been killed in their beds, then carried to the basement of their house, to the private living area known familiarly as the rec room, where they had been arranged on chairs and couches in Halloween costumes and masks. The family's two Scottish terriers were placed at their feet. The room had been festooned with black and orange candles and crepe paper streamers, and big orange bags of candy. Candy corn and gumdrops had been strewn about the place. Mark had no idea what music had been playing at this scene, but he'd made it "Night on Bald Mountain" in his novel, in deference to the fact that Mr. and Mrs. Carlin were classical musicians.

Michael Carlin, the world-famous conductor, had been decapitated, and the others had had their throats slashed. Mr. Carlin's head was in one of the orange candy bags with black pictures of pumpkins and witches and the legend TRICK OR TREAT! on the sides. A big jack-o'-lantern, crudely carved, had been placed on his severed neck, a big candle burning brightly inside it. They had been found there the next morning by their manservant, the housekeeper's husband, who had been away from the house for two days.

Because of Carlin's worldwide fame, and because his wife, Raina, had been one of the world's leading concert pianists, the incident took even longer than the first three to play itself out in the papers and on television. Mark glanced over at the silent former agent as he drove, trying to imagine the incredible frustration he and his colleagues had been feeling by that point. He couldn't imagine it, couldn't even begin, but he remembered his own feelings when he'd first heard about the Carlin family and, later, the Banes family in Brooklyn.

He had been devastated, horrified, and his first instinct was to go to Green Hills, to attend the highly publicized funerals with all the crowds of fans and statesmen and celebrities from the international music industry. The President of the United States had sent a wreath and a telegram, as he had for the Websters and Mark's own family. A movie star, a Fundamentalist minister, and two noted musicians had been killed, and even the White House had paid solemn tribute. But

Mark, after much soul-searching, did not go to Green Hills twelve years ago, nor did he arrive in Brooklyn for the Banes funerals. He was Mark Stevenson by that time, and Matthew Farmer had successfully disappeared into the ether. Nothing would be served, he decided, by revealing his new identity, by mourning with strangers whose families and friends had met the same fate as his own people.

He was thinking this as they arrived in the town of Green Hills just after nine o'clock. It was not quite a town, more what Mark would call a village, and it was very pretty. There was a main street with charming rows of shops lining it. The town was situated in a valley, surrounded by—Mark smiled in spite of his growing dread—hills thick with evergreen forest. Green Hills.

Then his smile disappeared. Scavenger was here, in this postcard-pretty town, and he had Tracy. Mark thought about her, and about the awful photograph in the black envelope. She had been bound and gagged, and possibly drugged, as he had twice been drugged. He wondered how Scavenger had managed to get her, and when. But these were secondary thoughts compared to his one overriding obsession. It consumed him now, in the car, and he reached into the pocket of his jacket to once more touch the cold, reassuring hardness, the reality of the revolver Ron O'Hara had given him.

He was going to kill Scavenger. Now, tonight. And nobody was going to stop him.

He looked over at O'Hara, wondering if the man could read his mind, if he knew what Mark was planning. If he did, he wasn't saying anything about it. Good, Mark thought. I don't want any interference, and I will brook no argument. Scavenger is dead. Period.

O'Hara drove straight through the town on Main Street and continued past it for about half a mile. Then he slowed, looking off to the right in the glow of the headlights, searching. At last they came to what he had apparently been watching for, a drive that led away from the road through the thick forest. It was a paved road, and the entrance was flanked by two high brick pillars. O'Hara nodded.

"There's the driveway," he muttered, more to himself than to Mark. Then he drove on, past the turnoff. As ever, Mark did not question his action, merely sat beside him, waiting to be shown what would come next. A couple hundred yards farther down the road, O'Hara once again slowed the car, peering off to the right. There was another road there, this one unpaved, a narrow dirt track between two large trees. O'Hara turned onto this, and the ride became rather bumpy.

"Service road," he explained, "for the farm closest to the Carlin house."

Even as he said this, the wall of evergreen trees to the left of the dirt road abruptly stopped. The car emerged from the forest, and Mark could see tall grass in the headlights, stretching off to the left as far as he could see. A field. Thick trees lined the right side of the road.

"Okay," O'Hara finally said. "We walk from here, and it's going to be steep."

He parked the car by the side of the rutted lane and got out. Mark followed him off the dirt track into the first stand of pine trees. It was dark, but O'Hara produced a penlight from a pocket that cast a tiny beam a few feet ahead of them. Even in the near-pitch-blackness, Mark could see that their way was sharply uphill. He took a deep breath and followed the big man into the forest.

"Stay behind me," O'Hara muttered. He continued to lead the way, and Mark followed by squinting at the weak wash of light a few feet ahead of him. Twice he collided with tree trunks sticky and pungent with pine sap, but he brushed himself off and continued on his way. It was slow going in the forest, especially with the upgrade that seemed to become steeper with every step. But he followed, silent and uncomplaining. Tracy was at the end of this journey. Tracy and Scavenger. The one he would deliver, and the other he would kill.

They made their slow way up through the trees for what Mark estimated was about fifteen minutes. He was just getting used to the disorienting journey, falling into the rhythm of the big man in front of him, when O'Hara came to an abrupt halt, holding out his hand to check Mark's progress.

"Whoa," he hissed.

Mark stopped, blinking. "What?"

In answer to his question, O'Hara shone the penlight over to his left. Mark didn't see anything in the darkness at first, but then the flicker of the beam caught a glint of silver. A small, camera-shaped electronic object was strapped in place on the side of a tree, a tiny prick of red at the center of what looked to be the lens. The light was directed off to their right. O'Hara slowly swung the penlight until he found what he was looking for: an identical object attached to a tree some twenty feet away. Neither he nor Mark had to be told that there were similar units mounted beyond that, circling the property. Off through the trees, perhaps the length of a football field above and in front of them, the lights of a big house shone brightly in the surrounding gloom.

"This is as close as we can get," O'Hara said, the disappointment clear in his voice though Mark could not see his face. "We'll have to go back the way we came, and around to the driveway. But even that is probably rigged."

Mark closed his eyes, feeling the damp wind whistling through the trees that pressed in at them from all directions. They were stuck here, prevented from a surprise approach by Scavenger's thorough protection system. Tracy might as well be a million miles away. He prayed that she was all right.

"What now?" Mark whispered to the dark shape beside him.

Although he couldn't see him, Mark was certain that O'Hara actually shrugged.

"We wait," he said.

49

His employer was playing the piano again.

Ivan Kolnikov, known to his quarry as Scavenger, sat on the over-stuffed couch near the center of the room, facing the Bechstein concert grand. He was clad in his usual uniform now, a black suit, white shirt, and black bow tie. The duster was hanging in his room upstairs on the third floor. As big as the couch was, he gave the impression of being too big for it, but he waited patiently enough, his hands folded in his lap, wincing at the terrible, stumbling rendition of a difficult piece by one of his native country's greatest national treasures. He frowned as he listened: for all his unswerving loyalty to this man, he wished he wouldn't desecrate Rimsky-Korsakov.

At last the selection was at an end, and the Massenet elegy began. It was his employer's favorite, judging from the number of times he insisted on playing it, but all the repetition had bred no familiarity with it. What should have been sad, soulful music was rendered sharp, discordant, comical. Ivan knew it was a song for the dead. He also knew his employer's late mother's famous recording of it. He wondered if that was why the man played it so frequently.

But so badly. Oh, well. . . .

He waited on the couch for his new instructions. He didn't mind the amateurish playing: it had never really bothered him, not in all these years. Besides, now he had something else to ponder. He was excited, filled with a thrill of longing that was almost palpable. He glanced down at his watch: eleven o'clock. Soon, he thought. Very soon.

At midnight, one hour from now, Matthew Farmer would come into this house, and Ivan would be ready for him.

Now the playing stopped. He looked over at his employer as he stood up and came around the piano to stand before him. He rose, awaiting instructions, noting that the man was smiling at him.

"It's almost time," his employer said.

"Yes," Ivan replied.

"Ms. Morgan?"

Ivan inclined his head toward the door beyond the archway under the main staircase. "They're getting her ready."

"Good, good." Ivan watched as the man smiled again and nodded, obviously pleased. He stood at attention, waiting for his employer to speak again.

"Well," the man said at last, "it's been quite a week, hasn't it?"

Ivan nodded. "Quite a week."

"You've done very well, Ivan. Very well indeed. You did everything perfectly, just as we envisioned it." He paused now, glancing away, and Ivan felt the first icy little stab of apprehension. He saw something in the man's eyes, in his demeanor, that hadn't been there before. He waited in silence. Finally, his employer continued.

"But I'm afraid there's been a little change in plans," the man said. He gestured with an arm toward the piano, a slightly pained smile on his lips. "A variation on a theme, if you will. I hope you don't mind too much, but your role in tonight's game has been . . . well, *rewritten.*"

Ivan stared at him, at the expression on his face. The man still would not meet his gaze, and he looked truly contrite, apologetic. Ivan heard the basement door behind him open. His employer was looking past him now, toward the sound. As Ivan watched him, he gave a single, curt little nod and moved away toward the piano. He sat down and began to play again.

The Massenet elegy.

In that moment, just as the mournful music began to fill the living room, Ivan Kolnikov realized that he had been duped. He knew it as certainly as he was standing there. He had been cozened, made promises by this man whose parents were responsible for Ivan's freedom, for his wife's freedom, for their very lives. This man whom he had served faithfully all these years had used him to achieve his own goals. Ivan had escaped prison, wandered endlessly through frozen tundra, *killed.* He had survived the worst event of his life, in this house, eleven years ago. And it had all come to this end. He thought these things in that single moment, and then he thought: Anna.

"Anna!"

He had actually spoken her name aloud, he realized. Still the sad music continued, the song for the dead.

Then Ivan turned around to see the two people coming slowly toward him across the room.

50

The waiting had been the worst part. Mark sat in the passenger seat of the car looking out at O'Hara, who stood leaning on the hood, smoking a cigar. They'd returned to the car in the lane beside the field and sat for two hours. Mark had told him everything that had happened to him in the last few days, from the moment he had left O'Hara's house in Georgetown and gone back to his parked car, where the black-wrapped cellular phone had been waiting for him.

Telling the story made him relive it in his mind, and he felt the cold anger, the murderous rage slowly growing inside him, permeating him, strengthening him. He remembered it all now in a series of vivid mental images: the computer disk with its bizarre letter, the house in Brooklyn, the mental institution in New Orleans with the tragic revenant that had once been Sarah Tennant, the cemetery in Los Angeles, his family's home in Evanston. His father's head: not the genuine article, but an amazing facsimile. He remembered the friendly nurse, Millicent Call, and the handsome police officer, and the photograph on the news program of Robert Gammon. Mark had not met him, only spoken with him on the phone, and the one time he had actually seen him he was dead, his face obscured by the jackal mask. But he felt the loss, the void Robert Gammon's death caused, just the same.

Most of all, he thought of Tracy. She was in that house, that fortress in the forest above them, being held captive by a crazy person.

No, *two* crazy people. At least two, possibly more. The blond woman might be there, and others he didn't know, could not imagine. Mark didn't care. With his fury came recklessness, a headlong tumbling feeling he was unable to check. He would kill them all, if it came to that. He would deliver Tracy from the evil that was Scavenger. And he had former FBI Special Agent Ron O'Hara here to help him.

Now he saw O'Hara drop the cigar, crush it out under his foot, and come back to open the driver's door, but he did not get in.

"Okay," the big man said, "here's how we're going to play this. You drive. I'll be in back, on the floor in front of the backseat. Those pillars will have cameras, probably, and the drive is about two hundred yards long. It's surrounded by forest until you emerge in the front of the house, the lawn. There's a bend about halfway up the drive. When you get there, slow down and I'll get out and go into the woods. I doubt there are cameras or alarms that close to the house. Anyway, it's a chance we have to take."

Mark looked at his watch. Ten minutes to midnight. He felt the thrill of anticipation, and of fear. "What are you going to do?"

"I'll be nearby," O'Hara said. "I can't come in with you, though. They might get nervous and hurt Tracy. You'll have to go in yourself, alone. Don't try any heroics: her life is at stake, and your life, too. Just—I don't know, try to stall them until I can figure out a way to join you."

Mark nodded and slid over into the driver's seat. O'Hara opened the back door, got in, and crouched down, wedging his large body into the relatively narrow space between the seats. Mark heard a grunt of pain or discomfort from behind him as he started the car. He turned it around and drove back through the trees to the main road.

"What about backup?" Mark asked the man on the floor behind him. "Your friends in the FBI, or at least the local police. . . ."

"Later," O'Hara said. "Not now. A crowd would just spook them, and then we'd have a hostage situation."

"We already *have* a hostage situation."

"Yeah," the big man said, "but not like we'd have if we called in the troops. Besides, this way we have something that may be better, that may actually save Ms. Morgan."

"Oh? What's that?"

"Surprise. They're expecting you, alone. They don't know I'm here."

"Of course they don't," Mark said. "They think you're dead."

The car arrived at the turnoff, the drive that would lead up to the house. When Mark made the turn, he looked out at the brick column on his left. There was a small video camera mounted on top of it, aimed down at the road. As the car passed between the pillars the camera moved, silently tracking its progress.

"You were right about surveillance," Mark whispered.

"Uh-huh," came the voice from behind him.

Then everything became very dark as he drove up the steep grade between the high evergreen trees. The headlights pointed straight ahead of the car, reminding him of his approach to Tennant House in the fog. The memory of that house, what he had found waiting there for him, sent another pang of fear through him. He came to the bend in the driveway and slowed to a brief stop.

"They'll be in the basement, I should think," O'Hara whispered. "That's where the family was. The entrance is under the main stairs on the far side of the living room from the front door. Remember: no heroics. I'll be with you as soon as I can get in."

The rear door opened and closed softly, and O'Hara was gone, melting into the shadows between the trees. Mark took a deep breath and drove on. Another turn, and then the car emerged into a clearing dominated by the big, dark house. A wide front lawn had been cleared from what must have once been forest, but he could only just make it out in the headlights and the single light that shone from the porch above the front door.

There was a two-car garage at the left of the house, but both spaces were taken up by vehicles, a black minibus and a red sedan. Mark parked at the end of the drive in front of the garage, first turning it around so that it faced the way he had come. Leaving the keys in the ignition for a likely fast escape, he got out and went up the walk to the steps that led to the porch, which ran the entire length of the front of the house.

Mark looked around as he went up the steps, noting that the front and side lawns ended abruptly in forest some thirty feet in each direction. O'Hara was somewhere in that wood, watching him, waiting. The thought was reassuring, but he couldn't rid himself of his terrible fear. The feeling grew as he arrived at the big oak door under the porch light.

It was standing wide open, and beyond it was black emptiness. He couldn't see anything. He stopped, staring into the gloomy depths before him, breathing deeply of the chill, moist night air. Tracy was beyond this door, and so was his enemy.

Scavenger.

Just before he moved, the door and the wall of the house he faced were briefly illuminated by a flash of light. It was followed about ten seconds later by the low rumble of thunder. The sound rolled over him, the house, everything, before subsiding, echoing away through the trees.

One more deep breath, and Mark stepped forward into the darkness. When his eyes began to adjust, he found that he was in a large entryway, a foyer not unlike his own in Evanston. This one was much more grand, and it was obvious at a glance, even in the dark, that rich people had lived here, much richer than his own family had been. The Farmers had been well off: the Church of the True Believers had been a source of great wealth for Jacob Farmer, and he had not changed his will to exclude his estranged son before he died. Mark had inherited everything.

Now he felt compelled to move. If he stood here in this place too long, he might lose his courage, whatever he had that was going to save Tracy from her captors. And he was going to kill them. He had accepted the fact, made it a part of him, and he would not be deterred. He would kill Scavenger, and he would kill anyone who was assisting him as well. He reached up once more to feel the reassuring bulk of the revolver in his jacket pocket.

Alone in this alien place yet feeling the eyes upon him, Mark Stevenson, who had once been Matthew Farmer, stepped forward into the house. He moved steadily out of the foyer, through the archway on his right into the living room. There was still no light anywhere, but he could make out the dark shapes of couches and chairs and tables, and a big black shape in one corner. The door he wanted would be on the other side of this room, O'Hara had said.

At that moment the French doors across the room were briefly lit up by another flash of lightning, and the thunder came only five seconds after it. The storm was getting closer. In that moment of light, Mark had seen the big shape in the corner clearly. A grand piano. And he'd noticed something else: the tables were set for games. He'd had a brief impression of a chessboard, and of some other kind of board game on another table, maybe Scrabble. Whoever lives here likes games, he thought grimly. He was obviously in the right place.

He walked slowly across the room, reaching out with his hands to avoid running into furniture, hearing the hollow echo of his shoes on the wood floor. Then he was on a carpet, and his footsteps were suddenly muffled. He wondered who was listening, who was waiting below him in the basement. Scavenger, certainly—but there were others. He was certain of it. And Tracy was there.

The staircase appeared before him in the gloom, and the door beneath it. He paused a moment, breathing deeply, preparing himself for whatever it was he would have to face. He readied himself to kill.

Tracy, he thought. Tracy.

Then he slowly opened the door and stepped onto the staircase that would lead him down, down, down to the basement.

51

She was sitting in the darkness, the tape across her mouth, breathing slowly through her nose. She had been trying to stop the tears that cascaded down her face, but it was useless. Whenever she thought of her plight, what was about to happen here in this dark room, she could only weep.

Tracy looked across the room, peering through the vast, shadowy place at the horrible scene near the stairs. She couldn't see much of it from her perspective, but it was enough, and the music only made it worse. With a shudder, she closed her wet eyes, sending a fresh trickle down her hot cheeks.

She wished they'd put her in a softer seat. It was a plain, armless wooden chair, and her hands were behind the back of it. The sharp edge of the back was biting into her elbows, and the circulation was seriously compromised. She could feel the dull prickling from her aching shoulders all the way down to her fingers, and she wondered how much longer it would be before her arms fell asleep. Her back and legs were throbbing as well, protesting the unnatural position she was in.

Worst of all, worse than the creepy music or the scene across the room or her discomfort, was the presence in the dark beside her. He stood next to the chair, waiting, and he had a big knife in his hand. A very big knife. The table beside him held something else, something she didn't understand. She stared at the object, wondering.

She wondered if she was going to die. She wondered if Mark was going to die. If they would die together tonight, here in this basement.

Mark. She knew he was here now, that he had entered the grounds, because one of the assistants had informed her host of the fact. They apparently had surveillance cameras in the driveway, and the blond man said he had seen him. Mark was alone, the man said, and he was driving a rented car. Only the man had not referred to him as Mark Stevenson. He had called him Matthew Farmer.

The two assistants had disappeared, were not here in the basement with them. She wondered where they were, what they were doing. This worried her most of all.

Maybe Mark isn't really alone, she thought. If he's been playing their game for a week now, maybe he's figured it out. Maybe he knows what this creature is planning for him. Maybe he's brought help. Maybe—

Then she heard it, and she heard the man beside her emit a single, soft hiss in the dark. He had heard it, too. It was directly above their heads, in what would be the living room, moving toward the entrance to the basement.

Footsteps. The footsteps of a single man.

She closed her eyes again and moaned, but the tape across her mouth muffled the sound. She wanted to cry out, to scream, to break free and run. But there was nothing she could do. She could only watch and wait, and pray. She trembled as she felt the man beside her move closer to her in the dark, and his sleeve brushed her bare arm.

The basement door at the top of the stairs swung open, and someone was coming slowly, cautiously down the stairs. She could only see the dark shape descending until it reached the bottom of the stairs and stepped out into the big room, into the light from the candles. It took her a moment to recognize him because of the blond hair, but then she knew.

It was Mark.

52

There was light at the bottom of the stairs. Candles. He made his way down, listening to the music emanating from the big room below him. "Night on Bald Mountain." The light grew brighter as he descended, and now he could see the scene. He came to the bottom of the stairs and moved toward it, staring.

This is bad, he thought. This is the worst one yet, worse even than the Christmas decorations and the reproduction of my father's head. They saved the best for last.

Four of them, the three women and the boy, were seated on two big couches facing each other, the coffee table between them. The women were dressed in black with tall, pointed hats on their heads and ugly green face masks with big noses and warts. The boy was dressed as a skeleton, the bone-white skull mask obscuring his face. There was a large, crudely carved jack-o'-lantern in the center of the table, surrounded by black and orange candles. Big orange bags filled with candy were on the floor near the two black dogs. Candy corn and gumdrops and bite-sized wrapped chocolates were strewn everywhere around them.

The women and the boy were mannequins, department store dummies, but the fifth figure in the tableau was real. He was seated in a big armchair at a right angle to the two couches, facing them, giving the appearance of presiding over the scene. His head, unlike Mr. Carlin's head twelve years ago, was still attached, but his throat had been slashed from ear to ear. Bright red blood soaked his white shirt and black bow tie. He was not wearing a Halloween costume, and his face was not masked, so Mark had no trouble recognizing him.

Scavenger. The tall man with the scar who had followed him,

drugged him, struck him. The man who Mark had, until hours ago, thought was the mastermind, the ringmaster, the inventor of the game. Scavenger was sitting here before him, dead.

Mark was still staring at his dead opponent when he became aware that another light had come on in the cavernous room behind him. Now he did not hesitate: he reached up and pulled the revolver from his pocket. He was not afraid, he realized. He was furious. Holding the gun firmly in his right hand, he turned around and looked across the room. As he did so, the music subsided in volume to a mere whisper. It continued very softly, as underscoring for what followed.

Tracy was sitting on a plain wooden chair some twenty feet away from him, bathed in the light from a single pinspot directly above her. Her hands were held behind the chair, and there was a strip of silver duct tape across her mouth. She sat unnaturally still, her wide, terrified eyes staring directly at him. And there was a huge silver blade pressed against her throat.

At first Mark thought the man who stood behind her was wearing a Halloween mask like the figures on the couches. He was wrong. As he walked slowly across the room toward them, he realized that one side of the man's face was grotesquely scarred. Mark had seen burn victims before, and he recognized the damage immediately.

The left side of the man's face was a splotchy red and purple welter of old burns. The left eye was smaller than the right, narrowed into a permanent squint, and closer inspection caused Mark to guess that the eyeball there was glass. The man's left ear was gone, only a stump remaining where it should have been. There was no left eyebrow, and the dark hair on that side of his head grew in random, coarse patches. In vivid contrast to the devastation on the left was the fact that the entire right side of his head was perfectly normal, even handsome. This made the effects of the long-ago fire somehow more jarring, more horrible. He was hideous.

Perhaps the ugliest thing about the man was the hand that held the knife. The hand, like the left side of the head, was a mass of burned flesh, gnarled and raw, ending at unnaturally short, pudgy fingers. But the hand, ugly and misshapen as it was, had a firm grasp. The other hand, which had also been burned, grasped Tracy's shoulder, holding her in place.

Mark arrived before them, his gaze riveted to the indentation at the side of Tracy's throat where the blade was pressing. He didn't have to be told: he slowly put the revolver back in his pocket and lowered his hand to his side.

The dark-haired man with the ravaged face gazed at Mark, a wicked smile on what remained of his lips. When he spoke, it was in the low, resonant voice from the phone.

"Good evening, Mark. I'm so glad you could join us for the final round."

Mark tore his gaze from the blade and forced himself to look directly into the man's eyes. "Who the hell are you?"

"First things first, if you don't mind. Please remove the weapon from your pocket and place it on the table. Then take two steps backward, away from us."

Mark complied, glancing down at the table as he did so. There was a large, flat box there wrapped in black paper, a black bow in the center. Beside it was a big portable CD player. He stepped backward, watching the man. "Let her go, and I won't kill you."

Now the creature laughed. His giggle, unlike his speaking voice, was high-pitched and girlish. Demented. "Oh, I don't think so. We have to finish the game!"

"Who *are* you?"

Holding the knife firmly at Tracy's throat, the man bobbed his head in a parody of a formal bow. "Seth Carlin, at your service."

Mark stared. "Seth Carlin? The other son? But that's impossible. Seth Carlin committed suicide years ago. Who *are* you?"

The man laughed again. He was obviously enjoying himself immensely. "Now, Mark, you're the journalist, so perhaps you can remind me who it was who said, 'The reports of my demise are greatly exaggerated.' "

Mark calculated. If he lunged for the hand holding the knife, he might not be fast enough, and Tracy would die. The gun was on the table a few feet away, but the same problem applied. He wouldn't reach it in time. He thought, Where the hell is O'Hara?

"You're Seth Carlin," he whispered, wondering how to keep the man talking until O'Hara arrived.

"Yes, Mark, I am Seth Carlin, and my initials are S.C., and I am the avenger." The high-pitched giggle again. "S, C . . . avenger. *Scavenger,* get it?" He continued to laugh, enjoying his joke, never once relaxing the grip of the knife.

Mark waved his arm, indicating the tableau on the other side of the room, the dead man with the scar. "If you're Scavenger, then who is *that*?"

Now the man stopped laughing. "Nobody. A servant. Expendable. He helped me with the game, and then I had no more use for him. And speaking of the game, I have a final gift for you, on the table there. Aren't you going to open it?"

Mark stared at the man, filled with loathing. Then, with a sigh, he took a step toward the table and reached down, his eyes on the gun.

"Ah! Ah! Ah!" Seth Carlin sang. "Not so fast, Mark. The *box*, not the gun, thank you."

Mark stopped himself. He picked up the box, stepped backward again, and tore off the bow. The paper came next, falling to the floor at his feet. The black-lacquered lid and the black tissue followed it. Mark reached into the box and pulled out a hardcover book. It was his novel, *Dark Desire*. He stood there, blinking at it.

"*Wait!*" Seth Carlin cried, sounding remarkably like a television advertisement. "*There's more!*"

Mark put the book down on the table and stepped back again, away from the gun. He reached once more down into the box and pulled out a silver-plated woman's hand mirror. He dropped the box and looked back at Seth Carlin.

"What the hell is this?" he said.

The man who was Scavenger continued to smile.

"Isn't it beautiful, Mark?" he said. "It belonged to my mother. It is the final article in our scavenger hunt. Hold it up and look into it."

Mark blinked at him, then did so. His own angry face looked back at him.

"*And there you have it, folks!*" Seth Carlin announced triumphantly. "Congratulations, Matthew Farmer. You've found The Family Man!"

53

The mirror fell to the floor, filling the basement room with the clatter of silver on concrete and the tinkling of smashing glass.

Tracy watched Mark's face.

"You're insane!" Mark cried, taking another step backward. *"You're out of your mind!"*

She shifted her gaze as well as she could, straining to look at Seth Carlin.

"Yes," Carlin said. "You're right, I *am* insane! And you, Matthew Farmer, are the reason. You killed my family—after you killed your own family. You killed them all."

Now she looked back at Mark. He was staring incredulously at the man beside her.

"What are you talking about?" Mark shouted. *"How can you say such a thing?"*

She felt the cold blade press even more firmly against her neck. When Seth Carlin spoke again, his voice was once more low, reasonable.

"It was the book," he said. "*Dark Desire.* Your so-called novel based on actual events."

Mark blinked. "My book? What about it?"

"What about it?" the other man echoed. "Well, let's see, how about page twenty-seven? Page one hundred fourteen? One eighty-nine? Two fifty-three? And there's always my favorite, page three hundred twenty-six! Do you remember them?"

Mark blinked again and glanced absently over at the book on the table. "Not offhand."

The blade bit into Tracy's flesh, and she closed her eyes.

"The scenes of the crimes," Seth Carlin said just beside her ear. She could feel his hot breath on her cheek. "You described them all so vividly, down to the smallest detail. Not like a writer would, but, rather like someone who'd been there. Someone who knew *everything*."

Tracy opened her eyes again and watched Mark.

"So?" he whispered, still obviously confused. "What does *that* mean? It was all reported in the media. I'm a writer; I did my research."

She knew without having to look that Seth Carlin was smiling again. She continued to watch Mark carefully as the other man spoke.

"Research," Carlin murmured. "Yes. But the media reports weren't good enough for you, were they? You decided to embellish the truth, didn't you? You added your own dramatic little touch to it. You're really *not* much of a journalist."

Tracy felt the hand on her shoulder clamp down more firmly, and the tip of the blade pressed into her flesh. She winced, not daring to move her head or even to swallow. If Seth Carlin's hand were jostled . . .

Mark was frowning as he stared at the damaged man beside her. "What the hell do you mean, you sick creep?"

She heard the sharp intake of breath beside her, and she braced herself for whatever was going to happen next. To her surprise, the hand on her shoulder was suddenly removed, but the point of the knife remained where it was.

"Now, Matthew, what did I tell you about your rudeness?" Seth Carlin said. His voice was once more calm, almost unnaturally so. "Look around you. This is where my family died. Everything is as it was that Halloween, but there's something else. Something that wasn't there. *You* put it there, in your *book*. Tell me, Mr. Matthew Farmer, what's wrong with this picture?"

As Tracy watched him, Mark actually turned to glance briefly into the darkness behind him. Then he turned back to Seth Carlin, his expression now wary.

"I don't understand," he said. "What are you talking about?"

The odd, high-pitched laugh from the man beside her was as cold as death. Without for a moment relieving the pressure of the knife, he reached down to the table with his other hand and turned up the volume on the portable player. The room was filled with the lush, agitated strains of "Night on Bald Mountain."

"Music," Seth Carlin said.

She saw Mark blink, still confused. "What about it?"

A click. The music stopped, and the damaged hand returned to rest on her shoulder.

"There wasn't any," Carlin whispered. "Not here, not anywhere. Why did you make that up?"

Mark blinked again, and Tracy saw that now he was annoyed. More than annoyed: arrogant.

"Of course there was music!" he cried. "That shows how much *you* know about it! *I'm* the one who found the bodies of my family in Evanston! 'Jingle Bells' was playing." He took a step forward, an expression of triumph on his face. His eyes glittered. "And what about 'Stars and Stripes Forever' in Los Angeles? And in New Orleans, 'When the Saints Go Marching In'? What about *that*? *What the hell do you mean, I made it up?*"

Now she saw him glance down at the gun on the table some three feet away from him, calculating his odds. Before he could move, however, Seth Carlin's voice stopped him.

"Thank you," he whispered.

Mark froze, and Tracy saw his eyes widen. *"What?"*

"Thank you," Seth Carlin repeated. "That's all I wanted to hear you say, Mr. Farmer. Mr. *Family Man!*"

Mark did not move, nor did he remove his astonished gaze from the man with the knife.

"What?" he cried again.

There was a moment of silence in the room, and Tracy was aware only of her heart pounding in her chest. Then Seth Carlin spoke again.

"The one thing only The Family Man could know," he said. "Only *you* could know. You, quote, found the bodies of your family in Evanston, unquote, so I guess you knew about 'Jingle Bells.' But how could you possibly know that there was music at the other places—to say nothing of precisely *what music was playing*—when nobody else knew about it? The music was the one piece of information withheld from the press and the public. Only the police and the FBI were supposed to know about it. *How did you know about it, Matthew Farmer?*"

Tracy was staring now, concentrating on Mark's face. Then, for the flash of a single second, she saw it. It was what she had been hoping, praying, she would not see.

Rage.

In that instant, she knew that Seth Carlin was telling the truth.

When he had told her, repeatedly, last night and earlier today, she had assumed he was insane. But he wasn't insane.

He was right.

Now Mark was looking at her, into her eyes, and she knew what was going to happen next. She closed her eyes again, bracing herself for it. The blade pressed in once more.

"You killed my family, Matthew Farmer," Carlin whispered. "You killed everyone I loved, and now I am going to kill the woman you love."

She had to see what happened next, but she could not open her eyes. She heard the sudden movement, and the click, and her lover's voice. It was cold, dead, completely uninflected. It was his voice, but not a voice she had ever heard before.

"No, you won't," Mark Stevenson said. "I will."

Then she forced her eyes to open. Mark stood before them, aiming the revolver he'd grabbed from the table directly at her chest. She looked up into his eyes: they were as dead as his voice had been. He wasn't Mark Stevenson anymore. He wasn't even Matthew Farmer. He was The Family Man.

He fired.

54

Mark fired at Tracy's chest. Then he swung the gun over and fired twice at Seth Carlin, directly into his grotesque, staring face. So much for *him*, he thought. Too bad about Tracy. I really did love her, but she had heard. She knew. Now I just have to find Ron O'Hara and get rid of him before *he* finds *me*, then get the hell out of here. The keys are in the car—

He stopped, blinking, then stared at the sight in front of him. He had just shot them, but they hadn't moved. Tracy sat in the chair and Carlin stood beside her, slowly lowering the knife to his side.

They were both looking directly at him.

As Mark stared at her, Tracy brought her unbound arms around from behind the chair and reached up to slowly pull the tape off of her mouth. She dropped the tape on the floor, still gazing at him. He saw tears in her eyes. Then, with a little sigh, she lowered her head and wept.

Seth Carlin still had the knife in his right hand, but he reached his left arm across Tracy's shoulders and held her gently.

"I'm sorry, Ms. Morgan," he said.

Mark looked down at the gun in his own hand.

"It's over, Farmer," said a voice behind him.

He whirled around, the useless gun falling to the floor. Ron O'Hara stood just behind him, aiming his weapon, loaded with real bullets, at Mark's chest. Just over his shoulder, Mark could see the big man with the scar, the man he had thought was Scavenger, standing silently by the chair in which he'd been sitting, removing something made of rubber from his neck.

"*You!*" Mark cried.

"Yes," the former agent said, his voice low and calm, his aim steady. "I told Mr. Carlin about the music when he first contacted me. He'd read *Dark Desire,* and he was curious about the music at the murder scenes. He asked if there had been music anywhere. That was four months ago: it took us that long to put together this little game for you. I hope you enjoyed it. I know *I* did. I'm going to enjoy watching you get the needle even more. I'm going to dance on your grave."

Mark stared at the man, and at the other man behind him. Then everything exploded. With a bellow of rage, Mark threw himself directly at O'Hara, pushing him over backward to the floor. O'Hara's head smashed into the concrete with a sickening thud, knocking him unconscious. The weapon fired, sending a bullet into the ceiling before skittering away. As plaster rained down on him, Mark lunged, snatched up the weapon, and scrambled to his feet. He aimed the gun directly down at O'Hara's slack face.

"Sorry, Ron," he said, "but *nobody's* going to dance on my grave." He took a deep breath, preparing to fire.

The eight-inch blade entered Mark's right shoulder, and the gun fell from his hand. He staggered backward, nearly falling as the sudden, unexpected pain tore through him. He looked blankly down at the black handle protruding from him, then up at the man who had thrown the knife from the other side of the room, the man with the scar. Into his eyes. They stood staring at each other for a long moment. Then the tall man with the scar took a step toward him.

In one swift motion, Mark bent down, picked up O'Hara's gun again, and fired twice at the big man. The man dived for cover, landing on one of the couches, toppling two of the mannequins to the floor.

Mark ran. He clutched the gun against his chest, wincing at the pain that was now spreading throughout him. He pounded up the steps, reaching up with his left hand to pull out the knife as he went. He ran across the dark living room, colliding with the edge of the coffee table in his flight. Fresh pain shot through him as he staggered, dropping the bloody knife on the carpet, then regained his balance and plunged on, knocking over the chess table on his way to the foyer. The heavy chessmen clattered to the floor behind him. His right arm was throbbing, but he managed to keep the weapon clutched in his right hand as he reached out with his left hand and threw open the big front door. He stumbled out onto the porch, thinking, The car. Just get to the car—

And he stopped short, staring.

The front lawn was no longer dark. It was lit by bright floodlights, and there were people there. He blinked in the sudden glare, looking wildly around him. Several men in blue uniforms knelt in a semicircle on the grass, aiming rifles at his chest. Beyond them, near the flashing police cars and vans on the lawn, he saw all the others.

Millicent Call, wearing a Kevlar vest over her white nurse's uniform, was aiming a handgun at him. Behind her, protected by Agent Call's body and a car, stood Sarah Tennant Gammon. The red-haired man next to Sarah was obviously her husband, Robert Gammon. The dead Los Angeles motorcycle cop was standing on the other side of the car, aiming a rifle. The blond woman from Chicago was behind the motorcycle cop, standing with a tall blond man Mark had never seen before.

The big, blue-uniformed man in the center of the rifle line raised a megaphone to his lips.

"*Matthew Farmer, drop your weapon and raise your hands above your head.*"

The second white explosion of rage in Mark's brain coincided with a bright flash of lightning. He was running through a rainy graveyard, pursued by the monster he thought he had destroyed. The pious, grasping, abusive bully who had tormented him in the name of God. But there was no God, not then and not now. As the thunder crashed, he threw back his head and screamed.

"*Fuck you, Jacob Farmer!*"

Then Mark stepped forward to the edge of the porch, bringing up O'Hara's gun and aiming it directly at the man with the megaphone.

This time, the eight-inch blade entered the back of his neck, severing his esophagus. The tip of the knife came out the front of his throat in a spray of blood as rifle bullets tore through his body. He felt the impact from both directions, a thousand explosions of pain.

And then he was falling. He tumbled forward down the steps and rolled slowly out onto the grass. He landed on his back, on the knife handle, burying the dagger in his throat. He lay there, no longer feeling the pain, no longer caring if he did. He could not see them, but he sensed the presence of the people moving silently forward to crowd around him, staring down at him. The last words he heard were uttered by Sarah Tennant Gammon.

"Thank God!"

His penultimate thought was of his father, and of the family who had turned their backs on him, deserted him, ostracized him. The reason for everything he had done. The reason for The Family Man.

His final thought occurred to him through a veil of red, as the sky finally opened and the first cold drops landed on his upturned face.

Yes, he thought.

Yes, of course.

Rain. . . .

55

Tracy could not weep anymore. A feeling of exhaustion, of numbness, was beginning to set in, replacing grief.

She did not look at Seth Carlin. She reached up and removed his arm from her shoulder. Then she stood up from the chair and went over to kneel beside former FBI Special Agent Ronald O'Hara, the man who had chloroformed her and bundled her into the van in New York City two nights ago. He was sitting up on the floor now, rubbing his head.

"Are you all right?" she asked him.

He nodded. "I'll be okay." As she rose and turned away from him, he added, "I'm sorry about all this."

She looked back down at him. "Don't worry. We made a deal: if you turned out to be right about him, I wouldn't press charges for kidnapping me. I won't." She headed for the stairs.

"Where are you going?" O'Hara asked.

She turned around again, and their eyes met. "I have to see."

He nodded again and looked away from her.

Then she went up the basement stairs to the living room. She had heard the sounds of gunfire, and she braced herself for the worst as she crossed the living room, kicking aside stray chess pieces from the overturned game table, and went out through the front door.

She saw that it was raining, and several of the people here, the civilians, had moved up onto the porch. The big man, Ivan, who had rushed from the basement after Mark, was standing at the top of the steps, looking down. She walked past him and down the steps to the lawn, not feeling the cold rain as it pelted her. The crowd of police and federal people turned to look at her, and they parted, silently moving aside as she passed, including the two federal agents she'd met earlier today, the woman in the nurse's uniform and the man dressed as a motorcycle cop. She knelt beside Mark in the rain, gazing down.

Still she did not weep. She stared down at his face, at his bloody neck, at his bullet-riddled body. The body she had loved, had made love with. She did not touch him. She merely stared, making a study of him for several long, quiet moments. Then she stood and went back up the steps to the porch.

Ivan was sitting on the top step now, staring at the body on the lawn. She could not read the expression on his face. The people on the porch, whom she had met a few hours ago, kept a respectful distance from her, avoiding her. She was the pariah here, the enemy. They respected her because she had finally, reluctantly helped them. But they despised her because she had loved him.

She looked over at them. The blond woman, Ellen Harvey, was a Hollywood makeup expert, recruited by O'Hara's wife, Wanda Morris, the movie star. Ellen had performed her magic on Robert Gammon in New Orleans and the "cop" in Los Angeles, going so far as to use pig's blood on his fake wounds, and she had created the head in the box in Chicago. Tonight, Tracy had watched as she gave a reluctant Ivan a very convincing slit throat, pouring a vial of blood from the local butcher shop over her handiwork. Blood has a distinctive, strong odor, she explained. A blend of corn syrup and food coloring was fine for the movies, but in the theater of the real only real blood would do. She had also told Gammon to wet his pants in the house outside New Orleans, for the same reason.

Ivan had been upset tonight because he had been promised by Seth Carlin that he would be the one to kill Mark in retaliation for his wife's death, and they had just told him that the plans had changed. They weren't going to kill Mark at all: they were going to arrest him, try him, convict him. Execute him. That had been the plan, anyway.

Well, Ivan had gotten his wish, after all.

The blond man next to Ellen Harvey was her husband, Fred, a freelance filmmaker and computer whiz. He had made the phony newspaper in New Orleans, and he'd filmed the phony newscast in Los Angeles with a friend of his, a Chinese actress named Sandra Chan. The guest house proprietor, Mrs. Mullins, and the hotel management in Los Angeles had cooperated with Seth Carlin and Ron O'Hara, delivering the newspaper and the closed-circuit television transmission on schedule.

Furthermore, the blond husband and wife had acted as spies, following Tracy's movements in New York and Mark's progress in Los Angeles and Chicago. Fred had also assisted Ron O'Hara in her abduction: he had been driving the van. Once here, he had filled Ivan's role as manservant until Ivan had returned from Chicago. Seth Carlin was paying the couple a great deal of money for all this. Tracy had heard their story over dinner with them in the dining room tonight.

The dark-haired woman was Sarah Tennant Gammon, who had so convincingly utilized her acting training in the Pontchartrain Clinic in New Orleans, where she had never been a patient. Seth Carlin had made a generous donation to the facility in exchange for the use of it for the afternoon. Now Mrs. Gammon came over to her.

"Thank you for believing us," she said. "I'm sorry for you, for what you've been through, but I'm not sorry about *him*." She blushed and looked away from Tracy, and the rest of her words were spoken in an embarrassed whisper. "Anyway, I—I just wanted to say thank you."

Tracy nodded mutely, and the woman moved away, rejoining her husband on the other side of the porch. She had a right to feel that way, Tracy supposed. Her family had been Mark's first victims.

Mark.

Matthew Farmer.

The Family Man.

She swayed slightly, reaching out to grasp the porch railing. She leaned against it, staring out through the rain as the Green Hills police zipped Mark's body into a body bag and carried him over to an ambulance. Millicent Call and the other FBI agent followed them.

She watched them go, and she looked around at all the other people assembled here, and she thought: I will survive this. I will get over this numbness, and the shock and pain that will soon follow it. I will go back to the city, to my life. To my mother and my work and my friends. I'll find something for the baby shower. I'll handle my authors. I will find Jared McKinley and explain this to him as well as I can, and I'll try to keep him from getting drunk when he hears it. Then I'll do the same with Carol Grant. But I will go on. I will *not* be The Family Man's final victim.

As the ambulance drove slowly away, she felt a hand on her arm.

"Come back inside, Ms. Morgan."

She turned around and looked at Seth Carlin. His scarred face seemed softer now, filled with concern for her. She forced a weak smile to her lips.

"Please, call me Tracy," she said.

He smiled, too. "Only if you'll call me Seth." He turned to the other people on the porch. "It's over now. Thank you for your help, but go home now, all of you." Then he turned back to her. "Come inside, Tracy. Mr. O'Hara is waiting for us. I have brandy, and Ivan will build us a fire."

She nodded. He reached out to take her hand, and she allowed him to lead her into the house. Ivan Kolnikov followed them inside, closing the door firmly behind him.

Yes, she thought as she went. Brandy, and a fire, and the long road back.

GAME OVER

It was nearly dawn now, but still he continued to read.

Seth Carlin had started the manuscript yesterday, and he had immediately printed out the pages he had written. He read it over dinner last night, oblivious of the comings and goings of his servant. He ate heartily of the food Ivan placed before him, and he drank several glasses of wine. When his meal was finished, he carried the pages here, to the living room. Ivan had brought another bottle of wine for him, rebuilt the fire, and retired to his rooms upstairs.

Seth was now comfortably ensconced in his favorite armchair, in the middle of his third reading of the opening chapter. He was working slowly, carefully, making certain that everything was there. He wanted his biography of Matthew Farmer to be as convincing as possible. He wanted everyone to know his version of the story of The Family Man. Most of all, he wanted to publish a fully detailed account of the game he had devised to trap the notorious killer.

He was calling it *Scavenger*.

Ronald O'Hara and his friends, "Nurse" Call and the "cop" named Barton, would assist him a great deal in this, as would the others: Sarah Gammon and her husband, Ellen and Fred Harvey, Ivan.

And Tracy. He smiled when he thought of her.

Seth had gone to Chicago last week and tracked down a relative of Judy Barlow, who agreed with his theory that Mark had drugged the girl to sleep that Christmas Eve, driven to his family home in the earliest hours of Christmas Day, done his business, and been back in bed beside her before she woke up. The relative, an aunt, also agreed with Seth's theory that Matthew Farmer had provided Judy with the overdose that killed her a few months later, in case she ever remembered his absence from the bed that night.

The director of the market research firm that had employed Matthew Farmer during The Family Man's reign of terror was a woman named Alice Powell. She would not agree to speak to Seth, so the theory he was going to describe in that part of the book—that Matthew had found the other four families, with complete descriptions of every family member including gender and age, in his own client base—was mere speculation. But it would make for interesting reading.

Seth would not speculate as to why Matthew had changed his *modus operandi* after killing his own family, why he had apparently changed his cutting implements and dropped the musical motif for the last two families. In fact, he wasn't going to mention this at all in the manuscript. After much thought on the subject, he had decided to leave it out.

He sipped his wine now, in the living room, and slowly read the completed pages. There was much more still to write: the murders of the five families. And then the scavenger hunt, from the moment Seth had heard about the book, *Dark Desire,* to the moment in April, two weeks ago, when Matthew Farmer had fallen, dead, on Seth's front lawn. This would be his own contribution to the legend, and he was proud of it. He had read *Dark Desire,* and he had called Ronald O'Hara in Washington. O'Hara had been convinced when Seth brought up the details about the music.

Thus the game had been born, devised mainly between Seth and O'Hara. Wanda Morris, O'Hara's famous wife, had helped them out considerably, bringing in her movie friends to set the scenes and spill the blood. Sarah and Robert Gammon were eager to be a part of it. The only facet of the plan that had caused disagreement between the two men was Tracy Morgan. O'Hara had initially balked at the idea of abducting an unwilling civilian—particularly one who was in love with their quarry. But Seth had worn down the agent's resistance, and everything had worked out as Seth had envisioned it.

O'Hara had added touches to the plan, for which Seth was properly grateful. The former FBI man had come up with the "divorce" story and gotten Miss Morris away from the action completely, for her own safety should Farmer figure out what they were doing to him. O'Hara had also placed his friend and former subordinate, Millicent Call—armed with a semiautomatic under her white sweater—at the meeting between Farmer and Sarah Tennant Gammon at the clinic.

And it was O'Hara who had suggested telling Matthew Farmer that Seth had committed suicide years ago, to prevent him from looking in Green Hills before they were ready for him.

Now he finished reading, reached for the wineglass, and drained it. Then he stood up. Yes, it had been a most satisfying game, and the manuscript was going to be a good one. But now it was time for sleep. Tracy Morgan had invited him to dinner at her favorite restaurant in New York City tonight, and he would be there. He would actually make a foray out into the world. It was time to get used to humanity's reaction to his face, and he liked Tracy very much. She was kind to him, and she never treated him in either of the two ways he hated: with pity for the death of his family—or as a freak.

A freak. The way his parents and his brother and sister had treated him. He would never forget the Institute twenty miles from here, where he had spent most of his teen years before his family died. The freak house. He glanced over at the photograph of himself at his first and only piano recital there. His mother and father had sat there in the "musical therapy" room among the paraplegics and mental defectives, listening to him play in embarrassed silence, and then they had left him there and gone off on another world tour. His sister and brother— musical prodigies, both—had not even attended, nor had they ever visited him there. Not once.

He looked over at the portrait of his mother, Raina Carlin, so beautiful in her satin gown and Fabergé necklace. Then he looked over at her piano, the Bechstein. She had refused to touch any other instrument.

Now the Bechstein was his, and he thought about his mother whenever he played it.

He picked up the pages and tucked them under his arm. Sleep, he decided, then dinner with Tracy in the city tonight. Ivan would be driving him there. Ivan had said he had business in New York that he could see to while Seth was with Tracy. Seth had smiled and nodded, wondering if Ivan was seeing a woman.

Well, Ivan deserved a night on the town. He had played the game well.

He smiled to himself, glanced once more at his mother's portrait, and made his way upstairs to bed.

Ivan delivered his employer to the restaurant near Gramercy Park. He held the door for him and and saw him safely inside with Tracy

Morgan. Then he drove around the corner and parked. A few minutes later he was at Tracy's building, ringing her buzzer. The ring was answered immediately, and he went inside and up to the second floor.

Ron O'Hara was sitting at the dining table in Tracy Morgan's apartment, and there was a woman with him. The woman let Ivan in, then went back to what she had apparently been doing before he arrived, crouched over some elaborate recording device, adjusting knobs. O'Hara stood up and shook his hand in greeting, then indicated the empty seat next to him at the table, across from the woman. Ivan sat down with him, and the two of them watched the woman work.

Ivan had not seen the former FBI agent since that night two weeks ago, and he had been surprised when the man had contacted him three days ago, asking him to come here. O'Hara had told him that Tracy Morgan had set up dinner in a restaurant with Seth Carlin at O'Hara's request, and that Ivan was to drive Seth into the city, then join him at her apartment. That was all Ivan knew, but he'd done as the agent had asked. As instructed, he had not told his employer about the rendezvous.

There were boxes of Chinese food in the center of the table. Without a word, O'Hara handed him a plate and silverware and a cold bottle of Tsingtao beer. Ivan helped himself to sweet-and-sour pork as he watched the woman working with the machine, listening to the two familiar, disembodied voices emanating from the speaker.

"The Cobb salad is good here."

"That sounds wonderful, Tracy. I'll have that, too, and the soup."

"So, how have you been? How's the book coming?"

"Well, I'm pleased to announce that I've just finished the first chapter. . . ."

Ivan put down his fork, looking sharply over at the other man.

O'Hara returned his gaze. "She's wired, and she's not alone with him. The people at the table next to them are friends of mine."

Ivan stared, then took a long pull at the beer and set the bottle on the table. "Why are you spying on Mr. Carlin?"

The former agent took a bite of lo mein, put down his fork, and leaned back, regarding him.

"Okay," he said, "here goes. Matthew Farmer killed the Tennants in New Orleans and the Websters in California and his own family in Chicago."

"Yes," Ivan said. "I know."

Now Ronald O'Hara leaned forward, looking Ivan straight in the eye. "*Period*. That was it. Those are all the people Matthew Farmer killed. He became a serial killer so he could get rid of his own family without being seriously suspected. Once he'd done the Farmers, he moved here to New York and assumed a new identity, Mark Stevenson. Do you understand that, Ivan? He *stopped*."

Ivan stared. He was suddenly finding it difficult to breathe. The room seemed to be closing in on him.

"What do you mean?" he asked, aware of the weakness of his own voice. It was nearly a whisper.

O'Hara reached out with his hand now, placing it gently on Ivan's wrist. "I now know where Matthew Farmer—perhaps I should say, Mark Stevenson—was that Halloween, and the following Easter. He was working for the *Post* then, and he was punching clocks. He didn't kill your employers, and he didn't kill the Banes family." He leaned toward Ivan, whispering. "He didn't kill your wife, Ivan. Seth Carlin did."

Ivan stared. His first instinct had been to laugh, but something in the other man's eyes stopped him. He was trying to take it in, but his mind was not fast enough. "*What?*"

O'Hara picked up Ivan's beer bottle and handed it to him. Ivan drained it, watching as the former federal agent opened a second bottle, took away the empty, and replaced it. Ivan took a swig from the second bottle, then slumped back in his chair, the Chinese food forgotten. He continued to stare at the other man.

"Do you have any proof of that?" he whispered.

"Yes," O'Hara said. "Oddly enough, it's the same proof we had on Matthew Farmer. When Seth Carlin called me last January, he said he knew Mark Stevenson was Matthew Farmer, and he thought Matthew Farmer was The Family Man. I hadn't read *Dark Desire* at that time, but he got me interested in it real fast. He told me about the music in the book, and he asked me if it had any basis in fact. Then he said an interesting thing. He said, 'There wasn't any music at my house, and there wasn't any in Brooklyn.' Those were his exact words: '*There wasn't any in Brooklyn.*' He never even noticed his slip. I immediately began telling him about the music at the first three scenes: it was classified, but I wanted to see where this was going. Then he told me his proposal, the scavenger hunt that would trip up Matthew Farmer. And I couldn't resist. I had one suspect who knew about the music at the first three scenes, and another one who knew there *wasn't* any music at the final two scenes. *Both* men knew too much—and, at the same time, not enough."

Then O'Hara told him everything he'd put together in the four months since Seth Carlin had first contacted him:

Seth had been badly burned in a fire at the age of fifteen, a fire that had started in the basement recreation room where the family later met their fate. Last January, O'Hara went to the Lowrey Institute, the place where Seth Carlin had lived at the time of his family's murders. He'd lived there almost constantly for six years, since the fire. What the powerful Carlins had kept secret, what even O'Hara had not discovered until now, was that Seth had started the fire deliberately in an attempt to kill himself and his entire family. The fire wasn't his first display of violent behavior. As for the Lowrey Institute, Seth's parents were its most generous donors, and information about Seth was not made available to anyone. His physical wounds had been dealt with as well as they could be, but his mental rehabilitation had obviously been unsuccessful.

Seth's actions on that Halloween and Easter, unlike Matthew Farmer's, were unaccounted for. He had not been at the Institute on either date. Some inmates, including Seth, could come and go as they pleased, and the new director of the Institute, who did not approve of the former administration that had catered to the Carlins, had shown O'Hara the sign-out sheets.

At the time of his family's murders, Seth Carlin had been dismissed as a suspect, mainly because of his physical condition. But a few weeks after his family was killed, he had been interrogated by federal agents when letters were found, letters from Raina Carlin to her husband in which she told him she was afraid to visit their son at the Lowrey Institute alone, because he had repeatedly told her he hated the family, and on at least two occasions he had threatened her life. He had also threatened the lives of his brother and sister. Seth had been questioned by the FBI about his mother's letters, but the interviews were perfunctory and inconclusive. Shortly after that, The Family Man had struck again. O'Hara and his people had gone back to their original theory of a random sociopath, and Seth was forgotten. Now, all these years later, O'Hara admitted his own error in not investigating him further.

The change in *modus operandi* between the first three scenes and the last two suggested not one killer but two. Whoever had committed

the final two crimes had used different knives and saws. More important, he had apparently not known about the music that had been
playing at the first three houses. The final two crimes followed the
Family Man pattern only generally, as it had been described in newspapers and on television.

The last detail that had convinced O'Hara that there were two
Family Men, he told Ivan now, was the market research firm in
Chicago where Matthew Farmer had been employed. The director, Alice Powell, had refused to talk to Seth for his forthcoming book, but
she had cooperated with O'Hara. She had shown O'Hara Matthew
Farmer's client list. It included the Tennants and the Websters, which
implicated Farmer, but not the final two families. Matthew Farmer
had not known those people existed.

Ivan stopped him here. "Wait a minute. How would Mr. Carlin
have found out about the family in Brooklyn?"

In answer, O'Hara got up and went over to Tracy's coffee table in
the living room. There was a briefcase on the table from which he
took two objects, a magazine and a big book that looked like a hotel
register. Ivan watched in silence as O'Hara brought them back to the
table and sat down again. He glanced over at the woman, who was
still monitoring the conversation in the restaurant a few blocks away.

"There's so much I want to tell you about myself, Tracy."

*"I'd like to hear about your family—if you don't mind talking
about them, I mean."*

"Oh, I don't mind . . ."

It was a *New York* magazine from a week in January eleven years
ago, two months before the Banes family in Brooklyn was killed—and
one week after Seth had been interrogated by the FBI. George Banes
smiled up from the glossy cover over the legend, SURGEON OF THE YEAR.

Ivan stared. "Mr. Carlin subscribes to this magazine. . . ."

"Yes," O'Hara said. "We know. The article inside describes the
Banes family in great detail, right down to the dog." He put the magazine aside and opened the register book. "This is an old record from a
hotel in Brooklyn, about four blocks from the Banes house. Last De-
cember I looked around the area again, because I figured Seth would
have stayed somewhere close to the scene of the crime. He *does* tend
to attract attention, you know. I went around to the local hotels—
there aren't many in that part of Brooklyn—asking if anyone fitting

Seth Carlin's description had stayed there that Easter. It was a long shot, but someone *did* remember him." He pointed at a signature.

" 'Stan Corbin,' " Ivan read. "That—that's his handwriting, I think."

"It is," O'Hara said. "One of the managers recognized a photograph of Seth Carlin. He was at the hotel four blocks from the Banes house from Good Friday to the following Monday."

Now the two men were silent, drinking their beers and listening to the disembodied voices.

"Would you like to go to a movie after dinner, Tracy?"

"Oh, gosh, I can't, Seth. I'm going to meet a friend of mine. How about next week? Friday?"

"Fine. I'll have Ivan bring me into the city next Friday. We'll have dinner again."

"That will be lovely. . . ."

O'Hara grunted, a sound Ivan interpreted as a laugh. "She's meeting a friend, all right! She's taking Jared McKinley to an AA meeting. She's seeing a lot of him lately. He hasn't touched a drop since the day he heard about Matthew Farmer."

Ivan was barely listening. He was trying to remain calm. He had believed that he had avenged Anna's death, but now he realized that he had not. The old rage welled up in him. And with the rage, more than the rage, was the confusion, the sheer bewilderment he'd felt since that awful morning twelve years ago when he'd walked into the basement of the house in Green Hills and found them.

"Why?" he cried. "What was the *point* of all this?"

O'Hara was watching him, an expression of sadness, of weariness on his face. He had once been in a line of work, Ivan knew, that brought him more than his share of human atrocity. Ivan had seen cruelty in his own life, more than most, but this was beyond him. It was not beyond Ronald O'Hara. He sipped his beer, rested his arms on the table, and leaned forward.

"Suppose you are an arrogant young man," he said, "who has decided to kill his entire family. How would you do it? Well, we have a peculiarly modern phenomenon that springs to mind: the serial murderer. Jack the Ripper was the first big star, but there have been many since: Crippen, Christie, Gein, Fish, Gacy, Berkowitz, Bundy, Dahmer. Many others. So you join them, become one of them. But you can't start with your own intended victims; that would be too obvious.

What do you do?" He shook his head. "You create a fantasy, a pattern that will accommodate the people you eventually want to kill: upper-middle-class, white, Christian. Parents, three young adult children, at least one pet." He leaned toward Ivan. "And if there's anyone else in the house—say, a housekeeper—well, you do them, too."

Ivan winced, feeling the prick of long-unshed tears at the backs of his eyes.

O'Hara continued. "So you find likely scapegoats, a couple of other families similar to your own, and you use them for practice. A curtain-raiser, if you will, warm-up sessions. Then you simply wait awhile and do the people who were your intended victims in the first place. You might be suspected briefly—Matthew Farmer was—but you've already created the illusion, the idea that some lone wacko is out there doing this. And, this being the modern world, with similar stories on television and in newspapers all the time, everyone is perfectly willing to believe it. We've heard it all before."

Ivan stared at the man, mesmerized by his voice, the almost complete lack of emotion in it. He listened, wondering what this man had seen.

"Now," O'Hara went on, "suppose you are *another* arrogant young man who has decided to kill his entire family. You have the same problem as Young Man Number One, but you have a distinct advantage. The first guy has already created the illusion for you. You follow the stories of The Family Man in the papers, and you see the remarkable similarities between the random victims and your *own* intended victims. Well, if you are arrogant enough, it is irresistible. You don't have to warm up: the other guy has already done that for you. All you have to do is kill your family and make it look like *he* did it. So that is what you do."

As if sensing his emotions, O'Hara put his hand on Ivan's wrist again. "You kill them all, including—including Anna. And nobody even thinks of suspecting you, especially if you happen to be . . . well, someone who's been in a fire, someone people will automatically feel sorry for in the first place. But then, weeks later, some letters come to light, letters that make the investigators look at you, focus on you with new interest. You panic, of course. And then you do the only thing you *can* do."

He reached over now and picked up the *New York* magazine. The two men gazed down at the smiling George Banes, the surgeon responsible for saving and prolonging countless lives, who had lost his own so violently.

O'Hara finished on a whisper. "You continue the illusion. You continue The Family Man. The investigators run off to the new scene of the crime, and you go on with your life."

Ivan nodded, and O'Hara leaned forward once more.

"But that isn't quite the end of it," he said. "Now, more than a decade later, you pick up a book, a so-called novel about the long-ago killings. You read it, and you realize that you have found him. The only other person in the world who knows that *you* are responsible for the final two scenes. The only other person in the world who can possibly understand or appreciate what you both have done." A grim smile came to his lips. "Well, wouldn't you just *kill* to meet that man? So you devise a way: a game. A scavenger hunt. And you bring the mountain to Muhammad, as it were. You meet—and, incidentally, *destroy*—the only other person on earth who knows your secret."

Ivan closed his eyes and sagged back in his chair, thinking of his own role in Seth Carlin's mad game. When he opened his eyes again, he saw that O'Hara was studying him intently. Then the former agent took a breath and changed his tone completely. He got down to business.

"I asked you here today because I thought you'd want to be in on this."

Ivan watched him. "In on what?"

In answer, O'Hara pointed over at the woman and the recorder. "I've got some circumstantial proof, but I don't have any *real* evidence. So I'm doing to him what he did to Matthew Farmer. I'm playing with him. Tracy is helping, because he likes her, and he doesn't seem to have any other friends."

"He doesn't," Ivan agreed.

"We'll have to get him to talk. I think he wants to talk. Maybe he'll tell Tracy something, in time."

Ivan stared. "Why would he want to talk about it?"

O'Hara shrugged. "Same reason he came up with the scavenger hunt. Same reason he's writing a book about it. Hell, the same reason he killed his family in the first place, using the Family Man pattern. He loves games. Part of him wants us all to think Matthew Farmer was the one and only Family Man—but part of him wants us all to know just how clever he is."

Ivan thought about it. It made sense, he supposed, as much as it would ever make sense. He leaned forward.

"What can I do to help you?" he asked.

"Well," O'Hara said, "your part in this is probably the toughest. I want you to go on just as you are with him. He mustn't suspect anything. You have to stay with him, help him, do whatever you did before you came here tonight. Do you think you can do that, Ivan?"

Ivan nodded. For Anna, he could do anything. Even this. But only on one condition.

"He's mine," he said.

O'Hara shook his head. "No."

"You overlooked my doing Farmer. You can overlook this, too."

"No," O'Hara said again. "We're not going to kill him."

"*You're* not," Ivan said. "*I* am. He's mine."

Ronald O'Hara regarded him in silence for a long moment. Ivan waited for his reply. The woman across the table continued to record the remote conversation.

At last, O'Hara sighed. "We'll see."

That was good enough for Ivan. "So what now?"

O'Hara leaned back and reached for his beer.

"We wait," he said.

NEW GAME

TOM SAVAGE is the author of three previous novels: *The Inheritance, Valentine,* and *Precipice.* He lives in New York City, where he divides his time between writing and working at Murder Ink, the world's oldest mystery bookstore.